LOVE'S CAPTIVE

"Unhand me. I'll not be forced to return to Sedgewick against my will. Nor will I allow you to decide what is best for me. I have been your prisoner for the last time. I surrendered to you last night but never again. You may be the Lord of Sedgewick Castle and command all that you survey but I am not your property. In my time, a woman belongs only to herself."

Katharina tried to extricate her arm from his viselike hold, only to find herself held captive by both arms. Kane pulled her against him, so close that their breaths mingled. Time seemed to stretch into eternity as they both became aware of the warmth spreading between them.

"Blast it, Katharina," Kane ground out. "What I do is for your own good."

A low moan of anguish escaped Kane as he surrendered to the torrid hunger that pushed all thought aside. The heat of his need for her incinerated everything in its path as it swelled him. He took her tempting mouth, ravishing her lips, savoring their sweetness as he enticed them to open for him.

Lady of the Night

Cordia Byers

LEISURE BOOKS   NEW YORK CITY

Welcome to the world, John-John, my adorable grandson.

A LEISURE BOOK®

July 1998

Published by

Dorchester Publishing Co., Inc.
276 Fifth Avenue
New York, NY 10001

ISBN 0-8439-4404-8

The name "Leisure Books" and the stylized "L" with design are trademarks of Dorchester Publishing Co., Inc.

Printed in the United States of America.

Lady of the Night

Prologue

England, 1480

"Please, my lord! Don't allow them to do this to me," Eleanor beseeched, falling to her knees in front of Lord Sedgewick. She raised her hands in supplication to the man staring over her head at the distant trees. The iron manacles circling her raw, bloody wrists slid back with the motion, ripping away more flesh from her festering wounds. Tears streaked her pallid, dirt-smudged face as she again cried, "My lord, you have known me since I was a babe. You know I do no harm with my herbs. I only give aid to those who suffer."

Lord Sedgewick remained mute to her pleas. The muscles in his throat worked, yet he stood stiff and unrelenting, refusing to look at the woman at his feet.

"Get up, witch," the priest commanded, stepping between Lord Sedgewick and the pleading woman. "You have been seen fornicating with the Devil. It is our duty to see such evil extinguished from the face of God's earth."

"I am no witch," Eleanor protested. "Tell them, my lord. You are the only man who ever came to my bed. I am a good woman."

"Be gone, witch! I'll not allow your vile tongue to defile this good, honorable man. Tell no more lies. Lord Sedgewick is a just man, a decent man with a good wife of his own whom he loves and cherishes. He need bed no wicked wench." The priest glanced toward the guards and gave a nearly imperceptible nod.

Two leather-clad men-at-arms responded immediately to the priest's silent command. They grabbed Eleanor about the arms and roughly hauled her away from the priest and Lord Sedgewick. Her chains rattled ominously through the still, misty morning air as they propelled her toward her destiny.

The sun crept over the treetops, spilling its bright light across the glade, illuminating the stake where the guards worked to secure their prisoner. Golden light bathed the cords of wood piled about her feet. Callused fingers struck flint, giving life to the flames that flickered briefly before greedily devouring the dry kindling.

Eleanor flashed one last desperate look at the man she had loved all of her life, the man who had shown her what it was to be loved as a woman, the man who had professed his undying love until he married Rosemond of Clive.

Eleanor glanced back at the granite walls of Sedgewick Castle. She knew Rosemond stood in the shadowy recesses, watching, savoring her triumph, pleased to be rid of her rival for Richard's affections. Rosemond was responsible for the accusations against her as well as the testimony from her neighbors. The lady of Castle Sedgewick had threatened the villagers with eviction from their homes should they choose not to confess their dealings with the witch.

Eleanor could lay no blame upon the villagers for their submission to Lady Sedgewick's demands. They were as helpless as she against the power of the lord's wife. Nor could she hold Rosemond totally accountable for her fate.

Anguish tearing at her heart, Eleanor looked back to where Lord Sedgewick stood. Richard had been too cowardly to try to protect her from his wife's jealousy. He had feared he would damage his own name if he told the truth about his relationship with a simple village girl.

Eleanor coughed as the flames and smoke rose about her. She squinted through the gray haze at the man who had turned his back on the scene. She drew in one last deep breath and used her remaining strength to speak above the crackling sound of the fire. "Lord Sedgewick, I die now for the love I gave you. And as God and you know, I am no witch. But I do curse you and those who possess the blood of you and the viper Rosemond. May they suffer the agonies of hell and the scorn of their fellow man because you chose the viper's lies over the beauty of the love we shared."

The flames swirled upward toward the clear blue of the morning sky. They wrapped themselves about the woman chained to the stake. Her life spiraled heavenward, leaving behind only a silver-gray cloud of smoke.

Chapter One

England, 1993

The black silhouette of Sedgewick forest stood in relief against the shimmering night sky. The approaching storm made a glimmering display in the distance, reminding Katharina of the sudden summer storms that rolled across the stark mountains of Utah. The unusually warm late-winter weather now clashed with the cold air moving down across the North Atlantic. The confrontation between the elements had created a titan battle that now reverberated across the English countryside, shaking Sedgewick Castle to its ancient foundations.

Katharina pressed her fingertips to her pounding temples, absently massaging the ache that had begun soon after their arrival at Sedgewick. She wished she was at home instead of in an English castle, ghost-hunting with her aunt.

Katharina grimaced when she caught sight of her eerie image in the leaded glass window. It wasn't a pleasing reflection. The distortion from the aged glass made her taut, drawn features appear ancient, more like an old witch who brewed bat wings and toads' eyes in an iron cauldron instead of a young woman of only twenty-six years of age. All she would need to complete the illusion was a black gown and a pointed hat.

Perturbed by the aberration in the glass, Katharina glanced over her shoulder at the woman dressing in front of the cheval-glass mirror. She could nearly hear Sidney's burst of laughter should she reveal her wild thoughts. Her aunt would shake her head in bemusement at her sensible niece's whimsy.

Sensible! Katharina ground her teeth together, creating another sharp pain in her temple. She loathed the description her aunt so often used when she boasted to her friends that it was Katharina's sensible, analytical mind that was responsible for Herbal Health, Inc.'s recent financial success. She gave her niece credit for the development of several new products that had helped give the company the foundation it needed to expand into the international market. Katharina took pride in the recognition; however, she couldn't stop herself from hating being called sensible when she knew otherwise.

Sensible! She wasn't half as sensible as Sidney believed or she would not have made a fool of herself by falling in love with that bastard, Kevin Fullerson. Sidney had never understood the attraction. And when Katharina had fallen head over heels in love with him, her aunt had warned her that Kevin wasn't the right man for her.

Katharina sighed. She loved Sidney, and admired the way her aunt always lived life to its fullest. But no matter what she said, she couldn't make Sidney understand that the very traits that had attracted her to Kevin were the same qualities her aunt also possessed. He had made her feel alive with his enthusiasm for life. He had also shown her what it was like to be a woman instead of just a socially dysfunctional girl. Because of him, she had quit hiding herself away in the research lab at Herbal Health, Inc., and had faced the fact that even with all her degrees, she was like other young women. She wanted to love and be loved. The lab had been her haven from the outside world, though it had also been her love from the moment she'd first entered it after graduating from college. Every moment she spent trying to find new ways to use plants and herbs made her feel that she was contributing something—not only to Herbal Health, Inc., but to mankind.

Katharina's enthusiasm for her research could only be surpassed by Sidney's. Her aunt's belief that herbs and other plants could heal every ailment known to man had rubbed off on Katharina early in life and had spurred her to seek a degree in botany with a minor in genetics. Katharina firmly believed that the only way to prevent the destruction of the world's rare plants was to duplicate them in the laboratory by genetic engineering. So many of the beneficial plants came from the vanishing rain forest and could not survive under different conditions unless their genetic make up was altered.

Katharina flashed one last glance at her reflection. She released a sigh. No matter what she accomplished in her professional life, her personal life was a mess. Unfortunately, she couldn't claim to be a social butterfly. For a short while with Kevin, she had felt she was beginning to make her way out of the cocoon of insecurities that had kept her isolated for most of her life. But Kevin had inflicted a nearly lethal blow to her self-esteem when he'd broken off their affair, admitting the only reason he'd dated her was because one day she would inherit Sidney's fortune.

After that devastating experience, it had taken her months to accept a date with any of the men Sidney seemed determined to match her with. And when she did, she felt they were seeing Sidney's millions sitting across the table from them at dinner instead of herself.

Katharina turned to watch Sidney adjust the linen collar concealing the indecently low-cut neckline of her gown. She smiled. Even with a throbbing headache, she found it amusing to see Sidney dressed like a seventeenth-century Puritan. The pious image and the truth were so far removed from each other, it made the entire scene ludicrous.

"Exactly what's so funny, Rina?" Sidney questioned, arching a perfectly sculpted brow at Katharina in the mirror while her nimble, well-manicured fingers readjusted the collar to give a provocative glimpse of her deep cleavage through the lace edging.

Katharina moved away from the window. "I was just comparing the real Sidney Ferguson to the image in the mirror."

Sidney turned to face Katharina. Her blue eyes twinkled with devilment and tiny dimples touched the corners of her full-lipped mouth as she smiled and shrugged. "So? Maybe I've not lived a puritanical lifestyle, but . . ."

Katharina shook her head as she sank down into a striped satin Queen Anne chair. "That is exactly what I mean. That is an awfully big 'but,' don't you think?"

Sidney feigned a snort of disgust and smoothed down her velvet skirts as she glanced over her shoulder at the mirror. She inspected her image carefully from head to toe. "I hope you're not implying I've gotten fat. The guarana you suggested I try has helped tremendously to curb my appetite."

Katharina couldn't stop her laughter and immediately regretted the impulse before the sound completely died away. A new wave of pain shot to her temples and careened through her, settling sickeningly in her stomach. It had been a long, tiring day that had begun in London at seven that morning. She'd spent nearly all of it with Sidney and her lawyers trying to help finalize the negotiations to ensure that an Herbal Health store would open within the next year in England. Fortunately, by five o'clock the contracts had been signed and she and Sidney had been on their way to Sedgewick Castle, their last stop in England before returning to Utah.

Katharina squinted against the piercing lamplight. Though the lamp only used a small-wattage bulb, what little light it gave sent agony splintering through her head. As the director of Herbal Health's research department, she firmly believed in the benefits of natural health remedies, but in her present state of agony, she wished she had one of the pharmaceutically concocted, over-the-counter chemical products to put an end to her misery.

"Why the frown, Rina? You need to smile. You look beautiful dressed in that gown. You look as if you'd just stepped through time from the seventeenth century. The burgundy velvet accents your dark hair and complexion as if it was made for you."

"I'm happy with the gown," Katharina said and

swallowed hard against another crushing pain.

"You're having another headache, aren't you?" Sidney asked, eyeing her niece with concern.

Katharina forced the smile back to her lips. She'd not allow one of her miserable headaches to ruin Sidney's night. Her aunt had been looking forward to the banquet in the castle's great hall for weeks. For a short time tonight, they would step back in time into the seventeenth century. Everything was to be authentic to the period, from the gowns they now wore to the feast being prepared in the kitchen.

Katharina's stomach churned at the thought of food but she resolutely shook her head and attempted to lie. "No. I'm just tired after such a long day. We've had a busy two weeks. But at least it's over now and we can enjoy ourselves without having to worry about business."

Sidney crossed the room to her bulging tote bag and began to rummage through it. A veteran traveler, she'd insisted Katharina pack a similar bag. It contained just about everything a woman might need or ever hope to need should she become lost from civilization for five years. The two totes alone weighed more than all the clothes they'd brought in four suitcases.

Retrieving a bottle Katharina immediately recognized as the feverfew her aunt's company produced for headaches, Sidney poured a glass of water from the crystal pitcher sitting on the bedside table and turned back to Katharina.

"Here, take this. It will help."

"I don't have a headache, Sidney," Katharina began, but her aunt's stern look silenced her denial.

"I'm fortunate your research isn't as poor as your lying. Now take the capsule and you'll soon feel better. I want to see the sparkle back in your beautiful blue eyes before we go down to dinner. You never know, tonight you might meet your Prince Charming."

Katharina obeyed her aunt's directives but she doubted the herb would have much effect upon the headache that was pounding at her skull with the force of an air hammer. And she also doubted there would be any Prince Charming foolish enough to be out in such freakish weather.

"Do you think we'll find one here?" Sidney asked quietly, casting an expectant look about the bedchamber.

With the pounding ache digging into her head, it took a moment for Katharina to realize her aunt had changed the subject to the reason for their visit to Sedgewick Castle. She drew in a deep breath before offering a tentative answer. "I truly don't know. If the brochures are right, Sedgewick is haunted by ghosts and goblins of all types and descriptions. Hundreds of years of witch burnings and other macabre events have supposedly left ghosts and monsters all over the castle and its grounds."

Sidney smiled, pleased. "I hope they are right.

I need to see at least one ghost before we have to return home."

"Does it really matter so much?" Katharina asked, massaging her temples.

Sidney clasped her hands in front of her. Her intelligent eyes seemed to examine every shadowy corner as if seeking out the specters mentioned in the brochure for the Haunted Britain Tour. "It does to me. I know you think I'm crazy to search for ghosts. But neither channeling, nor any of the other new-age methods, have given me any proof that there is life after death. And I must know, Rina. I'm forty-seven years old. I've lived a full, and as you say, less-than-puritanical life, and I'm not getting any younger. I've only maybe forty good years left before I die. If there is a right path, I want to set my soul on it before it's too late. In my heart I feel there is a higher being, but until I find at least one ghost, I can't completely convince my mind that what the ministers say in church every Sunday is true."

Katharina released a long breath. It would be futile to attempt to convince her aunt that by believing in God, she would find the faith she was searching for without any ghosts. Sidney would have to find her own faith. And as her aunt had done all her life, she'd do it in her own way and in her own time.

Katharina winced as another pain hit her temple. To be honest, she was in no mood to help

Sidney get to heaven when she felt like living hell herself.

Sweet lord! When will this end? Katharina thought, trying desperately to keep from telling their hostess exactly what she could do with all the witches, ghosts and monsters haunting Sedgewick's halls. The feverfew had helped ease her headache to a small degree but hadn't completely rid her of it. She needed to sleep to be really free of the migraine.

Katharina glanced to her right, where Sidney sat engrossed in the evening's presentation. She was completely absorbed in the elderly lady's tale of those who haunted the castle: one witch who had been burned to death for her crimes in the fifteenth century; several lords; a man with a cudgel; a sinister specter who might have been the victim of a murder; and several revelers who had been locked away in a secret room, condemned to eternal gaming and drinking until Judgment Day. There was also the legend of the vampire who was born into the Sedgewick family periodically throughout the centuries. By the tour guide's description, Sedgewick Castle couldn't be surpassed by any other building for its hauntings and macabre events.

Katharina closed her eyes to give them a moment of reprieve from the light. She should have taken a tablet of bee pollen along with the feverfew. It would have given her enough energy to make it until midnight, when they would tour the castle by candlelight.

"Rina, go up to bed. There is no reason for you to stay down here when you are feeling so miserable," Sidney whispered, placing an understanding hand on Katharina's.

Katharina opened her eyes to find Sidney leaning toward her. "I'll be fine. I don't want to disturb the other guests by leaving now." She glanced toward the small porcelain clock sitting on the intricately carved, Italian marble mantle. "We are to have a break just before midnight. I'll slip away then."

"Excuse me, ladies. Is there something you wish to ask?" the little gray-haired guide inquired, giving Katharina and Sidney a censuring look for interrupting her talk on the Sedgewick poltergeists, holy healing and wishing wells, curses and sorcery, and last but not least, the Little People who inhabited the woods.

Katharina felt her cheeks go crimson and shook her head as Sidney said, "No. Please, do go on. I find your stories fascinating. To date, Sedgewick has been the most interesting place on the Haunted Britain Tour."

Appeased by the praise, their hostess gave a brisk nod and continued her tale as if she'd only paused to take a breath.

Lowering her gaze to the soft burgundy velvet of her gown, Katharina had to admit Sedgewick

Castle had been the most interesting of all the places they had visited.

Katharina stroked the heavy fabric of her gown appreciatively. The garment had been beautifully designed, though it was cut more simply than gowns from other periods in fashion history due to the puritanical dictates of Cromwell's rule. The bodice came to a deep point at the waist and was laced down the front with satin ribbons. The neckline was cut low, but was covered modestly with an opaque linen collar edged in fine lace. The thick velvet of the skirt fell in folds to the floor, again giving the effect of stylish modesty.

Katharina smoothed the soft silk velvet. It was heavy material, but it felt good against the chill that had invaded the chamber soon after their hostess started her ghoulish tales. The castle had been renovated for central heat in the late sixties, but it was still cold and drafty.

The owners had also renovated the plumbing, but they had failed to add a private bath for each bedchamber. At present there was only one bath per floor, an inconvenience Katharina could well do without.

Katharina's gaze passed over the heads of the other tourists to the dark paneled walls and antique furnishings. Sedgewick's owners had loved the castle enough to preserve it for posterity. Every piece of paneling as well as all of the furnishings were original to the castle.

The daughter of an Anglophile, Katharina was

delighted just to sit amid the antiquities of Sedgewick Castle. She had grown up hearing British history discussed nightly over the dinner table. When Sidney had invited her to come to England, she had been thrilled. Instead of just reading about them, she would be able to see the places she'd heard so much about from her father.

Katharina's gaze once more swept over the room. Something deep within her could nearly feel a tangible presence left by all who had lived, loved and died here for over five centuries. What she felt had nothing to do with ghostly hauntings. It was the spirit of those who had helped shape the destiny of a nation.

So much history had transpired at Sedgewick Castle. It had sheltered many of England's leaders during times of war and peace. If the thick granite walls could talk, they could probably tell tales that would put the guide's ghost stories to shame.

Katharina shivered as a chilly draft of air brushed the back of her neck. Thinking of the history that had passed here could make even a sensible-minded person like herself get the willies.

"Now ladies and gentlemen, it is eleven-thirty. We will take a twenty-minute break before we begin the midnight tour. You will find refreshments in the drawing room. Should you need anything further, please feel free to ask one of the servants." The tour guide smiled politely and moved down the aisle to open the wide double doors that led into the hallway.

Katharina got to her feet, relieved. She could now escape to her room to find the comfort of her bed. All she wanted was to cover her head and sleep off the remains of her headache. Katharina jumped as a deafening roar of thunder shook the castle to its foundations.

"It would seem the weather is determined to make our midnight tour more interesting." Sidney laughed, standing at the same instant a strong burst of wind sent a downpour of rain crashing against the leaded windows.

"That's exactly what I was saying to my wife," a dignified-looking gentlemen said, pausing at Sidney's side. He glanced toward the windows and smiled. "It is a night made for ghost-hunting, wouldn't you agree?"

"I do hope so," said the petite woman at his side. She looked at Sidney and extended her hand. "I'm Alice Harrogate and this is my husband, Dr. Henry Harrogate. We're from Oxford."

"How nice to meet you. I'm Sidney Ferguson and this is my niece, Katharina. We're from the States."

"How nice of you to visit us. I hope you've found England pleasant."

"Yes, very much so. I only hope we can see a ghost before we have to leave. I'm fascinated by the prospect," Sidney said.

"If there is one to be found in Sedgewick, we

should see it. The conjunction of the planets tonight means that anything can happen."

Alice Harrogate smiled proudly up at her reed-thin husband. "Henry is a professor of astronomy at Oxford. He's been waiting years for this conjunction to take place. It only happens every hundred-and-seventy-one years. And during the six months it takes for the conjunction to conclude, Henry says that there will be major events taking place. Isn't he brilliant?"

Henry Harrogate blushed and placed a loving arm about his wife's narrow shoulders. He cleared his throat and said, "I believe my wife exaggerates my intelligence a wee bit, but I am looking forward to the conjunction that begins at midnight. It has been interesting to look back at the events which have taken place during past conjunctions. We are now dressed for the time of the one in 1651; not too long after the execution of Charles I. The one before that saw the discovery of your own country."

"How very interesting. This makes tonight even more exciting," Sidney said enthusiastically. Glancing to where Katharina stood, her smile faded at the wan look on her niece's face. "Go on up, Rina. You need to rest. I'll stay here and talk with Dr. and Mrs. Harrogate."

Katharina felt a burst of relief. She extended her hand to the Harrogates and gave them a weak smile. "If you will excuse me, I believe I'll go up to bed. I wish all of you much luck in finding your ghosts."

"We'll do our best," the Harrogates said in unison before proffering their good nights. As Katharina moved past them, Sidney had already drawn Dr. Harrogate back to the subject of the conjunction of Neptune and Uranus.

Relieved that Sidney wasn't alone, Katharina hurried up the timeworn stairs to her bedchamber on the second floor.

Intent upon getting to bed, she ignored the cracks of rumbling thunder overhead until the porcelain bedside lamp flickered several times, momentarily leaving her in the dark. When its weak light reemerged, Katharina flashed an exasperated glance at the small, delicately wrought lamp. "All I need to top off this miserable night is for the electricity to go out before I can change out of this gown."

Quickly retrieving her nightgown and robe from the armoire, Katharina hefted her tote bag over one shoulder and turned back to the door. For the first time since coming to England, she wished they had decided to stay in the hotel in the village with all its modern conveniences. With her head feeling like a swollen lump on her shoulders, she could well do without having to trudge about searching for the john.

Katharina closed the door behind her and turned in the direction the maid had indicated when they'd arrived. She'd not had time to locate the bathroom earlier. They'd only just had time to change for the banquet in the great hall.

Another loud crack of lightning split the atmosphere above Castle Sedgewick. The slow-moving storm she'd observed in the distance earlier had now reached them in all its glorious fury. The electric torches in the passageway flickered again, making Katharina catch her breath and speed up her steps. She didn't like the thought of being caught alone in the dark, in strange surroundings. There were so many different passages leading off the main hallway, she'd never find her way back to her bedchamber.

Katharina debated turning back to her room but quickly discarded the idea. She'd never make it through the entire night without heeding nature's call. Her decision made, Katharina determinedly readjusted the heavy strap of her tote bag and turned once more in the direction of the bathroom.

At the end of the corridor she paused, looking from right to left, uncertain of which way to go. Two dimly lit hallways led off in different directions, but she couldn't remember if the maid had instructed her to go left or right. Disgusted, her patience wearing thin, Katharina turned to the left. She'd go a short way and if she didn't find the bathroom, she'd go in the opposite direction. She couldn't wander around all night hunting for the facilities.

Another searing bolt of lightning split the sky

as she stepped into the tapestry-lined hallway. Katharina felt the floor tremble beneath her feet. The electric torches flickered and then went black, leaving her in the total darkness of the passageway. A strong, icy breeze whistled down the corridor, wrapping itself about Katharina, tugging at her hair and skirts.

Katharina suddenly felt the same sensation she'd experienced when she'd visited Carlsbad Caverns in New Mexico a few years before. She'd become totally disoriented when the tour guide turned the lights off to allow everyone to realize how totally black it was within the caves.

Katharina felt goose bumps break out on her arms. She reached out to steady herself, seeking the solid comfort of the wall. Her hand found only empty air as a wave of giddiness swept over her, leaving her light-headed and breathless. Cold sweat broke out across her upper lip and her stomach churned sickeningly with nausea. Feeling faint, Katharina drew in deep ragged breaths of air. She'd never fainted in her entire life, and she'd be damned if she would start now, lost in the dark in a haunted castle.

The word haunted seemed to reverberate through Katharina's mind as she stared into the pitch-black void surrounding her. She swallowed uneasily and felt the hair at the nape of her neck rise. She was Sidney's sensible niece, but even Sidney's level-headed niece, who didn't believe in ghosts or any paranormal occurrences, couldn't stop the tingle of fear that inched its way up her spine when she recalled Dr. Harrogate's prediction that anything could happen with the astrological conjunction taking place in the heavens.

"Don't be ridiculous!" Katharina said aloud, forcing herself out of the cavern of her imagination and back to reality. She wasn't lost. She was in Sedgewick Castle with fifty other people. The electricity would soon be repaired or someone would come along with a light to help her get back to her room.

At the same moment this thought occurred, her giddiness passed, the current of air stilled and Katharina felt a wave of relief as she spotted a pinpoint of light at the end of the corridor. She smiled as the tiny glow grew steadily into a circle of golden warmth surrounding a man still costumed in the seventeenth-century livery of a servant. He paused when he saw her standing in the hallway. He held the candle higher and scowled at her.

"What ye be doing in here? This be the private wing. No guests allowed."

Unable to understand completely his strong brogue, Katharina said, "Pardon me. I'm afraid I'm lost. Could you show me where the john is?"

A look of comprehension flickered across the man's wrinkled features. He muttered something about foreigners beneath his breath and then shrugged a thick shoulder. He pointed to the door down the corridor. " 'Tis no business of mine if 'e sends 'is soul to 'ell."

He reached for a candle on the table near the doorway and lit it from the one he carried. He handed it to Katharina and shook his head in disgust. "No wonder ye couldn't find yer way, wench, wandering around in the dark and all."

Giving no more thought to her, he turned, scratched an armpit and then shuffled away. Puzzled by the man's odd behavior, Katharina watched him until he passed from sight. She'd understood little of the grumpy man's speech; only his physical directions when he'd pointed. His less-than-hospitable reaction was completely different from the gracious service that the other servants had given Sedgewick's guests during the evening. Katharina shrugged off the thought and excused the servant's actions. He was probably as tired as she was after such a long day—a day that seemed to be stretching into infinity.

Recalling her own quest, Katharina raised the candle to inspect her surroundings. The soft light spilled over the tapestry-lined walls, thick Aubusson carpets and family portraits, before her gaze came to rest on the intricately crafted table that had held the golden candelabra. Strangely, she'd not noted any of the furnishings before the electricity failed. Nor had she seen the doorway only a few feet to the right.

Katharina let the thought pass as she moved toward her destination with relief. When she suffered a migraine, she didn't pay a great deal of attention to anything but the pain.

Katharina paused, startled. Her headache had vanished during the few moments she'd been left in the eerie darkness. She touched her temple in astonishment. She couldn't believe it. Her headache as well as her upset stomach were entirely gone.

"The thought of being lost in a haunted castle probably frightened it out of me," Katharina said, chuckling at the absurd notion as she opened the door to the john.

Chapter Two

Because she was intent upon keeping her meager light from being extinguished by the current of air coming through the doorway, it took Katharina a moment to realize she wasn't alone. When she looked up from the flickering candle, her breath caught in her throat at the sight of the room's other occupant. Naked as God had made him and as perfect as Michelangelo's *David*, he stood like a bronzed deity in the middle of an oblong brass tub. Droplets of water caught the soft candlelight, spreading an iridescent glow over his wet, male flesh.

Mouth agape, Katharina stood transfixed, boldly admiring the man before her. Broad shoulders topped his beautifully contoured body. Crisp dark hair velveted the heavily muscled expanse of his steel-hard pectorals. Velvet and steel. The combination of images tantalized Katharina's senses until she found herself fighting the urge to reach out and touch the stranger just to experience the contrast of textures.

Keeping her hand at her side, she managed to resist the temptation but allowed herself a moment more of pleasure before her curiosity sent her gaze roving down his tapered torso to the flat, hard plane of his washboard belly. Below his navel, a narrow trail of dark silk drew her gaze downward to his narrow lean hips and the apex of his long, muscular thighs.

Unbidden, Katharina's gaze moved to the ebony glen at the juncture where his masculinity lay tranquil amid soft curls. Shocked to realize she was staring at the man like a hungry wolf watching a lamb, she grew hot with embarrassment at her brazen behavior. She jerked her gaze up to the man's face and was mortified to find a knowing look in his piercing midnight eyes. Katharina opened her mouth to apologize for intruding upon his privacy but the words froze upon her tongue. Her insides seemed to dissolve slowly into jelly as a provocative, mesmerizing grin touched the most sensuous pair of lips she'd ever seen.

Shaken by her unusual response to the man, Katharina quickly decided it would be in her own best interest to put as much distance as possible between herself and the stranger. If she didn't, she feared she might make an even bigger fool of herself in front of him and start drooling. Katharina's mortification magnified when she realized her mind didn't seem to have control over her feet. She stood riveted in place.

"Wench, don't just stand there. Bring me a towel. I don't have all night. John will be here at any moment."

Katharina heard his words and understood them, but it took a moment for her mind to interpret them. Unlike the servant in the hallway, he spoke with a far more cultured dialect, but his speech was more heavily accented than any she'd encountered since her arrival in England.

"Wench, are ye deaf? Bring me a towel."

"I'm sorry, I-I," Katharina stuttered, gripping the strap of her tote bag like a lifeline. Face burning with embarrassment, she finally regained control over her limbs and began to back toward the door. She wanted to escape before she had to try to explain her intrusion and then her rudeness in ogling him.

Grin fading, the man stepped from the tub, grabbed the towel from the washstand and wrapped the linen about his narrow hips before he turned and stalked toward Katharina. Water dripped across the polished, oak parquetry flooring as his long strides closed the space between them. His well-manicured, long-fingered hand caught Katharina before she could turn and bolt through the doorway.

"Wench, I am master here and you will obey me."

Katharina stiffened as the word "master" penetrated her embarrassment. All the circuits in her brain seemed to overheat and begin to sizzle at the antiquated idea. She looked down at the hand grasping her arm and slowly raised her eyes to meet his ebony glare. She raised her chin and squared her shoulders, ready to do battle with the male chauvinist. She hadn't watched Sidney outfox the male competition over the past few years without acquiring some knowledge of how to deal with such arrogance.

"Sir, I would suggest you release my arm. I apologize for the intrusion upon your privacy, but I see no reason to be manhandled because I mistook your bedchamber for the bathroom."

The stranger frowned down at Katharina as if puzzled by her statement. "From which village do you hail, wench? I do not recognize your speech as local."

"For one thing, my name is not wench. And I come from the United States, not an English village. Now if you will kindly release me, I'll return to my room," Katharina answered, summoning as much dignity as possible while her insides trembled with several uncomfortable emotions.

The man's hand tightened upon Katharina's arm and the lines about his mouth deepened.

"Where is this United States of which you speak?"

It was Katharina's turn to frown. The man might be an Adonis in looks, but to ask such a question, he had to be an imbecile. There were only a few people left on earth who didn't know of the States, and they lived in Third World countries without any modern communication. The strong fingers biting into the flesh of her upper arm jerked Katharina's thoughts away from her captor's intelligence. She answered sharply, "In America, of course."

"America? What foolishness do you speak? There is no such place in the Colonies."

A chill rippled down Katharina's spine as she looked up into the black gaze riveted to her face. She saw only complete belief in the piercing depths of the man's midnight eyes. Katharina swallowed nervously. As the servant had said earlier, she'd intruded into the private domain of Sedgewick's owners and now was confronted by a man mentally deranged.

Forcing a wobbly smile to her lips, Katharina said, "Yes, you're right. Now if you will excuse me, I'll return to my room. It is getting very late and we have an early flight tomorrow." She made to step away but his hand remained firm on her arm, keeping her at his side.

"Desist in trying to play me for a fool, wench. You trespass into my home and think by spouting nonsense of your chamber and of growing wings that you'll succeed in convincing me you're a madwoman so I'll show pity upon you. But it will do you no good. I know people of your ilk and the reason you were sent here."

"Sir, I have apologized for trespassing upon your privacy and will immediately go back to my room if you will be good enough to release my arm," Katharina said, worried now that the man might also possess violent tendencies.

"You'll have no chamber at Sedgewick except the dungeon. A night with the rats might make you regain your senses and remember who sent you here to spy upon me and mine."

Fright fraying the last of her composure, Katharina tried to jerk her arm free. "This game of yours has gone on long enough. If you don't release me this minute, I will sue the pants off you and Sedgewick's owners.

"And as you already know, I am the owner of Sedgewick."

"At this moment, I don't really give a damn if you are the owner of Sedgewick or the Prince of Wales himself. I just want you to let me go. If you do, I'll forget this ever happened," Katharina said quickly, praying with every fiber of her being that she could escape the madman. At that moment, she was willing to do and say nearly anything just to get safely back to her room.

"You and your cohorts would relish using anything I might say or do to prove that I am a royalist, wouldn't you? Then it would be so easy to confiscate Sedgewick and the rest of my estates.

However, you have failed in your mission. My enemies will never get their hands on my land, nor will they ever know what happened to their beautiful, seductive little spy."

At the end of her rope, Katharina shook her head. "I'm not a spy. I only came here by mistake looking for the john."

Again a smile appeared on the man's sensuous lips, but Katharina felt none of the melting sensation she'd experienced earlier. To the contrary, the gesture sent alarm bells ringing through her brain.

"Wench, John's love for beautiful women is well known by friend and foe alike. But his loyalty to me can't be swayed, no matter how well you perform beneath the covers."

Katharina frowned up at the man before her eyes widened with understanding. A smile briefly touched her lips and she managed to suppress a chuckle at the awkward situation created by the diversity of the English language. "Sir, I believe we have come to the crux of our problem. I fear we do not understand each other."

"I understand perfectly, wench. I'm no one's fool, as Glenville well knows. He's tried more than one devious method to get his hands on my wealth."

"No. I'm talking about the john; nor your wealth or anyone called Glenville."

"As I said, I have John's loyalty. There is no use in trying to use your body to worm your way into his good graces in order to spy on me."

Katharina shook her head. "No. You don't understand. Where I'm from, we call the bathroom the john."

"There is no need to try to equivocate. Your lies become even more absurd with each passing moment," the man said, drawing Katharina toward the open doorway. He didn't pause as he dragged her, cringing and struggling every step of the way, down the hall to a narrow stone stairway. Unable to traverse the winding steps with Katharina in tow, he pulled her tote bag from her hands and tossed it aside before he picked her up and threw her over his shoulder. His actions served to knock the breath from her as her abdomen crashed against hard, male flesh. She gasped and momentarily went limp as she fought to pull air back into her aching lungs. Her captor paid no heed to her discomfort as he carried her downward.

"Simon," he bellowed as he paused at the base of the stone steps, in a huge shadowy chamber that smelled of unwashed bodies.

The scrape of metal against metal sounded as a door at the far end of the chamber swung open. A bear of a man ducked to avoid the door header as he stepped into the shadowy room. He grinned when he saw Katharina. "My lord, 'tis a fine-looking piece of baggage ye have perched on yer shoulder. Is there something ye require before ye settle down to enjoy yerself this night?"

"Take this wench to the dungeon and beware

of her tales. She spouts lies from her beautiful mouth so easily that she can nearly make you believe she can sprout wings to take flight."

Her captor abruptly dumped Katharina from her perch and she lost her balance as her feet came into contact with the cold, stone floor. His long-fingered hand steadied her before he relinquished her to the man he'd called Simon.

Simon looked from his lord to the beautiful woman and momentarily doubted his own hearing. His voice reflected his uncertainty as he asked, "Lord Sedgewick, are ye certain ye want her thrown into the dungeon? 'Tis been years since it's housed anything but rats and vermin."

"Do you disobey my order, Simon?" Lord Sedgewick asked softly.

"Nay, my lord. I only questioned my own understanding of yer order, nothing more. The last to be locked away there were the three gamesters who tried to cheat your grandfather out of his holdings in a game of chance."

"Aye. And if this wench doesn't soon tell me who sent her here, she'll suffer the same fate as those who tried to ruin my grandfather." Lord Sedgewick looked down at Katharina and smiled coldly. "They refused to admit they'd cheated and ended up starving to death."

An icy chill ricocheted down Katharina's spine. "Now listen here. This has gone far enough. If you wanted to frightened me, you've succeeded. I admit I trespassed into the private quarters of the castle, but that does not give you the right to torture me with threats of being locked away in a dungeon and being starved to death. All I want is to go back to my room, get a few hours sleep and then I'll be on my way back to the States. Now, does that make you happy? You've succeeded in scaring the daylights out of me, and I promise on a stack of Bibles ten feet high that I'll never set another foot in England till the day I die." Katharina raised her hand and made the Boy Scout sign. "Scout's honor."

Simon quickly made the sign of the cross across his barrel chest and gave an nearly imperceptible shiver as he muttered, "She be a witch, my lord."

"Speak no more foolishness, Simon," Lord Sedgewick said sharply. "I've heard enough nonsense this night to last me a lifetime. First she threatens to fly, and now you believe she can." Lord Sedgewick shook his head in disgust. "I have enough burdens without my own servants believing the rantings of a woman who has been sent here to spy on me and mine."

"I'm not here to spy on you. I came with my aunt to search for ghosts," Katharina said, growing more desperate with each passing moment.

Simon's eyes widened again and he glanced uneasily at Lord Sedgewick. He swallowed hard against the trepidation rising in his throat. Though nearly six feet tall and stoutly built, his unusually deep voice squeaked as he uttered, "My

Lord, are ye certain she be no witch?"

"As certain as I am that she *is* a spy for Glenville. Now put her in the dungeon and we'll see if she'll be more willing to confess by the time dawn lightens the morning sky. I think a night with the rats and vermin will bring some sense to her wild rantings. Then you will see she's no witch, only a wench paid to seduce John into betraying me."

Simon flashed another doubtful look at Katharina.

"Bloody damn, Simon. Are you going to follow my orders or stand here all night like a cowering fool? You and the rest of my retainers know there are no witches at Sedgewick. No more than there are ghosts and vampires. Now be done with it. Lock the wench up for the night. And then make sure George has my mount ready."

Simon nodded. His grip on Katharina tightened as he turned to lead her toward the thick iron-bound door through which he'd entered the chamber earlier.

Katharina strained against the strong hands pulling at her. She shook her head and tried to dig her heels into any crack or crevice that might prevent her from being taken further into the bowels of Castle Sedgewick. "No!" she shouted. "This joke has gone on long enough. Let me go. You can't do this. I'm an American citizen, and you just can't lock me up for going into the wrong room! My ambassador, my congressman and even your prime minister are going to hear about this. I'm warning you."

"Shut yer trap, wench," Simon said, dragging Katharina through the doorway and into the damp, vile-smelling black void beyond. The only light to penetrate the darkness came through the doorway, allowing Simon to see his destination. The rusty metal protested with an anguished squeal as he forced opened the ancient lock and opened the barred door. Before his captive had time to start babbling again in her strange evil tongue, he shoved her inside and swung the heavy door closed, relieved that she'd not put a curse on him during her rantings. He made the sign of the cross again and turned back to the light.

Katharina stumbled from the force of his push. She threw out her hands to try to protect herself from the fall as she stumbled to her hands and knees on the slime-coated stone floor. Something wiggled beneath her palm. She gave a cry of revulsion and shot to her feet.

Heart pounding and breathing heavily, she panicked. All thoughts of imitating her aunt evaporated under mind-numbing fear. Turning back to the door, she began to pound on the rough wood with both fists. "Let me out. Let me out. Someone help me. I'm being held prisoner by a madman."

Kane wiped the rainwater from his face as he strode into the tavern. It was well past midnight, and his mood was as stormy as the night beyond the walls of the tiny hovel that served as a haven for rogues, thieves and other miscreants whose lives depended on the anonymity they enjoyed at the Fox and Hound. Neither the taverner nor anyone else cared who you were or what you did as long as you had the coin to pay for his services.

Scanning the dimly lit, smoky interior, Kane glanced toward the fat jowled man behind the bar, gave a brisk nod and then strode up the narrow, steep stairs. Light filtered from beneath the doorway as he tapped upon the splintered panel. A moment later the door swung open and he was immediately embraced in a fond hug.

Laughing dark eyes gazed into his as he was pulled into the dank little room where a meager fire kept the chill of the wet night at bay. "It's about time you got here. I had begun to fear a mishap might have befallen you."

Kane swept off his dripping hat and made a graceful bow. "Majesty, this night has been full of mishaps, but none to keep me from our meeting."

Charles II lifted an ebony brow in question and glanced toward the door. "You come alone? Where is Sir John? I thought from your message I would be meeting with you both."

"That's exactly what I assumed as well, Majesty, but Sir John has seemingly disappeared from the face of the earth."

A look of concern flickered over Charles's swarthy features. "Has he been harmed?"

Kane shook his head as he untied his soggy cape and shrugged out of it. "I have no idea. He was at Sedgewick earlier in the evening, but when it was time for me to leave, he had vanished. I had the castle searched, certain he'd be found in some serving wench's bed, sound asleep from all the wine he'd consumed earlier. However, he was nowhere to be found."

Charles crossed to the small fireplace and held out his hands to the weak blaze. He frowned down at the naked, jewelless fingers he extended to the scanty heat and clamped his jaw tightly together, hating the anonymity, the hiding, the secretiveness of sneaking into his own country in the guise of a pauper in order to see his friends and supporters.

He stared for a long moment at the orange and yellow blaze before he cocked his dark head to one side and looked at Kane. His frown marred his handsome features, and his eyes reflected the seething tempest churning his insides at the injustice his family had endured at the hands of the Roundheads and their leader, Oliver Cromwell. "Bloody damn. Do you think Glenville has anything to do with his disappearance?"

Kane nodded. "I fear Glenville has again set about to try to find a connection between us. I caught one of his spies at Sedgewick tonight. She is now enjoying herself in the dungeon."

Charles's lips crinkled beneath his perfectly shaped moustache. "She?"

"Aye. From what I could gather from her wild raving, she'd been sent to seduce John. Glenville well knows my cousin's penchant for beautiful women."

Charles chuckled. "Aye, John is much like myself. He can't resist tumbling a beautiful wench when one's available. However, he'd never divulge anything that might harm either of us. He may drink and carouse, but his loyalty is without question."

" 'Tis true. 'Tis why I fear for John's safety. 'Tis unlike him just to disappear. Should he not return to Sedgewick by tomorrow morn, the wench will tell me what has happened to him or she'll pay with her life for accepting Glenville's coin. I love John like a brother."

Charles's smile faded. "How is young Richard?"

Kane looked away from his king's scrutinizing gaze. He drew in a long breath and said evenly, "The same. He will be sixteen on the thirty-first, and 'tis growing harder for him by the day. He has a quick mind and his body is young and healthy. He yearns for all the things men want from life."

Charles placed a comforting hand on Kane's shoulder. " 'Tis hard to live with such a curse."

" 'Tis harder for Richard." Anguish filled Kane's solemn eyes as he looked back at the man who he prayed would soon reclaim the English throne. "Of late I've caught him watching the maids from the shadows. I pray I don't have to begin locking him away to keep him from them."

Charles's fingers tightened on Kane's shoulder as he tried to give silent reassurance. No words could ease the shame and pain of the Sedgewick family. Only those closest to Lord Sedgewick knew the secret he carried. Rumors had surrounded the Sedgewicks for nearly two hundred years, but only a handful of people knew the truth: that they were not rumors.

"You'll do what is right for your family, as you've always done. And you know you have my support in whatever you choose to do," Charles said at last. He gave Kane a brotherly pat and then stepped away, ending their personal conversation. "Now 'tis time to discuss what's to be done about Glenville." He eyed Kane shrewdly for a long moment before he smiled. "Perhaps the wench you imprisoned this eve can be of far greater service to us alive than dead."

"How so?" Kane asked, wondering at his sovereign's scheme. The man had been through so much in the past years; anyone less strong than Charles II would have succumbed long ago. However, Charles carried his burdens easily upon his young shoulders. His quick mind pounced upon an opportunity when it was presented to him, and he didn't let go until he had succeeded. A determined man, he had vowed upon the death of his father to reclaim the English throne for the

Stuarts and would do so, no matter what he had to do or say.

"If she's in Glenville's service, then she can tell us what we need to know to bring about his downfall with Cromwell. Any little chink can create a crack in the bastard's hold on England. From that will come my reclaiming the throne."

A knock sounded at the door, abruptly silencing the two men. Withdrawing his sword, Kane moved to the door, ready to defend his king. Charles eased into the shadows beyond the sagging bed as Kane called out, "Who's there?"

" 'Tis I, Churchill."

A sigh of relief seemed to fill the room. Kane opened the door to his friend. " 'Tis about time you showed up. All I need tonight is for another friend to disappear."

Bowing to his sovereign, Churchill frowned. "Sire, is Kane having a problem with his friends?"

"Aye, to a certain extent," Charles said. "He's lost John."

Churchill arched a dubious brow. "I doubt you've lost the old rogue. He's curled up in some wench's bed without a thought to the destiny of England."

"So I also thought. But I've looked everywhere. He's not to be found."

"Perhaps the wench in your dungeon is a witch who made John disappear in a puff of smoke," Charles laughed.

"What wench?" Churchill questioned, wondering if his friends had not been enjoying the tavern's rum a little too much before his arrival.

" 'Tis a long story. I'll tell you about her later," Kane said, giving his monarch a disapproving look. "And there are no witches at Sedgewick."

"I am one who would never have thought such things existed until of late. After the witch hunter Mathew Hopkins was convicted of witchcraft and hanged, I thought we'd heard the last of witches. Now I've learned there is a woman in the village who swears she can make the crippled walk and cure a person of his ails with her chants and herbs."

" 'Tis nonsense, as you well know," Kane said, shifting uneasily. He wanted no rumors of witches and black magic circulating anew. Should that happen, he'd be faced once more with renewed talk about the Sedgewick curse.

"I'm not so certain of what I believe. However, it is of no consequence tonight. I must finish our business as soon as possible. Young John has come down with the croup, and I need to fetch the physician back to the manor."

"The boy is ill?" Charles asked, concerned. A lover of children, he well understood Churchill's need to be with his family when his son was ill.

"Aye. He's normally a healthy little hellion, but he's had a touch of the croup that he just doesn't seem to be able to rid himself of."

"Then let us finish. I am on my way back to France tonight. I will leave it to the two of you to learn what can be done to begin my last journey home. Cromwell's hold on my people must be broken as soon as possible. I now have Scotland with me. All we need is England's support again."

"You will have it, sire. Soon those who were too cowardly to support your reign will see that until Cromwell releases his hold on England, we cannot live as free people. They will throw off the Puritan yoke," Churchill said.

"I believe it will happen in the future. But there is still much to be done before I can return to claim my throne."

Kane nodded his agreement. Unlike Churchill, he knew it would take time to bring Charles II back to his throne. The civil war wasn't a distant memory. People wanted to rest, to regroup, to live normally for a time before again having to side against each other.

Charles crossed to the two men and gave each a comradely hug. "My friends, you are my future. Your loyalty is what sustains me when I look from France toward English shores."

"We will have you home, sire," Kane said. "I give you my word."

Charles nodded. His dark eyes looked suspiciously bright as he quickly donned his cape and opened the door. His last words came softly before he slipped into the shadow of the hallway. "God be with you, my friends. My life is in your hands."

Chapter Three

1993

A cold draught of air extinguished the candle. Icy fingers raced up John's spine as a wave of dizziness swept over him. Suddenly disoriented, he reached out to steady himself against the wall, wondering at the effect of the last glass of brandy that he and the maid had shared before he'd had to leave her curled up in the center of the down mattress. Running an unsteady hand over his sweat-dampened brow, John shook his head in an effort to clear the fogginess from his brain.

"Damn me, but that drink had the punch of a pugilist," he muttered, annoyed with himself for allowing his pleasure to come before duty. In his present state he'd be of no help to Kane on this night, and tomorrow he'd catch bloody hell from his cousin for his indulgence before such an important rendezvous.

A tiny smile touched John's full lips and he shrugged. At least Charles understood his weakness for pretty wenches and good brandy. Himself a rogue, England's king enjoyed the same pleasures as often as his loyal subject, John Edmond Clive.

John's smile faded. The same couldn't be said about his cousin, Kane. The man was dedicated to his country and family, and he'd allow nothing to come between his loyalty to either. John ran his fingers through his hair and pushed himself erect. He could do nothing to change things. It wasn't in his power. All he could do was give Kane his support. John grimaced. And before he could do even that, he'd have to take a brief nap to sleep off the brandy.

With no candle or moonlight to illuminate his path, John felt his way along the cool stone wall of the hallway, searching for an empty bedchamber in which to lie down. He needed only a short rest and he'd be as good as ever. John opened the first door he found. After stumbling over several pieces of small furniture, he felt his way to the high four-poster, pulled off his shirt and pants, kicked off his boots and pulled back the covers. He crawled into bed. His last coherent thought as he pulled up the soft sheet and burrowed beneath the pillow to shut out any noise was gratitude that his cousin kept the household in such good order. John had never smelt such a fresh lavender scent on any bed covering before. At last the brandy had its way with him. John drifted off into the deep sleep of intoxication.

The wind and rain still lashed at the walls of Sedgewick Castle. Sidney set the crystal glass on the side table and yawned as she watched the Harrogates acsend the stairs arm in arm. It had been a full day. She'd gotten the deal she'd wanted for her expansion into the British market, enjoyed herself thoroughly since her arrival and had made wonderful new friends. The professor and his wife had been the icing on the cake. After the ghost hunt at midnight, they had returned with her to the parlor for a nightcap.

Smiling, Sidney picked up the brandy decanter and poured the sparkling amber liquid into her glass. Feeling a light buzz from her previous drinks, she raised the crystal glass as she bid the Harrogates good night. Flushed and warmed by the heat of the liquor, Sidney picked up the candle the maid had left for her to light her way to her room. Still smiling, she made her way up the stairs and opened the door to the bedchamber she shared with her niece. Peering into the darkened room, all she could see of her niece was the lump under the covers. Quietly, she undressed and blew out the candle. She didn't want to disturb

Rina's sleep. The girl had been tireless in her efforts on behalf of Herbal Health, Inc., and she needed her rest.

Making every effort not to move too much and awaken Katharina, Sidney pulled back the covers and slipped beneath. She curled on her side and in moments drifted off to sleep.

Chapter Four

The creaking of the door's rusty hasp jerked Katharina from her exhausted stupor. She came to her feet, disoriented, and instinctively raising an arm to shield her eyes against the blinding glare from the torch.

"Yer free to go, wench," Simon growled, relieved to be rid of the noisy, unnerving woman. She had howled like a creature possessed until the early hours of the morning. Simon shivered. Lord Sedgewick had forbade him even to think his prisoner was anything but a spy sent by Lord Glenville, but it wasn't an easy command to obey.

The hair at the nape of Simon's neck rose and he rubbed a hand restlessly across the prickly bristles as he eyed his prisoner suspiciously. She could very well be a banshee sent to foretell a death to come. Appearing from nowhere in the middle of the night, she had spoken of all sorts of strange things.

Simon clenched his jaw. No matter what His Lordship said, there was something far more different about the wench than just her odd way of speaking. Another tingle of fear crept up Simon's spine and he suppressed another shiver. He'd be more than happy to see the last of her. There were far more than enough strange things that went on at Sedgewick without adding a screeching woman.

Unable to comprehend little more than the word "free," Katharina squinted at her beefy jailor. Exhaustion had dampened the fear that had left her nearly paralyzed after being tossed into the vermin-infested hellhole. Now it reasserted itself, making her hesitate.

"Have ye made yerself deaf with all yer caterwauling, wench? I said yer free to go!" With each word Simon raised his voice until his shouts echoed off the stone walls.

Unable to stand the reverberating sound, Katharina shook her head and shouted back, "I'm not deaf."

"Then get yerself gone before me lordship changes his mind and decides to treat ye like ye deserve."

Katharina glanced at the open doorway and took a hesitant step forward only to realize she had no earthly idea how she could accomplish the guard's order. She didn't know where she was, much less how to find the castle's guest quarters.

Too eager to be free of the woman, Simon gave Katharina no time to ask directions. Noting her moment of hesitation, he grabbed her by the arm and forcibly propelled her out of the cell, on through the adjoining chamber and along the corridor to an iron-bound door. He didn't release his hold upon her until he opened the portal and shoved her outside. He slammed the door firmly closed behind her and breathed a sigh of relief as he made his way toward the stairs. He'd report his actions and then he'd let Lord Sedgewick handle the rest of it. He could follow her if he chose, but Simon wanted nothing more to do with the Lady of the Night.

Katharina had no time to protest the man's callous treatment. His push sent her toward the edge of the stone steps, and it took all of her concentration to keep her balance. She caught only a brief glimpse of the clear blue sky overhead before stumbling toward the bottom of the stairs. She managed to make her way down the time-worn stones without falling, but her luck ended there. Her foot caught in the hem of her soggy gown and she fell to her hands and knees in the mud.

She was trembling from a mixture of emotions, and angry tears streamed down her dirty cheeks as she drew a hand out of the mud. She watched the slimy ooze drip down her fingers with only one thought in mind: Revenge. The madman whom the guard had called Lord Sedgewick would pay dearly for what he had done to her. She'd see him arrested and condemned to a mental institution where he belonged. Katharina pushed herself to her feet and grabbed up the hem of her soiled velvet skirts. The mud sucked at her feet, pulling off one shoe as she tried to extricate herself.

In that moment, Katharina thought she would explode into a million pieces from the burst of fury that possessed her. It did little to cool her anger to find several dirty-faced children watching her misfortune. Simmering with mortification at how she must appear, she forced a weak smile to her lips and gingerly put her foot back into her muddy shoe. She pulled the slipper out of the morass and took another step. Again the mud claimed her shoe. The sound of the children's giggles ended what little control she had. Exasperated, Katharina gave her shoe a rough yank with her toes, sending the filthy missile over the heads of several men who stood gaping at her, as dumbfounded as the children.

"Haven't you ever seen a woman before?" she snapped before stamping her way, shoeless, out of the mire.

Katharina caught only a brief look at the spectators who had gathered to watch her misfortune. She didn't note the man following her as she glanced around her barnyard surroundings, seeking some way to get back to the main entrance of the castle. The sight did little to improve her already deteriorating impression of the lifestyle lived by the inhabitants of an English castle. From what she had seen, once out of sight of the tourist, they lived much like they had three hundred years ago.

Chickens, pigs and goats mingled among the workers, grunting and squawking for their share of the slop that had been tossed into the yard without thought of the vile morass of evil-smelling, shoe-devouring mud they created.

"No wonder they can put on an authentic medieval banquet," she muttered, making an unconscious moue of disgust. She was perturbed to think she had eaten food prepared in the castle kitchens. From the appearance of her surroundings as well as the spectators, there was much to be desired in the way of cleanliness. She was certain the British health authorities weren't aware of the filth at Castle Sedgewick or they would have already closed down its tourism business.

Katharina pushed the thought from her mind and headed for the postern gate. In just a few short hours, this would all be behind her. She would report the madman to the English authorities and then she and Sidney would catch their flight back to the good ole U.S.A. The U.S.A that she intended never to leave again!

That comforting thought speeding her steps,

Katharina made her way back to the front of the castle. Flustered and intent upon finding her aunt, she failed to note the odd looks she received as she made her way across the courtyard and up the steps to the tall double doors at the entrance. She burst through, passing the startled inhabitants, and headed toward the stairs. She wanted to find Sidney and then get as far away from Sedgewick Castle as possible.

But before she reached the stairs, a well-remembered voice asked, "Wench? Where do you think you are going?"

As if jolted by a current of electricity, Katharina came to a halt and turned to face the madman. Bolstered by the knowledge that she was now surrounded by other members of the Haunted Britain Tour, making it impossible for the villain to harm her further, she balled her hands on her hips and raised her chin defiantly. She'd show the monster that he couldn't frighten her now that she was no longer at his mercy. Steadily she met his piercing black gaze and answered, "I am going to call the authorities and have you arrested for your assault upon me, as well as have you charged with abduction."

"You are a brazen wench. Or a very foolish one. I know not which. But it is of no great matter. You seem to be determined to remain at Sedgewick instead of returning to your own village. If that is your wish, it is mine as well." Lord Sedgewick glanced over Katharina's head to the guard who had followed her from the rear of the castle. "Have her taken up to the tower room. I will question her later."

"Now you wait just a damn minute. This isn't going to work a second time. Last night you had the advantage, but now it is mine. No one here will allow you to mistreat me again, especially my aunt. She'll have you locked up if you lay another hand on me."

Lord Sedgewick shook his head and smiled at the two men who now stood beside Katharina. " 'Tis sad to see such beauty house such a devious nature. The wench would do well upon the stage were we allowed to have theatrical performances. She plays the fool very well, don't you think?"

"Aye," the guards agreed in unison.

Lord Sedgewick looked back at Katharina. "You should have accepted the freedom I offered, wench. It will not be offered again until I have the truth from you."

Katharina ground her teeth together in frustration as she glanced around the hall, seeking a familiar face among the spectators. She frowned. She didn't recognize any of the people watching her so oddly. Her frown deepened. Why were they all still garbed in the costumes from the previous night? She looked back at Lord Sedgewick. "I don't know what's going on here and I really don't give a rip-roaring damn. All I want is to find my aunt and leave." Before anyone had time to stop her, Katharina called out, "Aunt Sidney, help!

Everyone has gone mad. Aunt Sidney!"

"Take the wench," Lord Sedgewick ordered, ignoring her outburst. From the way the girl had reacted to everything else, he wouldn't be shocked by anything she did. Glenville should be proud of her. She played the fool to the hilt.

Katharina resisted the guards' efforts to capture her, but her struggles were futile. After only a few seconds, her arms were firmly held and she was lifted completely off her feet. The two men carried her between them, ignoring her continued pleas for help. They echoed through the corridors as the men wound their way up the narrow staircase to the tower room. Without a word of explanation, they shoved her inside the chamber and locked the door behind them.

"I don't believe this can happen a second time," Katharina muttered as she stared at her bleak surroundings. A narrow poster bed, a chair and a small table comprised all the room's furnishings. A cross-slit window allowed the morning sun to stream into the circular room, illuminating its bareness. Katharina ground her teeth together to hold back the scream of frustration threatening to choke her. She clenched her fists at her waist and closed her eyes in an effort to regain control over her emotions. The fright she'd managed to force into the background earlier now threatened to turn into a tidal wave, making her heart pound against her breastbone like the ocean surf under a full moon. Katharina drew in several deep breaths. She had to remain calm. Hysteria at this point was totally useless. Something had gone terribly wrong during the night, and she had to remain coherent in order to understand what had happened.

"My God!" Katharina breathed, her eyes flying open, her face paling. She'd not thought of Sidney's welfare until this moment. During her few hours in the dungeon, the madman and his cohorts had done something to the other guests. Katharina clamped a hand over her mouth to keep from screaming at her terrifying thoughts.

That was the only explanation for the strange events of the last harrowing hours. The madman and his henchmen had harmed Sidney and the other guests, or he'd locked them away as he'd done Katharina. That had to be the reason for Sidney's lack of response to her pleas. Otherwise Sidney would have been there to fight for her. Her aunt would have torn down the castle walls to get to her.

Katharina crossed to the narrow window, wondering at the motives behind the weird actions of her captor. Dressed like a lord of the 1600s, he surely couldn't believe that people wouldn't notice when he took charge of Sedgewick Castle. And the only reason she could find for kidnapping the entire castle's inhabitants was to use them as hostages.

"Hostages?" Katharina said out loud as her

gaze moved over the courtyard below. "Why would he need hostages?"

A chill rippled down Katharina's spine as myriad reasons flickered through her mind. Besides, the crazies in today's world didn't really need a reason for their deadly schemes.

Katharina bit her lip and drew in a shuddering breath as she looked down at the courtyard before allowing her eyes to drift to the stables near the edge of the walls. A hay wagon with shafts high in the air was being unloaded while several horses were being groomed near the wide doors. Again her captor had outfitted his men in attire from the seventeenth century. The sight only confirmed what she already knew of him: He was completely mad. Katharina focused her gaze on the fields and meadow beyond the tall walls. She had a magnificent view from the tower. She could see the winding lane that led up to Sedgewick. An oxcart wove its way along the narrow dirt path toward the castle gates. To the right of the road, sheep grazed peacefully unaware of what had transpired a few hundred feet away. On the left side of the lane, a large plot of land had been turned, awaiting the spring planting.

Perplexed by the peaceful scene, Katharina's brow furrowed with her frown. The scene below was tranquil, but something wasn't quite right. She stared at the ox-drawn cart, trying to find the reason for her feelings. Her expression went blank and she slowly shook her head, unable to comprehend what her eyes saw. Only yesterday the narrow lane had been a paved roadway, wide enough for two cars. Her gaze swept to the castle walls. When they'd arrived at Sedgewick, there had been no gate or walls. The tour guide said the walls had been taken down during the eighteenth century when Sedgewick was no longer needed as a fortification.

Katharina again shook her head and pressed her eyes closed as she prayed the hallucination would be gone when she looked once more from the window. Drawing in a bracing breath, Katharina opened her eyes to the view. Nothing had changed. The gate, the wall, the ox-drawn cart were still there.

Katharina felt faint. She gripped the cold stone of the window facing. Her eyes had to be playing tricks upon her. It was impossible for things to change overnight. Katharina drew in a steadying breath and nodded to herself. A weak smile touched her lips as she peered down at the courtyard.

"Nothing has really changed," she reaffirmed aloud. "I've just been locked away in a part of Sedgewick that overlooks a different courtyard from the one we entered yesterday."

Her words rang false in her own ears. She could be viewing a different courtyard, but that did not explain the gate and walls. Their height would make them hard to miss even from a different entrance.

The hair at the nape of Katharina's neck seemed to stand on end as Dr. Harrogate's words echoed through her mind. "Tonight anything could happen. The conjunction only takes place every hundred-and-seventy-one years."

"This is ridiculous," Katharina said aloud in a effort to reassure herself. "There is a logical, reasonable, believable explanation for the strange things happening here. No one can go back in time, not even with the conjunction of Uranus, Neptune and Saturn or the other six planets combined. All the hokey astrology garbage in the universe can't create an opening into the past or future. All I need to do is to find out what is truly going on and what the madman has planned for me."

Katharina rubbed at the chill creeping up her arms and wondered how she would find out anything locked away in Sedgewick's tower. She flashed one last glance toward the oxcart and then turned her back on the scene. She crossed to the chair and sat down, her back straight, arms hugging her waist. She sat there, tense and perplexed, unable to reconcile the illusion beyond the window to what she knew as reality. And she waited, waited for someone to come and tell her that what her eyes saw and her imagination had conjured up were impossible.

The morning sun slowly slipped from the room as the day lengthened into afternoon. Katharina did not move from her perch on the edge of the chair. Her stomach rumbled from hunger as the hours passed, but she made no attempt to call for food. She sat and listened to the unfamiliar dialects drifting up from the courtyard. As the day wore on, she managed to comprehend more and more of the strange-sounding language. The meaning and the words fell into place, allowing her to gather bits of information from the smattering of conversations that came through the window. The people talked of ordinary matters, everyday occurrences within a large household, yet Katharina realized they could not be discussing the events in a twentieth-century household.

The idea was far more paralyzing to Katharina than her experience in the dungeon. Then she had thought herself held captive by a madman. That experience could logically happen in today's world. Now she didn't know where, much less what time in history, she'd blundered into during the course of the night. And if her mounting suspicions proved true, how could she ever go about getting back to where she belonged?

"My God." Katharina caught her breath. She had to be going mad herself even to contemplate such an occurrence. It was impossible, she told herself, even as she heard the bar across the door being raised.

"You smell good enough to eat," the very British, sexy male voice murmured as Sidney arched into the caress of a wide, callused masculine hand. She breathed a sigh of pleasure, enjoying her dream. It had been far too long since she'd last experienced an erotic dream, much less enjoyed the actual act itself. She savored his warm breath as his lips trailed a path of teasing kisses along her neck and his hand cupped a breast. His lips teased her skin as his thumb did likewise to her nipple.

Again Sidney gave an audible sigh as a hard thigh eased over her legs, gently separating them to make way for the hand that followed caressingly from her breast, down over her rib cage to her belly and then to the dark glen at the apex of her thighs where it urged her to open fully to him.

Blood racing, Sidney obeyed, arching toward the pleasure of his touch even as her mind began to shed the last remnants of what she had believed to be a wonderful, powerful dream. She raised her arms about his neck and opened her eyes to the man who had set her body on fire with his touch. Her heart nearly stopped as she looked up into his devastatingly handsome face. Instead of being frightened that a stranger was in her bed, she felt dizzy as she peered into the piercing depths of the man's eyes and saw her own desire reflected there.

In that moment, Sidney could no more have said no to his gentle, caressing entreaty than she could have stopped breathing. In that moment, there were no morals to build a shield between them, no argument that society could make against what she was allowing to happen. It was fate; nothing could stop her from enjoying the pleasure her mysterious lover offered.

He smiled down at her as he felt her thighs part for him and lowered his mouth to hers, taking her lips in a firm but gentle kiss that made Sidney's blood simmer. She gave a primitive whimper of surrender and thrust her hips upward, beckoning him to take her. She was already on fire. Had awoken on fire and needed him to quench the heat searing her body before she exploded into a million cinders.

Her entreaty did not go unnoted. Her lover deepened his kiss as he covered her body with his hard masculine form and entered her moist, welcoming flesh. They moved together, savoring the wild ride. Mature and experienced, neither was hesitant, each striving to give as well as receive pleasure from the other. They moved together, their breath and hearts in unison as they claimed each other, wildly devouring the sweet ecstasy of their union.

Their lips parted only when each became so lost in the wonder of fulfillment that they could not contain their cries. Sensation blanked out the world surrounding them, exploded through their bodies, myriad feelings that left them breathless, with every muscle pulsating with pleasure.

Sidney reached up and clasped the intricately carved headboard, arching against the hard, turgid flesh filling her and felt him explode within her, filling her body with his seed. Electricity seemed to shoot through her and she knew in that moment that she had found what she had been hunting all of her life. Breathlessly she opened her eyes and looked up at the man panting heavily from his own climax. He was too beautiful to describe; she raised her hand and touched his cheek gently. Still too awed by what they had shared to allow the realities of the world to intrude upon them and far too content even to consider her rash actions in giving herself to a total stranger, in having unprotected sex, Sidney could only say a soft, "Thank you."

A tender smile momentarily played over her lover's full lips as he gazed down at her. His gaze seemed to delve into the darkest corners of her soul and see what she was now experiencing. After a long moment, he gave a shudder as if to push aside the tenderness within his own heart and his lips curled into a provocative, roguish grin. He arched one dark brow as he moved away from Sidney. "No need to thank me, wench. I know you're a bit long in the tooth, but you're as good as any wench half your age. Like myself, you've learned that getting older does have some benefits that the young can never understand."

Sidney could nearly hear her dreams of tenderness and passion shatter around her. The piercing shards released the liberated woman who had momentarily lost her way into a world that she knew only existed in the female imagination. She sat up and jerked the sheet up to shield her naked body from his gaze. The CEO of Herbal Health, Inc., looked directly into the stranger's eyes, intent on giving him a put-down that he'd long remember. Her fury raged as she eyed the monster before her. Every vile word she'd ever learned came to her tongue but she caught herself before uttering the last: Rapist.

Hating herself for the honesty she'd always prided herself in possessing in her business as well as personal life, Sidney looked away from the man who stood regarding her silently. How could she call him a rapist when she'd been a fully consenting adult?

"Wench, what has fired your temper?" the stranger asked, reaching for the pants he'd tossed onto the floor beside the bed. "You have nothing of which to be ashamed."

"Ashamed," Sidney choked out, her eyes snapping back to her lover's face. "If anyone should be ashamed, it's you, not me."

The stranger eyed Sidney as if she'd lost her mind and ran a long-fingered hand through his dark hair. "Ashamed? Me? Wench, you are brazen. You come to my bed and then expect me to be ashamed of taking what is so enticingly offered me when I awake and find you curled at my side, your arms about me and your head on my chest."

Sidney spluttered and scrambled off the bed, dragging the sheet with her. The liberated woman whose self-control didn't allow anything to affect her vanished, leaving only feminine ire. She faced her accuser, her blue eyes brilliant with anger. "How dare you! This is my room and you—" Sidney glanced about the room, searching for her niece. Her passionate episode with the stranger had made her forget entirely about Rina. She looked back to the man eyeing her as if she'd grown two heads. Eyes narrowing with suspicion, she asked, "What have you done with my niece?"

John looked down at the beautiful, rumpled woman before him and wondered at her sanity. True, he'd never laid eyes on her before this morn; true, he'd found more pleasure with her than he'd ever experienced in all his adventures with the opposite sex, but no matter how lovely or enticing the wench might be, he'd not allow her to accuse him of anything more than what had transpired between them. "Wench, I know not of what you speak. Be gone. Your hysterics tire me, and I have an ache in my head that makes me feel as if a herd of horses have run over me."

Sidney reached out and grabbed John by the arm, "Damn your headache. If you've harmed my niece, you'll have far more to worry about than just your head. Now where is Rina? She was right here in this bed when I came up last night."

"Wench, you begin to tire me. I know nothing of this Rina of whom you speak, and the bed was empty when I claimed it last eve." John's eyes widened as he recalled the previous night and the rendezvous at the Inn. He jerked on his shirt and

74

grabbed up his boots. He had to find Kane and apologize. Drinking and wenching were no excuse when so much was at stake. He started toward the door.

"You're not going anywhere until I know what has happened to Rina," Sidney challenged, following at his heels. She blocked his path before he could reach the door. Holding the sheet tight against her breast, she leaned back against the exit.

Exasperation flickered over John's handsome face as he looked down at her. "Woman, I have never laid an angry hand upon a female in my entire life, nor do I ever intend to do so. However, there are far more important matters to attend than your hysterics. Allow me to pass and we will part now with sweet memories of each other."

"Damn you. I don't care what matters you have to attend. I want to know where my niece is." The hysteria that he'd accused her of was now truly forming. "What have you done with Rina?"

John reached out and took Sidney by the shoulders. He set her aside as if she weighed no more than a bit of fluff as he muttered coldly, "Wench, you try my patience."

John opened the door and closed it in Sidney's face before she had time to regroup. He rubbed at the throbbing ache in his temple as he moved down the hallway to the staircase. He paused at the landing and frowned. The brandy he'd consumed the previous evening had been far more potent than he'd realized. His head felt as if it would leave his shoulders at any minute. And to complicate matters further, he was also having a hard time recognizing the furnishings of the castle he'd visited since childhood.

John shook his head to clear it but found nothing had varied from the moment before. The staircase wound downward to white and black marble tiles. The marble tiles he recognized, but that was the end of it. From the large chandelier hanging over the foyer to the intricately crafted table and chairs that offered a quiet resting place for visitors, nothing looked familiar.

Shirt flapping open, exposing his wide, bare chest, John made his way downstairs. He stood for a moment observing his surroundings. His face lit when he realized the reason for his lack of recognition. "Damn, I was far more into my cups than I thought. No wonder I don't recognize anything."

He chuckled to himself. He could now understand the accusations of the wench upstairs. Somehow in his inebriation, he'd managed to end up in the wrong castle and in the wrong bed. There was no other explanation. Somehow, he'd left Sedgewick in a drunken stupor and had come here. John glanced around and muttered, "Wherever here is."

Feeling far better, he strode toward the tall double doors. He didn't have any time to waste or to learn who his host for the night had been. Nor was he in any mood for a duel should it be required of him when the master of the household learned of what had transpired upstairs this morn. He just wanted to find his mount and get as far away from the mystery surrounding him as fast as possible.

The sunlight blinded John as he stepped outside. He raised a hand to his brow to shield his eyes against the brightness as he made his way down the steps. The loud blare of a hundred trumpets brought him to an abrupt halt.

"What the devil," John muttered as he turned and squinted in the direction of the terrible, head-splitting noise. It took a moment for him to focus his gaze. John felt his blood run cold. He swallowed hard, unable and unsure of what his next move should be. A bright red monster stood only a few feet from his legs, growling low in its throat, ready to attack.

At forty-eight years of age, John prided himself on the honors he'd won for bravery in battle, yet at that moment, staring down at the gleaming thing with silver teeth and burning eyes, he, John Edmond Clive, found cold sweat breaking out across his brow. He stared at the monster, unable to make a brave show with his heart trying to break free of his ribs.

"Will you get out of my bloody way! We have a tennis tournament to attend and we're already late!" the driver of the Jaguar shouted at John.

Heart pounding furiously, John forced his gaze

away from the mighty monster and to the voice. He gaped at the man and suddenly felt as if the brandy he'd consumed the previous night had done far worse to him than what he'd first assumed. He stared at the man riding the monster, wondering at his own sanity.

"Are you deaf, man? We're in a rush. Be a good sort and take yourself off!" the driver said, giving John a flippant wave of his hand.

John slowly raised his gaze to stare at his surroundings. Something like a scream of terror rose in his throat as he turned and vaulted back up the steps, burst through the doorway and ran back up the stairs. He slammed open the door to Sidney's room just as she was zipping her soft wool slacks. He looked about the room, searching for anything familiar, but found that his only reality was the woman who now walked toward him, anger sparkling in her eyes.

John closed the door behind him and locked it before turning back to face Sidney. He leaned back against the portal, making certain with his own weight that no one could come through. Ignoring the angry look in Sidney's eyes, he said, "What in the hell is going on here?"

"I'm not the one who is going to answer questions. You are. I want to know what you have done with my niece. She was here last night when I came to bed."

"Bloody hell with your niece, woman! I find myself in a strange bed with a strange woman and then think to leave this place and find myself confronted by monsters and demons." John eyed Sidney suspiciously as he took in her strange attire. Again he felt his blood chill. By some foul means he had managed to land himself in the hands of a witch. That was the only explanation to his quandary.

John stiffened as Sidney took another step toward him. He shook his head vehemently from side to side. "Stay back, witch. I'll not allow you to bewitch me further with your seductive beauty. I'll not allow you to take my soul in exchange for the pleasure of your body."

Sidney paused, suddenly questioning the man's sanity. From his expression, he seemed totally convinced that she *was* a witch. Shaken by the thought that he could be insane, she paused, wondering how to handle the situation without endangering herself, as well as finding out what he'd done with Katharina. She gave John a smile that she hoped was reassuring and spoke softly. "I'm not a witch. My name is Sidney Ferguson and I'm from the States."

John felt the urge to make the sign of the cross at the sensuous curve of her beautiful, enticing lips. She had to be a witch, because no woman had ever had such an effect upon him in his entire life. John stiffened visibly.

Noting his reaction, Sidney's smile faded. She could see he didn't believe a word she'd said, and she knew she had to convince him or she might never see Katharina again. "I'm no witch. You must believe me. All I want from you is to find out where my niece is. Did you put her in some other room, perhaps?"

"*No witch!* You bring me here during the night without my knowledge and then seduce me with your beauty before I have time to realize your intentions. Then you have your familiars set upon me when I try to escape."

Realizing that she wasn't breaking through his madness, Sidney knew she had to get help before he could do her harm. Once the man was in the hands of the authorities, then she could get Katharina's whereabouts from him. She smiled weakly and hoped she could appease him long enough to get past him and out the door. "I'm sorry you feel that way, because I assure you, I know nothing of witchcraft. However, I think all this can be straightened out if we go downstairs and see the manager. I'm sure she'll be able to explain everything to your satisfaction."

"I'll not move from this room—nor will you—before I know you won't send your familiars after me."

"How can I do that when I don't honestly know what has upset you?" Sidney asked, ready at that moment to do anything he asked in order to appease him.

"Look from the window. Your familiar is there. Call him away and I'll leave."

Wondering what in the world the man considered her familiar, Sidney crossed to the window and peered down at the courtyard, where several of the departing guests' cars were being loaded with luggage. She frowned. There were no cats or even dogs that could be a witch's familiar about the courtyard. "I'm afraid I don't see what you are talking about."

Gaining courage, John crossed to the window. He watched for a moment as the bellmen loaded the trunks and then grimly said, "There." He pointed down at the courtyard. "Your minions now feed the beasts."

Though she knew there was nothing funny in her present situation, Sidney couldn't stop herself from smiling at the absurdity of the man's accusation. She looked up at John's handsome face and felt a twinge of sadness. It was just her luck finally to find a man who could fulfill her every dream, and he turned out to be as crazy as a bedbug. Now all she could do was to convince him that he had nothing to fear from the automobiles that seemed to frighten him so much. Perhaps then she could get him to talk about what he'd done with Katharina.

"Do you mean you haven't seen an automobile before?" Sidney asked.

John glanced down at her. "No, if that is what your familiar is called. Until now I didn't even believe in witches. I thought Mathew Hopkins was insane for his belief, but no more. I am no longer a foolish innocent where evil is concerned."

"Honestly, I am no witch. Nor are the cars you see below my familiars. They are only machines that carry people from place to place. Surely you remember riding in one."

The sincerity in Sidney's voice touched John, oddly soothing his fear. He drew in a deep breath. "If you are no witch, explain how I came here when I was on my way to meet with my cousin last eve."

"I have no explanation for how you came to Sedgewick Castle."

"Sedgewick! Now you play me for a fool. Do you think I would not recognize my own cousin's home?" John pointed to the green lawn. "Look there, wench. Sedgewick has walls twelve feet thick surrounding the castle. Surely you cannot think to make me believe I am at Sedgewick Castle?"

Sidney's brow knit as she once more looked up at John. "This is Sedgewick Castle. The tour guide said the wall had been taken down during the eighteenth century because the castle was no longer needed as a fortress."

A chill rippled down John's spine as he looked sharply down at the woman beside him. An eerie sensation made gooseflesh rise on his arms as he quietly asked, "What day is this?"

"This is Saturday, February the thirteenth, 1993."

John paled and slowly shook his head in denial. " 'Tis impossible. Only last eve I was to meet Kane and—" John stopped himself before he could reveal his intended rendezvous with Charles II. He eyed Sidney critically for a long moment and fought the truth in her words. "You lie, wench. I have not traveled through time. No such thing can happen. The date is Wednesday, February 10, in the year of our Lord, 1651."

"It is impossible," Sidney said more to herself than her pale-faced companion. She, too, was fighting the concept that something strange had taken place. Dr. Harrogate's words flickered through her mind and she shook her head, denying what her eyes now recognized as the differences between her own attire and the man's standing next to her. He was dressed similarly to the men who had attended the banquet the previous night. However, his clothing seemed to have been made for him. And for the first time during all that had transpired between them, she realized that his pattern of speech was unlike any other that she'd encountered across England.

"No," she muttered, rubbing her temples as if to wipe out the dawning truth. As John had said, no one could travel through time—no matter what astrological conjunction transpired.

Watching her expression, John felt a sinking sensation. He glanced once more down at the courtyard and watched as several people entered the monsters and then drove away with no harm coming to them. There were no such contraptions in 1651. John looked back at the woman at his side. Their gazes met with the recognition of the truth. In unison they spoke: "It can't be."

Chapter Five

Katharina didn't move as the door swung open to reveal her captor. She felt helpless as he closed the portal behind him and crossed the chamber toward her. She had blundered into another time and had no earthly idea how to explain her presence to this man who accused her of being a spy. An apprehensive chill shimmered down Katharina's spine when he paused in front of her and folded his arms across his wide chest. He eyed her speculatively.

In the modern world Katharina felt she could have easily dealt with such an imposing man. She would have mimicked her Aunt Sidney. Sidney knew how to deal with the opposite sex in any situation. However, at the present moment Katharina wasn't so certain that even Sidney could hold her own with such a man and in such a time. In his world there was no women's rights movement, no equality among the sexes. And with the exception of a few remarkable women who had found their way into the history books, in this day and age women were considered little more than chattel by men. Independent females were ostracized from society and often accused of witchcraft.

Katharina drew in a steadying breath and glanced uneasily down at her clasped, white-knuckled hands. Until that moment, she'd forgotten about the legends surrounding Sedgewick Castle. The first witch had been burned at Sedgewick during the fifteenth century. The tour guide had emphasized how the woman had cursed the Sedgewick family as she died in the meadow only a short distance from the castle. Supposedly her curse had been the beginning of all the paranormal events that had followed throughout the centuries.

Katharina swallowed nervously. She might have blundered into a far worse situation than she'd first surmised. Her captor now believed her a spy sent by his enemies. To make him understand that she was innocent of his accusations, she'd have to tell him how she'd come to be in his home.

Katharina's confidence sank even further and her heart began to pound against her ribs at the irony. She was absolutely certain that her captor, a man born and reared in a time when people believed in witches, would immediately believe her explanation of traveling from the twentieth century because of some strange astrological conjunction.

The muscles in Katharina's belly constricted with dread as her imagination conjured up the image of the flames that would rise about her. The truth would not set her free. It would be the first step toward a fiery death. Katharina fought to control her shudder as fleeting bits of history flashed into her thoughts. Women had been accused of witchcraft for far less than saying they'd traveled through time. They had been tried and condemned for consorting with the devil if a neighbor's cow's milk dried up after they passed by the pasture.

A bubble of hysterical laughter tickled the back of Katharina's throat and she drew in a deep breath in an effort to keep it from escaping. She couldn't allow herself to give the man further evidence to use against her. She had to remain calm. She had to survive until she could find a way to return to her own time.

"Are you now ready to tell me who sent you here?"

Katharina glanced up at Lord Sedgewick, who stood so close that she had to bend her head back to look him in the eye. She swallowed back the truth and shook her head. "I am not a spy."

"Then, my mysterious lady, who are you and what were you doing roaming about my home uninvited?"

Katharina glanced nervously away from his scrutinizing gaze.

"Wench, I will have answers from you, one way or the other. I would prefer that you willingly give me the information that I desire, for I would not like to have to make my dungeon your permanent home."

Katharina jerked visibly at the threat. Kane smiled as he added softly, menacingly, "If you are not truly mad when you're put back in the cell, you will be in the near future. Strong men have lost their minds when the rats and vermin began to nibble at their flesh."

Unable to contemplate returning to the dungeon, Katharina rose to her feet and moved away from her captor. She needed space in order to breathe. His size and his unrelenting scrutiny seemed to press down on her like a heavy weight, making her thoughts bound here and there like a rabbit trying to avoid a hound. She had to get far enough away from him to remain coherent.

"Wench, you can't escape me. I will know the truth."

Katharina paused at the narrow window and glanced back at her handsome captor. "I don't know what to tell you. I can only assure you that I'm not a spy. My name is Katharina Ferguson."

A flicker of exasperation crossed Kane's face

and his lips tightened. "Then why were you sneaking about my home?"

"I don't know," Katharina answered honestly. She had no earthly idea why fate had suddenly gone berserk and sent her back in time.

Hearing the ring of truth in her voice, Kane frowned more deeply. "You mean you have no recollection of how you came to be here?"

Katharina nodded. It was true. She didn't know how she had come here. The only clue she possessed was what Dr. Harrogate had said about the astrological conjunction that had taken place the previous night.

"You have no memory of anything in your past?" Kane questioned. He had heard of such things happening to people. Often a loss of memory occurred when someone had suffered a hard blow to the head.

Katharina seized upon the excuse her captor had unwittingly given her and affirmed his statement with a nod. It was the only way. She would have to pretend amnesia until she could find a way to return home. "I know only my name."

For a long, thoughtful moment, Kane gazed down at her through his thick lashes. He searched Katharina's features one by one before he arched a dark brow in question. "Then why did you pretend to be mad?"

Katharina glanced away from Kane's black, assessing gaze and took in the bucolic scene below. "I was frightened," she answered, without voicing the rest of the thought: And I do feel as if I've gone mad.

Again Kane heard the truth in her voice and accepted her answer. He had seen things far more unusual than an overwrought female. And she was a woman. He'd learned females did tend to react strangely when under stress.

Kane glanced past his captive to the open fields beyond Sedgewick's granite walls. He had far more important matters to attend than to play nursemaid to a witless female, no matter how lovely. Because of her, he'd already postponed his meeting with Churchill to discuss their plans for the future. It was only a matter of time before they would rid themselves of Cromwell and his Roundheads. After a short rest to recoup from the past years of war, the aristocracy would put the religious fanatic where he belonged: six feet under the earth that had soaked up so much loyal English blood. His duty to his king was to ensure that when the time came, everything would be in place for Charles to return to England permanently.

Kane returned his gaze to his captive. He had no time for Glenville's schemes. And even should the wench be lying, she could do him no harm now. He had found her out before she could learn anything for Glenville to use against him. And once John returned from his carousing with his latest wench, everything would be back to normal.

Normal, Kane mused, turning his troubled gaze once more to the peaceful scene beyond the window. His eyes moved over the meadow past the field. That was where it had all begun. Because of the curse, his life had never been normal. He had been born one of the cursed Sedgewicks. Shaking the thought away, he said, "If you speak the truth, I see no reason for you to remain at Sedgewick."

A burst of relief swept over Katharina for a fraction of a moment. She was free. She was free to leave Sedgewick. Reality returned with the force of a physical blow. She couldn't leave Sedgewick if she ever hoped to find her way back to the twentieth century. She felt sure the key to her time travel lay within its ancient walls, and she had to remain here to find it.

"I can't leave," Katharina blurted out before she realized she'd spoken her thoughts aloud.

Kane frowned down at the woman he'd just freed. No matter what she said, she had to be slightly mad. She had protested her imprisonment; now she protested her freedom.

"Wench, I have no time for this game you play. There are far more important matters that need my attention. Be grateful for the freedom I have given you and be gone from Sedgewick."

Katharina reached out and placed her hand on Kane's velvet-covered arm. She moistened her dry lips and asked, "But where will I go?"

Kane shrugged. "Anywhere that pleases you."

"Surely you are not so cruel as to send me away when I can't remember where my home is or who I am." Katharina's voice reflected her mounting apprehension as she gazed up at Kane, her eyes beseeching his understanding.

Kane felt his blood stir as he gazed down into her beautiful face and wondered at his reaction to her. He'd thought he'd managed to conquer his emotions in the past few years. He'd sworn never to marry or to bring another Sedgewick into the world to suffer the curse. To keep his vow, he'd thrown himself into the politics of his nation, involving himself in every dangerous mission and every battle to fatigue his body and mind into forgetting that life offered far more than a lonely bed for men who did not have the Sedgewick name.

Now, after only a few minutes in her company, his mysterious captive had made his defenses crumble with a mere look. Even in her bedraggled state, she stirred him as even the well-dressed beauties of his acquaintance had never done.

The lines at the corners of Kane's lips deepened as he took hold of Katharina's hand and removed it from his arm. He straightened his sleeve, pretending a nonchalance he was far from feeling. He drew in a steadying breath and fought to regroup his defenses. He opened his mouth to refuse her plea, but the words that came out were far different from the ones he'd intended. "You may remain here for a few days in order to try to regain your memory. But then you must leave.

Your sudden appearance during the storm in the dead of night has already set tongues to wagging. And I need no other complication in my household. Is that understood?"

Relieved, Katharina smiled up at Kane. "Thank you. I will do everything in my power to leave here as soon as humanly possible."

Stunned by the power her smile had upon him, Kane cleared his throat. "Then I will bid you good day. I will have your evening meal sent up to you this eve. As for the morrow, you may leave this chamber, but I warn you now, I will not have you trespassing into my private quarters, nor disrupting my household with your wild tales."

At any other time she might have taken exception to his orders, but at that moment Katharina would have agreed to anything. Her need to remain at Sedgewick castle overrode her twentieth-century sensibilities. Katharina opened her mouth to thank Lord Sedgewick again, but he turned and strode from the chamber before she could voice her gratitude. She watched the door close behind him before she gave way to the trembling in her knees. She managed to cross to the bed before they collapsed beneath her. The past few minutes had completely drained her. She fell back on the bed. Mind and body numb, she stared up at the heavy beams overhead, unable to think or feel anything but relief. After a few minutes, her eyes closed and she slept.

* * *

Only a pale streak of gold remained of the long, tiring day as Kane unlocked the door and made his way down the corridor. Weary to the bone, he rubbed the back of his neck and stifled a yawn. After leaving his beautiful, unwelcome guest, he'd met with Churchill and then had set out to find John, to no avail. He'd ridden across the countryside, visiting every cottage and inn that might house his cousin. Unfortunately, there had been no sign of him. John had seemingly vanished off the face of the earth.

Spying the aged woman seated next to the closed door at the end of the hallway, Kane wondered what he or his family would have done without her and her family. She had been the anchor that had helped keep his life steady in many a storm. She had served Richard and himself loyally and without fear, just as her grandfather had done for the Sedgewick ancestor that had been the curse's last victim. Other than his King, Tilly and her son were the only people to know that the Sedgewick curse had again claimed another victim. Tongues wagged with rumors of the strange happenings at Sedgewick, but no one except Tilly and her son could ever confirm the truth of them. He need have no fear of such an event ever happening. All the gold in Britain couldn't bribe Tilly or Joshua to betray him, and he loved them like family for it.

Kane paused beside the chair and looked down at his old nanny. Gray head bowed, her double chin rested upon her ample breast. Her age and the long day had taken their toll upon her, and she snored lightly. Kane bent and gently placed a kiss upon her head. Instantly roused from her light doze, she jerked and blinked up at him, her rheumy eyes fighting to focus upon his features. She smiled in recognition and made to rise.

Kane laid a hand upon her plump shoulder. "Be still, Nanna. You've had a long day."

Tilly nodded, beaming up at the man she had tended since his birth thirty long years before. "Aye, me lord. 'Tis been a frightfully long day. He's been anxious to see you since learning of the spy you caught prowling about the castle last eve."

Kanè released a weary breath. He'd hoped the old woman hadn't carried the tale of his beautiful guest to his brother. It would have made his evening far less tiring. Now he would have to relate everything that had transpired to Richard, including their cousin's sudden disappearance and his unsuccessful attempt to find him. After the day he'd spent, Kane felt little like humoring his younger sibling. The eventful day had drained him emotionally as well as physically.

"There isn't anything to tell, Nanna. The girl isn't a spy, as I'd first believed. She's only a witless lass who's had some mishap to take her memory. She can only remember her name."

Tilly looked up at Kane and gave a doubtful "Humph!" She levered her plump body from the chair and picked up the walking stick that rested against the door frame before she continued mildly, " 'Tis a good-enough tale if ye believe her."

"And I do," Kane answered, hoping to put an end to the conversation about the woman who had managed to stir to life feelings he'd thought long dead.

His answer brought another "Humph" from the old woman. "It's to be expected. Young men have a way of overlooking certain things when a beautiful woman is involved." Tilly raised an arthritic hand and waved Kane toward the door. She smiled, revealing yellowed teeth. "Even if the gel is a spy, I'm pleased to see yer taken with her. It's about time some female roused yer senses. I'm not getting any younger, and I do want to hold yer babe in me arms before I meet me maker."

"Nanna, I'm afraid I'm going to disappoint you if you thought there was something between me and our mysterious lady of the night. The girl means nothing to me. No more than any other female under my roof. She will abide at Sedgewick only until she regains her memory," Kane said, unnerved by his elderly nanny's accurate accessment of his feelings. She'd had that ability since he had been a toddler. The woman could read him with a mere glance. It was uncanny how she could sense his moods, his pain. She knew his decision about marriage and family but she stubbornly refused to give up her dream of holding his child. And she made it known to him at every convenient opportunity.

"Me lordship, I hear yer words with me ears, but me ole heart hears other things. But no matter." She gave another wave toward the door. "Go on in to Richard. Me babe is expecting ye. He's on the prowl like a caged beast. He needs ye to calm him, to take his mind off other things that he finds to his liking."

"It's getting worst, isn't it, Nanna?" Kane said, all thoughts of his beautiful guest gone.

The old woman nodded sadly. "Aye. He feels things just like any other man. It breaks me old heart to watch him stare out the window as the maids pass. I'm afraid the time is nearing when neither of us will be able to appease him."

Kane hugged the old woman protectively. "I'm afraid of the same thing, Nanna."

Tilly patted Kane comfortingly on the shoulder. " 'Tis hard to carry such a burden. 'Tis also unfair. Yer a good man who deserves far more than you've been given."

Kane chuckled and released Tilly. "And you, old woman, have a biased view of me. I fear sometimes that you believe I could walk on water. I'm far more the devil than the saint."

Tilly gave another "Humph!" and said, "I know what I know. Now be gone with ye. I need to make certain that Joshua has prepared the blood pudding to me poor babe's taste."

Kane watched her waddle down the hallway toward the secret passage that led through the family crypt to the base of the thick castle walls. There an entrance to the tunnel had been constructed as an avenue of escape should Sedgewick's walls ever be breached by the enemy. However, the tunnel's exit, which lay hidden in the meadow, had served a far different purpose throughout the cursed generations of Sedgewicks. It seemed only fitting anyone leaving the castle by that means would find himself in the meadow where everything had begun so long ago. Many a bowl of blood pudding and other foodstuffs had been smuggled into the castle to keep the cursed Sedgewicks alive. It also served as a means to keep the family secret. Only his monarch and a few trusted retainers, such as Tilly and Joshua, knew of the passageway and how it was used.

Kane opened the door and stepped inside the dimly lit chamber. The glow from the fire and a candle on the side table were the only light. The heavy velvet drapes had been drawn over the windows to shut out the evening sunlight. The oppressive atmosphere did little to improve his mood as he crossed to the high-back chair in front of the fireplace. He paused and looked down upon the dark head bent over a book. Intent upon the volume, his younger brother had failed to hear his entrance. "What has you so enthralled this eve, Richard? You usually meet me at the door."

As Richard raised his head, Kane caught the

first glimpse of his brother's face, revealing star-tlingly beautiful eyes and a well-shaped brow and nose. However, as the light lit his features further, the horror of his grotesque mouth overshadowed the deep-set black eyes. Two huge teeth pro-truded through malformed lips, dwarfing the teeth that had never been allowed to form prop-erly because of the restriction of the jawline.

The look in Richard's eyes offset his mouth's evil twist. They smiled up at Kane in welcome. "Brother," Richard slurred, his frozen features making it impossible for him to speak normally, "this is a marvelous volume. Shakespeare has a way of seeing all sides of life. Good and evil."

"Aye. That he does," Kane agreed, crossing to the opposite chair. Too weary to carry the con-versation, Kane dropped into silence and stretched out his tired legs to the warmth of the fire.

Richard watched him, noting the lines about his mouth and eyes, the elegant play of firelight upon his handsome face. He admired and loved his older brother. He also envied him for his un-tainted beauty. And he wondered far more now, after today's reading, what it would be like to be able to go about in the world, to have women, to ride in the sunlight instead of under the full moon. Richard, his young body stimulated by his thoughts, quickly turned to the gossip Tilly had conveyed earlier. "Nanna said we have an unex-pected guest at Sedgewick."

Kane shrugged and nodded. "An unwelcome one."

"Why so?" Richard asked, wiping at the dribble of excess saliva that speech always created.

"I believed her a spy for Glenville until this afternoon. However, I'm not quite so certain now. She says she has no memory of who she is or where she came from and denies any charges of spying."

Richard's eyes lit with laughter, though the sound that escaped from him sounded more like a snort of disapproval. "Would you tell your enemy that you were a spy?"

Kane smiled at his brother, once again amazed by the boy's perception and humor. The world had smashed him in the face with horror, but he didn't feel sorry for himself. "I suppose you're right. But I still don't believe the wench is a spy. There is a certain honesty about her that I just can't explain. She's unusual."

Richard's raised brows made Kane shake his head in denial. "Not you, too! Not ten minutes ago, Nanna was nearly accusing me of having fallen in love with the wench."

"Well?"

"Well!" Kane burst out. "Well, hell's spells. Can a man have no peace? The wench has been under my roof for less than twenty-four hours, and you and Nanna have me in love. Can I not generously share the accommodations of my home with a mindless female without being harangued by the two of you?"

"I believe ye protest too much," Richard said, enjoying watching his brother squirm.

"And I believe I'll burn all your volumes by Shakespeare if you don't watch how you misuse his verse."

"What is this mindless wench's name?" Richard asked, slightly perplexed by his brother's reaction to his small jest.

"Katharina Ferguson," Kane said rising to his feet. He braced his hands against the intricately carved marble mantel and stared down into the flickering flames, leaving his back to his brother.

"Ah, Katharina. Another of Shakespeare's beauties. Is this one as beautiful?"

"How would I know? I've been too busy looking for that rogue cousin of ours even to consider the wench's appearance. This time John has gone too far. He's up and disappeared without a trace."

"John must have found himself a new wench and wants not to be disturbed." Richard chuckled.

"Disturbed. I intend to see that he tells me his every move once he comes back like the prodigal son, looking for my blessing for missing our meeting with Charles."

"John missed the meeting? 'Tis unlike him. Women and drink he will have, but he would not disappoint our King," Richard said, knowing much about Charles's quest from his brother's stories. Kane was his eyes to the world, since he was unable himself to take part in the history-making events.

"Aye. John disappears and the mysterious lady turns up on the same night. I only pray that one of our enemies has not lured him to his death with an enticing wench."

Sobered by his brother's revelation, Richard rose from the chair and crossed to his brother's side. He placed a hand on Kane's shoulder. "Do you believe the wench had anything to do with John's disappearance?"

Kane stared into the flames, remembering the look in the girl's eyes as she spoke. He shook his head. "No. I believe she is as bewildered as to how she came here as we are. I can only hope her memory returns and John shows up with that silly, sheepish grin that he always wears when he's done something we disfavor."

A tap sounded at the door, interrupting the brothers' conversation. The door swung open to reveal Tilly's huge son. Kane forcibly stilled a shudder of disgust when he saw the tray Joshua carried. The food was little more than gruel mixed with blood pudding.

Kane gave Richard's shoulder a brotherly squeeze. "Chasing after John has wearied me to the bone. I believe I will retire early tonight."

The light in Richard's eyes faded. "I had hoped we could go riding tonight. I need to be free of these walls, Kane."

"I understand how you feel, Richard, and I regret it. However, tomorrow night we will go. And I'll race you across the moor. The winner will name his prize."

Richard stuck out his hand, anticipation rekindling the warm expression in his ebony eyes. "Agreed. The winner will name his prize."

Richard watched his brother close the door behind him before he turned back to the tray of food. His belly rumbled from hunger and his loins ached for the prize he would name. Taking up the bowl, he turned his back to Joshua and began to slurp down the contents of his evening meal.

Her own scream jerked Katharina from the nightmare. She bolted upright, sweat pouring down her face, her mind clinging to the terrifying images of the dream. She rubbed at her wrist. The dream was still so vivid in her mind that she could feel the pressure of the ropes that bound her to the stake. Flames rose about her, eating at the hem of her gown as grotesque faces beyond the ring of fire and smoke taunted her with, "Burn, witch, burn.

Shaken, Katharina drew in a shuddering breath and buried her face against her knees in an effort to shut out the horror. She had thought herself capable of facing anything life could dish out, especially after losing her parents in the plane crash. But nothing had prepared her to confront beliefs that could jeopardize her very life.

Her mind still imprisoned by the nightmare, Katharina failed to hear the scrape of the wooden bar as it was raised. Nor was she aware that Kane had entered the chamber until she felt a gentle hand upon her bowed head. Katharina jerked and looked up at him, eyes wide and glassy, her face pale with fear.

The look on Katharina's face touched something deep within Kane. He had seen similar expressions on other faces when people realized he was one of the accursed Sedgewicks, one of the devils whose seed spawned vampires and witches. Men often feared him, believing he possessed powers far beyond those of mortal men. Women either found him repugnant or intriguing.

A rueful smile tugged at the corner of Kane's shapely mouth. He had found that being a Sedgewick could be either a curse or a blessing. While his heritage had ruined any chance of having a normal, happy future, *however* it had also kept his enemies slightly intimidated, because they feared that he possessed powers that could destroy them. Glenville was a prime example of such a man. He never attacked outright but used other devious means to accomplish his goal of gaining the Sedgewick fortune. The girl now looking at him as if he were a monster might be using just such a devious means.

Kane shook the thought away. No matter how mysterious her arrival at Sedgewick seemed, he didn't truly believe her to be in Glenville's employ. Call him a fool, but he believed her when she said she didn't know how she had come to be at Sedgewick. However, her strange speech as well as her reaction to him and her surroundings suggested that she was far from ordinary. She was beautiful and intriguing, and Kane again found himself physically responding to her presence though he had only entered the chamber out of concern for her welfare. Drawing in a deep, calming breath, he let his hand fall to his side. "I heard your cry. Is something amiss?"

Katharina moistened her lips and slid away from Kane. She needed to put as much distance between them as possible. In her present state, his gentle expression could easily be her undoing. With the horror of her nightmare still teasing her senses and the truth of her situation preying on her mind, she desperately needed comfort and reassurance. Everything within her urged her to surrender to her needs and seek out the comfort she craved, but she couldn't allow herself to be so foolish. She had to remember who she was and where she came from to survive. This man could condemn her to death as readily as he now offered comfort.

Katharina wiped the moisture from her upper lip and shook her head. "There is nothing amiss. I had a bad dream. Nothing more."

Kane smiled in understanding, recalling the terror that often accompanied his own sleep. He'd lived with it for sixteen years. The images often jerked him awake, sweating and trembling. Unfortunately for Richard and himself, the nightmare didn't end upon his awakening. He lived with the curse day in and day out.

Before Kane could respond, the clatter of china drew his attention to the doorway, where a young maid had come to an abrupt halt upon seeing the master of the household with the strange woman. She stood uncertainly upon the threshold, nibbling at her lower lip and balancing the large tray she carried. Facing the master of the house always made her nervous; seeing him with the beautiful woman in the tower, she was nearly speechless. She'd never seen a real, live witch before. Nor had she imagined them to be so lovely. She'd always thought witches to be vile-looking crones, like old Faline, who used to threaten her and her brothers when they threw rocks at her as she passed their cottage with her menagerie of animals. A chill went up the girl's spine. Her grandmother had warned them not to taunt the witch, but they'd not heeded her warning until her oldest brother, Luther, had come down with a strange ailment that had nearly taken him to his grave. Her Mam had had to call upon old Faline and give her their cow in exchange for her help to heal Luther. The thought made the young kitchen maid tremble.

"Chole, set the food on the table before you drop it, girl. I would hate for our guest to think we serve everyone off the floor." A smile touched Kane's shapely mouth as he glanced back at Katharina.

"Aye, me lord," Chole muttered and hurriedly crossed the chamber to the small table. The china clattered again as she set the tray down and turned back to the two people across the chamber. She bobbed a slight, awkward, hurried curtsey and nearly ran from the chamber, as if she too were being chased by Katharina's nightmares.

Easily recognizing the look on the girl's face, Kane's smile faded. His lips settled into a grim line. Chole's face reflected her fear. He'd not have her or any of his servants afraid of him or anyone else at Sedgewick. He had enough problems keeping Richard's presence a secret without rumors about a witch in residence. He looked back at Katharina. "Your evening repast, my lady. I'm sure you will feel far better after you've eaten. Perhaps by tomorrow you will be able to recall where you come from and can seek out your family."

Kane's gaze swept over Katharina once more, taking in her muddied, disheveled appearance. He frowned at the dirt encrusted upon her skin. "I'll have a warm bath sent up for you," Kane said before he turned and left the room, leaving a shaken and grateful Katharina staring after him.

Katharina heard the bar fall across the door at the same moment her stomach gave an angry growl of hunger. She realized suddenly how long it had been since she had eaten. Because of her headache the previous night, she'd only swallowed a few bites of the lavish meal. The last time she had truly eaten had been at breakfast in London, nearly thirty-six hours earlier.

"Thirty-six hours and a couple of hundred years," Katharina muttered at she scooted to the edge of the bed and got to her feet. Barefoot, she crossed to the table and looked down at the food the young girl had brought for her. She smiled appreciatively as the aroma of herbs touched her nose. The food looked exactly as it had at the banquet. Relieved that she'd not been served something that she didn't recognize, Katharina settled herself in the chair. Her mouth watered as she picked up the two-pronged fork and knife. She sliced through the meat and popped it into her mouth. The food came out as fast as it had gone in. She made a moue of disgust as she looked down at her plate, wondering if her captor had intended all along to poison her. The meat was spoiled. The cook had tried to use herbs to cover the strong, unpalatable taste of what she suspected to be venison.

Katharina picked up the glass of wine and took a deep sip, hoping to rid her mouth of the nasty taste of the meat. She clamped a hand over her lips to keep from spewing the liquid back out. Again her taste buds revolted from the assault. The wine, a deep, red ruby–colored drink, was far more potent in taste than the California wines she was used to drinking.

Katharina forced herself to swallow the mouthful and stared down at her plate. How would she ever survive to find her way back to the twentieth century if she didn't have food to eat? She picked up the piece of bread and looked it over carefully to ensure that no mold speckled its hard, crusty surface. She answered her own question aloud. "I won't."

Determination and her growling stomach ruling her, Katharina bit into the thick slice. She chewed with difficulty. It was a brown bread, crusty and tough. Without twentieth-century processing, it wasn't soft inside like the loaves she purchased at the bakery near her apartment. However, after a short time, Katharina began to enjoy the rich, natural wheat flavor.

She chewed and savored the bread as she tried to recognize the foods on her plate. It wasn't easy. She suspected the white round objects to be either potatoes or turnips. But the dark green mass she couldn't name unless she tasted it first. It was some sort of vegetable, of that she was certain. However, Katharina wasn't brave enough to confirm her beliefs.

Contenting herself with her meal of bread, Katharina wondered how long she could exist on bread alone. She prayed it would be long enough to find her way back to the twentieth century and fast-food restaurants.

Katharina chuckled to herself again at the irony of her thoughts and took another bite of the bread. An advocate of natural foods, she normally detested preservative-embalmed hamburgers and hot dogs. Now she'd give anything for a fat-laced cheeseburger and fries. Throw in a milkshake and a large slice of double chocolate pie; she'd be in heaven.

Katharina glanced about the chamber. It was twilight and the corners of the room had begun to darken, much like her thoughts. An iron holder held the remains of a burned torch, but she had no way to light it, nor any way to light the dark future she saw for herself should she be unable find her way back.

Chapter Six

The sun slowly sank into the west. Sidney sat staring at the man whom fate had mysteriously drawn through time. He stared back at her. After their acknowledgment that some strange occurrence had thrust him several hundred years into the future, they had mutually decided that it would be best not to tell anyone but Katharina of what had transpired. A hollow feeling settled in her stomach when she recalled searching for her niece earlier in the day. Katharina had vanished as mysteriously as the man across from her had appeared.

Sidney feared that Katharina's disappearance stemmed from the same weird phenomenon that had brought John into her life. Now, hours later, she had no earthly idea how to go about setting things to right, returning John to his time and bringing her niece back to the twentieth century where she belonged.

A pang of something akin to loneliness tightened in Sidney's breast. During the past hours, the bond she'd first felt between herself and her mysterious time traveler had grown. Logically, Sidney realized the emotions he had aroused couldn't be real, yet she had never experienced anything so powerful between herself and any other man. It seemed that time had separated her from her other half. Just being in his presence eased the longing that had been left unfulfilled even with all her success. And now fate was playing some malicious game with her, giving her a taste of contentment before snatching it away. She had to choose between the happiness she knew she could have with this man and the niece she loved like a daughter. It was unfair, but in truth she had no choice to make. She would have to find a way to send this man back to his time in order to bring her niece home. Katharina was a woman of the twentieth century and couldn't survive in the seventeenth.

A half sigh escaped Sidney as she pulled her gaze away from John's handsome face and looked out the window to the mixture of deep mauve and rose blending with the gold clouds to create a magnificent, bejeweled sunset. Her day had begun with the beauty of John's lovemaking, and now it ended with a beautiful sunset and the poignant knowledge that she had fallen in love with a man who would only be in her life for a short time.

"Sidney, 'tis time that we decide what must be done," John said quietly. He, too, was experiencing pangs of emotion that he'd never felt before. It was irrational how he felt about the woman he'd only known for a few hours, but everything that had transpired since his awakening in this new world had been illogical. He was still stunned by the things he'd observed from the window and found within the four walls of the bedchamber. He was emotionally and physically drained. While Sidney had searched for her niece, he'd viewed and heard things that his mind couldn't totally comprehend or accept. Sidney had tried to explain the strange phenomena he'd seen. Like the candle that sat next to the bed. She'd called it an electric lamp, telling him that something called electricity provided its light. In some manner they had fashioned a glass dome to cover the candle. Like any other candle, it was hot to the touch; however, the thing he found so odd was how it burned without fire being placed against the wick. He couldn't unravel that mystery and his mind wouldn't accept another explanation for the sudden burst of light that came with a flip of the fingers. There were other things that were equally as mysterious, but for the present, John didn't even want to consider them. He glanced at

113

the strange contraption sitting on the table beside the lamp. Earlier in the day, the small bells inside had rung and rung until Sidney picked it up and held it against her ear. A voice from the devil or some other ungodly place had come from it, but Sidney had seemed unruffled. It was truly too much for John to comprehend in only a few brief hours. He knew women, war and courtly intrigues, but for the life of him, he didn't know something as simple as how the people in this time had managed to make a candle without wax or had no fear of the growling monsters in which they traveled about.

Sidney glanced back at the man who had stolen her heart and nodded. "I know. And I've been thinking. The only person who might be able to help us understand this situation is Dr. Harrogate."

John lifted a questioning brow.

"I met him and his wife last night. He said that if anything strange was going to happen, it would be last night during the astrological conjunction." Seeing the puzzled look in John's eyes, Sidney smiled. "I'll explain all of it to you later. During the past few hundred years, many things have been discovered. However, at present, I need to find Dr. Harrogate. I pray he can give us the answer we seek."

"What if he can't? What will we do then?" John asked.

Sidney shrugged, unable to give a firm answer.

"We will do the best we can. I don't know what else we can do under the circumstances."

John could add nothing more. He was helpless to help himself. He was completely out of his element. He was an Englishman in England, but those who now inhabited Sedgewick were as foreign to him as if they had come from another world. A wry grin touched his shapely mouth. They did come from another world, one over three hundred years into the future.

Sidney got to her feet and crossed to the phone. She dialed room service and ordered their dinner. She glanced back to John as she put the receiver back on the cradle and smiled ruefully. "After dinner, I'll go and find Dr. Harrogate. I just hope he'll have the answer we need to get you back to where you belong."

John glanced around the room before he looked back to where Sidney stood. "Oddly, in some confounding way, I feel I belong here."

The warm look he gave her made Sidney's heart race. The breath caught in her throat and her stomach tightened. Sidney cleared her throat and said softly, "I have that same feeling."

A knock at the door broke the spell that had fallen over Sidney and John. She hurriedly answered it, and within moments John was seated before the small table that had been rolled into the chamber. He eyed the sparse offering on the plate the young man uncovered with something akin to disbelief. A man who had enjoyed all the bounties of life, John heard his belly rumble with the hunger of over three hundred years. He stared at his plate. He was being offered little more than a few crumbs of salmon scattered with a sprinkling of sauce and parsley. Relief swept over him as he realized that the bit of fish must be only the first coarse of the meal. He could wait another few minutes for the more hearty fair to be served. Satisfied, he cut the salmon in half and popped a piece into his mouth. His nose wrinkled in distaste at the mild taste. Even with the herb sauce, the flavor could not be compared to the fresh salmon that had been served at Kane's table.

John stilled at the thought of his cousin. Until that moment, he'd been so concerned with his own welfare that he'd forgotten how Kane would react to his disappearance. When Kane realized that he could not be found, he would immediately suspect Glenville of treachery. And then when his cousin Kane realized that Glenville wasn't responsible for his disappearance, his cousin would come to believe that he had deserted him and their mission.

John didn't like the idea of being viewed as a deserter to the cause, but he had learned early this morning that he had little choice in what fate decided to do with him. He shrugged—he could do nothing to change things at the present time. He needed to focus his energy on finding a way back to his own time. And he needed more than just a few bites of fish to preserve his strength.

John looked at the woman seated across from him. "Will the boy bring the rest of the food in a few minutes?"

Her thoughts on her meeting with Dr. Harrogate, Sidney looked at him, momentarily puzzled by his question; then she smiled. "I'll order something that will stick to your ribs a little better than this nouvelle cuisine."

Jon didn't know what nouvelle cuisine meant, and didn't ask. As long as Sidney ordered more food, he'd be satisfied.

Dr. Harrogate stared at the beautiful American. The previous evening he'd thought her highly intelligent. Now as she related her wild story, he questioned her sanity. He was certain she believed the man in her bedchamber had traveled from the seventeenth century, but it wasn't plausible. People couldn't travel through time, no matter how many different occurrences took place during the previous night's conjunction. History offered proof that the alignment of the three planets had often affected events previously. However, what Ms. Ferguson was telling him was totally impossible. No. Time travel was pure science fiction.

"Ms. Ferguson, I know you believe what you are telling me, but I must tell you it's impossible. Unlike some fictional space transporters, matter can't be transposed from century to century. And even if it could, it would throw everything out of

117

kilter when nothing filled the gap left by the disappearance of the time traveler. You see, there must be parallelism. Something must compensate for the absence of the matter," Dr. Harrogate said, assured his logic would make his new friend see the impossibility of her belief.

"How can you say it's impossible when you, yourself, came here to try to see a ghost? If the spirit of the dead can transcend time and space, why can't a human being do the same? And as for equality, my niece, Katharina, has been missing since our time traveler's arrival. I suspect she is the matter that you say must compensate for John's departure."

Dr. Harrogate shifted uncomfortably in his chair. The woman's own logic had him squarely boxed into a corner. He had to admit her theory might be right. Something as powerful as the conjunction might create a rift in time. He had come to Sedgewick expecting to see a few paranormal occurrences or some other extraordinary thing because of the meeting of the planetary giants. Now if what Ms. Ferguson said was in fact true, he had stumbled onto something far more exciting than seeing a mere ghost. Such findings would make him renowned in the scientific community. He envisioned his name engraved upon the Nobel Prize medallion; his heart pounding with surging excitement, Dr. Harrogate smiled at Sidney.

When she saw the doubt fade from Dr. Harrogate's eyes, relief swept over Sidney. "You believe me, don't you?"

Dr. Harrogate chuckled. "Do I have any choice? Alice has taken a liking to you, and she'd never forgive me should I accuse you of being deranged." He stood and proffered his arm to Sidney. "Shall we go? I look forward to meeting your young man." Dr. Harrogate chuckled again and patted the hand Sidney placed on his tweed-covered arm. "I believe I misspoke. If in fact he has come through time, he certainly couldn't be considered young."

Sidney's lips curled up at the corners and her eyes twinkled with mischief. "That is true, but he certainly wears his age well. He doesn't look a day older that forty-eight or -nine, give or take a few hundred years."

The two strolled up the stairs to Sidney's bed-chamber. Sidney tapped on the door and smiled reassuringly at Dr. Harrogate. A long moment passed before the door swung open to reveal the man Sidney had spoken about. Dr. Harrogate eyed John critically, searching out anything that might prove to Sidney that the man before them was only pretending to come from the seventeenth century. However, Dr. Harrogate could find nothing about the man to challenge Sidney's theory. If his clothing were only a costume bought to perpetrate the ruse, he had done a marvelous job. His clothes looked authentic down to his buckled shoes.

"Is this the man who's to help us?" John asked, eyeing Dr. Harrogate suspiciously.

Sidney nodded. "John, I'd like to introduce you to Dr. Harrogate. He is a professor of astronomy at Oxford."

Sidney's introduction didn't alter John's expression. "That's impossible. I don't know what this man has told you, but a professor at Oxford would be burned for such beliefs. It's witchcraft."

"Men!" Sidney said in exasperation. She tapped the heel of her hand against her forehead and looked at the two men eyeing each other warily.

John flashed her a puzzled look. "This man can not be who he claims. It has been many a year since I studied at Oxford, but things have not changed that much. If anything, since Cromwell usurped the king, the scholars adhere even more strictly to God's laws. The Puritans do not believe in astrology, nor many of the other sciences."

Sidney shook her head. This wasn't going to be as easy as she'd first assumed. She'd managed to convince Dr. Harrogate that she had a time traveler in her room. But how was she going to convince John of the changes that had occurred during the past three hundred years? "John, there isn't time for me to give you an English history lesson. We have far more important matters to attend, such as finding a way to get you back to your time and bringing my niece back to where she belongs."

Dr. Harrogate's excitement increased with each

word muttered by Sidney's visitor. It had taken a
few minutes for him to understand every word
that the man spoke, but it was becoming easier
with each passing moment.

"Excuse me," Dr. Harrogate said, interrupting
the two before an argument ensued. "It doesn't
truly matter what is now taught at Oxford. My
understanding of this spectacular happening is
that we are now missing Ms. Ferguson's niece. I
am assuming, as did Ms. Ferguson that she has
taken your place in your time."

John ran his fingers through his hair and
stalked toward the window. "I haven't the foggiest
idea about how I came to be here or of what is
now taking place in my absence." He looked back
at Dr. Harrogate. "Is there anything we can do
about this?"

Dr. Harrogate lifted one shoulder in a shrug. "I
don't really know. I need to do some research on
the matter. To my knowledge, nothing like this
has ever transpired before."

"How long do you think it will take?"

Dr. Harrogate shrugged again. "As you said so
eloquently a few moments ago, I don't have the
foggiest idea. All I do know is that if the astrological conjunction of last evening had anything to
do with your being here, we have only six months
before it ends."

"Six months!" John exploded. "I can't wait that
long. I have important matters to attend. Kane
needs my help."

"Well, sir, at present, you can forget about any other matter beyond trying to get you back to your time. Our every waking moment needs to be spent trying to discover how this phenomenon took place and how we can reverse it."

"Damn, you don't understand. England lies at risk. If Charles is not brought back to the throne, there may not be a time to go back to. Cromwell will destroy England."

Dr. Harrogate smiled. He could do one small thing to ease Sidney's time traveler's worries. "You need not fear for England, sir. The royal family still sits on the throne, and has since 1661."

John's dark brows drew together. He frowned darkly, suspiciously. "How do you know of such things?"

Sidney could contain her laughter no longer. "John, it's all in the history books."

John's face lit with understanding. "You mean that I can know the future of England from books?"

"No," Dr. Harrogate said bluntly, suddenly uncertain of what he'd just revealed. If he could help this man go back to his time, he must not take information back with him that might alter the course of history. Should such an event occur, the world as they knew it might disappear.

"What do you mean? You just said it is written down in books," John said, glancing from Dr. Harrogate to Sidney.

"Yes, it's written down, but until we better understand how you came here and how we can send you back, it's best that you just understand that for England's sake and your own, you must not know more than I've already mistakenly divulged. We can't alter the past, or we may regret it far more than any of us could ever imagine."

Comprehension widening her eyes, Sidney agreed. "He's right, John. We mustn't tamper with anything that could change history as we know it."

"Aye," John said, doubtfully, his curiosity eating away at him. It wouldn't be easy to remain ignorant when it could be so easy to learn the future of his family and country by only looking into a book. However, he didn't want to tamper with anything that might create a problem for him in his present situation or for those he'd left behind.

Dr. Harrogate breathed a sigh of relief. He'd have to be far more cautious in the future. Glancing at Sidney, he saw the same look of relief on her face. He smiled. "Then all that's left is to get started. I need to telephone one of my assistants and have him bring several of my books on cosmic phenomena down from school. Then we can begin to look for a way to reverse this strange happening."

Sidney looked from the aged countenance of the professor to the handsome face of her time traveler. Her heart ached at the thought of never seeing John again, but she was resigned to the

fact that she had no future with this man. She had
to keep concentrating on Katharina's welfare and
not her own happiness. It was the only way she
could accept losing John.

Chapter Seven

"I have to admit that she is a beauty," Churchill said, turning away from the window that overlooked the garden where his friend's houseguest sat in the warmth of the late-afternoon sun. He crossed the study and seated himself in the high-backed chair in front of Kane's mahogany desk. "But are you certain she is telling you the truth? 'Tis a strange tale to be sure."

"I'm as certain of her honesty as I am of anything else in this world gone mad. There is something about her that makes me believe her, though I am wise enough to have her every movement watched."

"I'm glad to hear it. I had wondered if she had put a spell upon you with her bewitching looks.

'Twould be hard to resist such a temptress."

"You think so? I hadn't truly noted," Kane lied, wanting to change the subject. Churchill's inquiries were coming far to close to the truth of how the girl affected him. His friend had not been the only one who had observed her when she visited the garden or strolled through the gallery looking at the centuries of Sedgewick family portraits.

Kane shifted uneasily as his body responded to the thought of his intriguing guest. In a way, she *had* bewitched him. He was intrigued by everything about her—from her manner of speech to the way she carried herself, so open and free. She seemed oblivious to the arts of seduction that every female of his knowledge had been taught from the cradle. She strolled freely about, never taking the demure little steps that women used to make their skirts sway in just the right manner to attract males.

Katharina was unique and far more interesting than any woman he'd ever encountered. And in that lay the danger. She had only been in his household for a week, and he found himself torn between his desires and his vow. Until her mysterious arrival, he'd thought he could easily master his male urges. He wanted no other to suffer as Richard and he had done during the past sixteen years. Kane shook the thought away and looked up to find his friend smiling down at him.

"I never thought to see it. But, damn me, she has gotten under your skin. I've often wondered when some female would capture your eye."

"Damn me, Churchill," Kane said, pushing back his chair and rising. "Can I not have peace in my own home?"

Before Churchill could answer, a noise at the door drew both men's attention. Completely unaware that the master of Sedgewick and his guest were in the study to overhear their gossip, the scrubwomen set to work in front of the double doors that stood slightly ajar.

" 'T' isn't natural, I tell ye. She be a witch, I vow. Showing up here in the dead of the night like a ghost or goblin. Now her's a-traipsing all over the castle like she owns it. I says she's bewitched the master, she has." The splash of water and a grunt accompanied the swishing of the scrub brush against the black and white marble tiles as the two women bent to their task.

"Aye," the second maid answered, her young voice reflecting agreement with the astute observations of her older friend. " 'Tis awful strange. Have ye watched how she keeps going about? As if she's searching for somethin'. 'Tis said she even counts the stones in the walls."

"Be off with ye!" said the first maid and gave a coarse crack of laughter.

" 'Tis a foolish witch she be if that were so. And 'tis only a fool that would think it. She's nay counting the stones in the walls. She be hunting the passageway to the underworld to bring up old Satan hisself. I've heard me mam speak of it. 'Tis said that Sedgewick was built over the doorway and Satan hisself cursed the family because the first lord wouldn't let him live here. Ole Nick needs a helpmeet to find the doorway and to let him free."

" 'Tis not what me pap said. Said a witch cursed the family, not the devil," the younger maid answered.

"No matter who put the curse on the Sedgewicks, I'm glad me bed is in the village. I want no part of ole Nick or that witch. Witches be evil souls, no good to man nor beast. They serve the devil and us poor weak mortals can only pray that they don't put a curse upon us."

"But why would His Lordship allow her to stay if she's a witch?" the younger maid asked as she slopped more water onto the tiles.

" 'Is Lordship is like any other man when it comes to a pretty wench. No matter how odd or evil a female be, a man is a weak creature when in heat. And I'm warning ye now, beware of His Lordship's lady. She can pretend sweet ways and no memory in that pretty head of 'ers, but she's a dangerous one, she is. Just listen to the way she talks. 'Tisnt nothing like the people talk here."

"How can ye be sure she's a witch, Maud? She talks different from the rest of us, but she is kind. She spoke to me so nicely in the hallway last eve. Acted just like I was gentry. Even His Lordship don't grace to speak to me."

"Aye, she be as pleasant as she is beautiful.

That's the way of a witch. They seems just like the rest of us poor souls until they gain their power over us. Then we either obey them and do their evil bidding, or they curse us God-fearing souls whose only sin is to work hard and have a few swigs of gin on fair day."

"Do you really, Maud? Me mam would skin me alive if I ever tasted such."

" 'Hat ye Mam don't know won't hurt 'er." Maud laughed. "Ye have a lot to learn, Smiggin. And I'm the one to teach ye. Let's finish here and go visit the kitchens to get a bite to eat. Perhaps 'Is Lordship's new stableboys will also have come in for a bite of cook's fresh bread." The maids' conversation drifted away as they hurriedly finished their chore and made their way to more interesting pursuits in the kitchens.

Kane sank back into his chair and began shuffling the stack of papers in front of him. He laid them neatly on his desk as the silence lengthened uncomfortably. Finally, he looked up at his friend and found what he feared. Churchill sat still, his face pale.

A chill of dread shimmered down Kane's back. Damn the blasted, superstitious maids and their inane chatter. In only a few moments, the gossip-mongers had managed to resurrect every ghost and goblin, demon and witch that he had fought to bury. And he could see evidence on his friend's face that even he was succumbing to the rumors.

Kane forced a smile to his lips and valiantly

tried to laugh off what they had overheard. "Well, it seems you're not the only one who has an opinion of my lovely house guest."

Churchill shifted uneasily in his chair. The hair at the nape of his neck stood on end. The realization that his earlier jest could well be true explained many things.

Lord Sedgewick, his longtime friend, was as much a mystery to him today as he'd been a decade earlier when they'd first met. Kane was a loyal man, dedicated to friend and country, yet he never allowed anyone too close to him. He protected his privacy as fiercely as he protected his king.

Churchill often wondered what drove Kane to live such a secluded life, and at times had even teased him about his reclusive nature. His friend had laughed at his jest, saying that he'd look to his personal life once Charles was back on the throne.

Churchill understood Kane's reasoning though he, himself, could not be as strong willed. He needed his wife and children about him. They gave him comfort where politics could not.

Churchill's thoughts veered from his mysterious friend to the small babe that lay in the elaborate cradle Churchill had made with his own hands. His son lay now wheezing and coughing his small life away. At times he turned blue from lack of breath. Another shiver raced up Churchill's spine. The physician said there was nothing more he could do. The babe would either outgrow the condition or die from it.

Churchill shook off the terror of his thoughts, determined to use every ounce of his willpower and his faith in God to see that his son lived and prospered to become one of England's great men. His tiny face might now be shadowed with sickness, but Churchill could see the future. He didn't doubt the outcome if only God answered his and Elizabeth's prayers. God had the power to protect the weak against the devil and his disciples.

He jerked as Kane slammed his fist down on the desk and rose to his feet.

"This is ridiculous," Kane snapped, crossing to the side table where a crystal decanter sat amid a circle of crystal glasses. He sloshed the amber liquid into a glass and lifted it to his lips. The brandy burned his throat, yet it eased some of the tension that had his muscles tied into knots.

Finding his voice at last, Churchill asked, "Could it be true, Kane? Could the girl be a witch?"

"Have you lost your wits, Winston? The girl is no witch, only an unfortunate soul who has no memory of her past. Nor are there any witches or goblins anywhere else in my home. They only exist in the tales that the villagers spout around their fires late at night."

"Kane, I am your friend and would see no harm come to you. You must realize that 'tis strange the way you have allowed the girl to come into your home. 'Tis best for all concerned that you soon rid yourself of her."

Kane flashed his friend a heated look before downing the last of the brandy. He calmly set the glass back on the table before he crossed to his desk and sat down. He looked at Churchill for a long, tense moment before he quietly asked, "Do you dictate who I shelter under my roof?"

Churchill's color rose. "I didn't mean to suggest such a thing, Kane. I only had your best interests in mind."

"Then allow the matter to rest, Winston. The girl is my concern and no one else's. And I will suffer the consequences if I have misjudged her. We have been friends for well over ten years, but test not our friendship again on this matter."

"Forgive me, Kane. I know Glenville would feel no compunction at using the most devious means to destroy you, even to the point of asking the devil's help if necessary. He'd sell his soul to see you brought down."

"I am aware of his hatred for me. I will not give him the opportunity to destroy me, especially if he thinks a woman's charms can do such a thing. No woman can sway me from what we have set out to accomplish. I work for the good of England and Scotland. None of us has a future if we don't succeed. Cromwell will destroy all of us if he continues to rule England."

"I understand, but I still have concerns. Yet I

will not voice them again. I have far too many other worries to attend."

"Young John?"

"Aye. The babe is no better, and my lady fears the worst. The illness seems to consume his small body a little more each day." Churchill balled his hand into a fist and struck the chair arm. "I know not what to do. The physician said he might grow out of the illness if he can manage to live that long."

Churchill got to his feet. He needed, wanted, to do something to help his son, but he was helpless against the enemy that ate away at his child's life. He reached for the wineglass sitting on the small table beside his chair. Like his friend only moments earlier, he downed the liquid in one gulp.

" 'Tis my turn to ask your pardon, Winston. I should not have chastised you when you have so much upon your mind. You and your family will have my prayers."

Churchill smiled and extended his hand to Kane. "It seems this day has us both on edge. 'Tis best that I say my farewells before either of us manages to insult the other completely. I will send word as soon as I hear from our friend in France. And should my contacts learn anything about your cousin's whereabouts, you will be notified immediately."

Kane's frown returned. "I have begun to fear the worst. In truth, Winston, I fear I shall never see John again. In all his dallying, he has never stayed away this long. Our enemies will pay for their treachery. Be assured, John's death will not go unpunished."

"I will be at your side when needed. John was my friend as well. Now I bid you good day."

"Give Lady Elizabeth my regards and tell her my prayers are with you."

"Thank you, old friend," Churchill said as he picked up his high-crowned beaver hat and settled it upon his head. Its jaunty angle was a silent protest to the Puritan clothing and lifestyle demanded by the Roundheads. He gave Kane an equally jaunty smile before closing the study door behind him.

Kane watched his friend through the window as he passed through the gate and turned his mount in the direction of home. He knew his friend was right. He had to rid himself of his beautiful houseguest before her wanderings took her into the east wing. Kane frowned and absently rubbed at the furrows across his brow. Katharina seemed to have brought life back into Sedgewick merely with her presence. And in all honesty, he hated to see it go back to the gloomy old pile of stones that had existed before her arrival. But he had no choice. Tomorrow he would speak with her. The day had progressed too far for him to put her upon the road. Though he had to be rid of her, he didn't like the idea of her being caught in the dead of night without a roof over her head.

Satisfied with his decision, Kane turned to the task of finding information that would lead him to his cousin. The day was still young enough for another search.

Katharina watched the two riders cross the meadow and disappear into the woods beyond. Though it was close to midnight, the light from the full moon illuminated the meadow as if it were day. She could easily discern the master of Castle Sedgewick even from such a distance. His powerful physique dwarfed those who served him. In the short time she'd been a guest at Castle Sedgewick, she'd noted only a few of Lord Sedgewick's servants who could claim such stature. However, it was not only her host's height that set him apart from his men. He held himself with an inborn pride. He possessed the confidence of those born into a privileged class.

Katharina watched the empty meadow for a moment longer, wondering what it would be like to have such confidence. She couldn't stop another thought from teasing her mind: What would it be like to be loved by a man such as Lord Sedgewick?

Katharina tried to push the thought away. She'd done her best to avoid it since the night she'd seen Kane Sedgewick in all his naked glory. Her life was complicated enough without having her heart involved with a man three hundred years her senior. However, she couldn't deny that

Kane Sedgewick roused an infinite range of emotions—emotions that she hadn't known to exist. She'd never felt the fire that seemed to course through her veins just at the thought of her intriguing host.

Lord Sedgewick was a man of mystery. Since being given her freedom of his home, she'd learned little about him. No one volunteered any information about her host or his family. However, she had learned one thing: Kane Sedgewick, the master of Sedgewick Castle, had the loyalty and respect of those who served him.

Katharina frowned. It was odd that such a man didn't have a pack of females baying outside his window day and night. Money and power—with the added benefit of a face and body to die for—would make most females drool. However, from her observations, he seemed a lonely man who wasn't close to anyone, male or female. He kept to himself much of the time. After seeing to his daily affairs about his estates, he secluded himself in the east wing, where no one was allowed except a few trusted servants.

The east wing. The thought set Katharina into action. Resolutely, she turned away from the window and crossed to the door. Quietly, she eased it open and peered into the hallway beyond. As she had hoped, all was quiet. No guard had been posted at her door, nor was there any sight of the maid, Chole. Chole had dogged her footsteps since she'd been allowed to roam freely about Sedgewick.

Freely! Katharina nearly snorted in disgust. She'd been allowed her freedom as long as she didn't want to visit the castle's east wing, where Lord Sedgewick's quarters were located. And that was exactly where she had to go. It was only logical, if such a thing as logic still existed in her upside-down world, that she would find her way back to her time in the same place where she'd arrived in the seventeenth century. That had to be where the passageway existed.

Katharina felt like a mouse scurrying furtively along the hallway. She'd had no luck getting to the east wing during the day, though she'd tried every excuse that Chole might find believable. She'd failed. Chole's loyalty was to the master of Sedgewick Castle, not to the strange woman who'd appeared out of nowhere. Now all that she could do was pray she'd not be discovered trespassing in Lord Sedgewick's private domain once again.

She could well do without another sojourn in the dungeon. The thought made Katharina shiver, but it didn't slow her steps. She had to take any risk to get back to 1993. Her stomach growled in accord.

Nerves on edge, Katharina found herself holding her breath at each tiny creak of the floorboards beneath her feet. Her heartbeat drummed in her ears, drowning out all sound as she neared the end of her journey. Sweat beaded her brow and upper lip as she came to the door that led into the east wing.

Hand shaking, Katharina turned the latch. The well-oiled door swung open to the shadowy hallway. Thick Aubusson rugs silenced her steps as she made her way along the passage in search of the doorway to Lord Sedgewick's quarters.

"Please," she murmured as she paused outside the chamber where she'd first seen the master of Sedgewick Castle, "let me find the passage here, tonight."

Illuminated by the light from the beeswax candles burning in the gold candelabra on the side table, the hallway looked as it had a week earlier. Katharina began to explore every nook and cranny that might hold her escape. She looked behind portraits and tapestries. Finding no passageway hidden there, she began looking at each stone, searching each crack. She explored the rough surfaces with her hands, trailing her fingertips along the grooves where the stones had been joined. Finding only mortar and granite, she became frantic. Heart pounding against her ribs, she pushed against the wall. "It has to be here. It has to be here."

"What has to be here?"

Katharina tensed with dread as she slowly turned to look at the man who stood scowling at her. Completely absorbed in her search, she'd failed to hear the door to Kane's chamber open behind her. She swallowed hard at the piercing look of condemnation he directed at her. In the ebony depths of his gaze, she could easily read the accusation and the fate that was to follow. Panicking, Katharina stuttered, "I-I-I can explain."

"Perhaps you could, if given the opportunity. However, you have trespassed upon my generosity for the last time, wench. I offered you the hospitality of my home, and you have gone against my direct orders. I vowed to see you in the dungeon should I learn you had played me false with your tales. I gave you my trust only to find betrayal at the first opportunity."

"No," Katharina said, shaking her head vehemently from side to side. "I didn't lie to you. I'm not a spy."

Kane's long-fingered hand shot out to capture Katharina's arm. Feeling a sense of déjà vu, she instinctively jumped back out of harm's way. She couldn't allow him to imprison her again. Once she was in his power, she knew what would happen. She'd find herself in a far worse predicament than when she'd first come to Sedgewick.

"No," Katharina said, backing away from Kane. "You have to let me explain."

"The time for explanations is over," Kane said, blocking Katharina's path before she could bolt down the hallway. He captured her easily, his long fingers grasping her upper arms. His black-ice gaze seemed to pierce her soul as he looked down at her. "I was a fool once because I believed your wild story of not being able to remember. Your tales will not work again. Glenville will find his hireling hanging at the fork of the road. Your corpse will serve as a warning to the next spy he despatches to Sedgewick. It will become a gruesome reminder to those who seek to destroy me and mine."

Katharina surrendered to the fear destroying all logic. She threw herself against Kane and wrapped her arms tightly about him. "Please. I'm no spy. And I don't know how I came here, because I'm not from your time. I'm supposed to be in the twentieth century, and I want to go home. I just want to go home."

The tears she'd been holding at bay for so many trying days now surged forth with the force of a volcanic eruption. She buried her face against Kane's chest and sobbed. She'd tried to be strong, to be like Sidney, but she needed comfort, needed to feel protected against the nightmare she couldn't escape: the horror of finding herself in a time and place so unfamiliar. Like a child lost from her parent, she didn't care who gave the comfort, only that she received it.

Startled by her outburst and the sudden reversal in who held whom captive, Kane stared down at the shining head pressed against his chest. He hadn't understood a word she'd uttered, but her sobs seemed to pierce his very soul and then echo throughout his lonely body. Bewildered by the strange surge of emotions filling him, Kane stood transfixed. He didn't know what to do or say. This was an entirely different situation from any he'd ever faced in his life. He had fought many a battle for his king and country. He had seen death and mutilation, seen his friends blown asunder by cannon fire. He had dealt with life as one of the cursed Sedgewicks, yet nothing had ever prepared him for the utterly helpless feeling that this one woman created. She held onto him as if he were a safe harbor in a storm, not her enemy.

Something seemed to break within Kane. Her sobs reached deep within him, wrapping themselves around the lonely man hidden beneath his confident, aristocratic exterior. They overpowered the extacting control he maintained over his life, sweeping away everything except a spiral of heat that melted everything in its path. With each breath she released through trembling lips, the man born of flesh and blood emerged. The saint, the tortured heir of Sedgewick, fell to the wayside as the hunger for life claimed him in its unmerciful grip. The need to feel alive, to feel himself deep within the desirable woman who clung to him, overshadowed all vows to end the Sedgewick curse. No longer able to deny himself or the emotions he'd managed to keep buried within his soul, Kane, too, surrendered.

He enclosed her in his arms, pressing her tightly against his pounding heart. He dropped tentative kisses upon her head as he murmured,

"Hush, sweeting, you're safe. No one will harm you."

Katharina's tears slowed as she savored the comfort he gave. She snuggled closer, her body molding itself against his as if they were two statues carved from the same block of marble. All thoughts except those of the man who held her vanished into the night. She felt no fear, no need to find her way back to the twentieth century. And she realized with a dawning of understanding that within this man's arms she could feel secure through eternity.

Slowly Katharina raised her face to look at Kane. Lashes bedewed with tears, she gazed up into his eyes and found the answer she sought. Within the ebony depths that only a short time ago had held only icy rage, she saw a fire to equal the one that now burned within her own soul. Her heart raced as she raised her hand to touch the cheek that had only a short time ago looked made of inflexible steel as his expression showed anger and distrust. She touched him, awed that steel had turned to warm flesh. She caressed him, rubbing the pad of her thumb against the stubble of dark beard that shadowed his cheek.

Katharina thrilled at the response she felt and saw. Like a magnificent animal, Kane closed his eyes, savoring her touch. His arms tightened about her, pressing her even closer to his aroused body.

For the first time in her life, Katharina experienced the overwhelming power of her femininity. Never had any other man made her feel so totally a woman.

Kane's reaction to her touch made her realize what had been lacking in all her previous relationships. There had never been the pure animal magnetism that drew her and this man together. It was completely natural—as natural as the wolf or the eagle finding its mate. They needed no courtship, none of the games civilization had ordained to take place before allowing consummation. All the essential elements were already there. And all that was necessary to meld their two souls was their physical union.

Freed completely by the knowledge that fate had inexplicably entwined her destiny with this man's and that it felt totally right, Katharina whispered, "My Lord Sedgewick, will you make love to me?"

Eyes warm with desire, Kane looked down at Katharina. Something akin to a shy smile touched his lips in answer. He could not verbalize what he wanted to say. The emotion constricting his throat was too great. He lifted Katharina into his arms and carried her across the threshold into his chamber. He kicked the door closed behind them and strode to the tall four-poster canopied bed. The candle on the bedside table flickered as he laid her upon the soft down mattress. For a long moment he stood beside the bed, looking down at her, savoring her beauty as well as the emotions she'd aroused within his soul.

She lifted a beckoning hand to him that he could not deny. He went to her, pulling her into his arms. He took her lips for his first taste of her.

The joining of lips sent a current of molten fire sizzling through Katharina and Kane. Like the lava in a volcano, it came from the very core of their beings, forming new worlds that neither had ever known, new feelings that neither had ever experienced. As new and pure as the beginning of time, they came together. There was no need for foreplay: they were already at the height of arousal. Buttons snapped and seams opened as they disrobed each other in haste. They tossed their clothing unheeded to the floor. Centuries had kept them separated but they would not allow another millionth of a second to keep them apart.

Kane covered Katharina with his hard body and she opened to him, drawing him deep within her. Arms entwining his corded neck, she moved with his thrusts, savoring each as it took her toward fulfillment. A cry was torn from Kane as he arched his back and thrust into Katharina to release his seed into her welcoming womb.

Katharina's own moan of ecstasy accompanied Kane's as waves of pleasure radiated outward from the core of her femininity. It seemed to encompass her entire being as she held onto her lover, pulsing with it, stroking and caressing Kane intimately as he, too, pulsed within her.

Breathing heavily, Kane lay over Katharina,

afraid to move away, fearful that any movement would end the dream and he would awake to find that everything he had just experienced had been only an illusion born of his loneliness.

Savoring the glow left by their lovemaking, Katharina gently stroked Kane's dark hair back from his damp brow. She entwined an ebony strand about her finger as she gazed up at the thick velvet canopy overhead and savored the thought that she had at long last found a man worth loving. Kane Sedgewick was a man to whom she could freely give her heart, without fearing he was using her to get at her aunt's wealth.

Then reality crashed in with the force of a sledgehammer, shattering the golden glow left by their lovemaking. Ugly shadows descended, obscuring the future that might have existed had she come from the same time as the man in her arms.

Katharina's fingers stilled in Kane's hair, and hot tears of grief crept to the corners of her eyes. They ran down the sides of her cheeks to dampen her hair as she lay holding the man she loved.

What she had just experienced was a momentary illusion. How could anything come from it when they were separated by hundreds of years? She had blurted out the truth, but so much had transpired in such a short time, she wasn't certain if Kane had truly comprehended her confession. It was nearly an irresistible temptation to allow him to believe she was a woman of his own time. She had found the man of her dreams, but she was wise enough to realize that nothing could be built on a foundation of lies.

After what she'd just experienced, she had no desire to go back to the plastic world of the twentieth century. She had found her destiny. However, she didn't know what fate had planned for her in the future, and she had to make Kane understand how she had come to be in his life. It was the right thing to do.

Kane felt Katharina's tension and eased his body to her side. He raised himself on an elbow and looked down at the woman who claimed his heart and soul. She might be all he suspected, but he couldn't deny his heart. He had fallen in love with the woman his servants had named the mysterious lady of the night.

A frown knit Kane's brow. He'd failed to honor his vow to end the Sedgewick line. He had taken this beautiful woman to his bed and had spilled his seed within her. Even now another Sedgewick might be growing within her womb. A moan of something akin to horror escaped Kane. He couldn't stand to look into her eyes and know the damage he had done to her. His lack of control might have sentenced the woman he loved to a life of hell on earth.

Feeling the need to bolt, Kane rolled away from Katharina and rose to his feet. His demons ate away at his heart as he strode across the chamber and poured himself a glass of brandy from the crystal decanter on the mahogany side table. Unable to look at Katharina, he stared out into the moonlit night. In the distance, he could see Richard and Joshua returning from their midnight ride. Kane closed his eyes and clenched his jaw against the sharp pang of guilt that shot through his chest.

Wounded by the look she'd seen in Kane's eyes as he left her alone in the tall bed, Katharina realized she had to make him understand that she hadn't meant to lie to him, that she hadn't betrayed his trust. Crossing to where he stood with his back to her, she wrapped her arms about him and pressed her cheek to the tanned expanse. "Forgive me, Kane."

Kane did not turn to look at her, but Katharina felt him draw in a shuddering breath before he said, "I am the one who ought to ask your forgiveness, Katharina."

The tone of his voice sent a chill of apprehension rippling down Katharina's spine. "No. I need your forgiveness for lying to you. But I didn't know what else to do in my confusion. I wasn't even aware of what had happened until after you had me locked into the tower room. Then I feared you'd have me burned at the stake for witchcraft should I tell you the truth of my situation."

The furrows across Kane's brow deepened with his confusion. "What drivel do you speak? I would never have you burned at the stake. I protect what is mine, but I am no barbarian, Katharina."

"I know that now. But when I first arrived, I

could not be certain of anything. I am completely out of my element in the seventeenth century. It's bewildering to find yourself three hundred years in the past. And I understand that it's hard for you to accept what I say because of my pretending to have lost my memory. But you have to understand, it was the only way I knew to protect myself. You thought me a spy come to harm you, and I had no idea how or why I had come here. Now I think I know. It was to find you."

Kane unclasped Katharina's arms from about his waist and turned to look at her. He stared down into her eyes, searching for the madness that made her speak of the impossible. Yet he found only the soft look he'd seen as they made love. Another pain ripped through his heart as he pulled Katharina into his arms and laid his cheek against her shining, tousled hair. Tears came to his eyes. He was the cursed Sedgewick; not Richard. Beyond having to carry the secret of his brother to his grave, he now had given his heart to a woman whose madness equaled that of his ancestors.

In that moment, Kane felt like raising his clenched fist toward the heavens and cursing God. This beautiful creature had been sent into his life only to add to his torment.

Katharina sensed Kane's agony. She leaned back and looked up into his tortured face. "Kane, you do believe me, don't you? You understand why I said what I did. I couldn't tell you that by some quirk of fate I had managed to travel more than three hundred years back in time."

Kane nodded and forced a smile to his lips. "I believe you, if that is what you believe, Katharina."

"If that is what I believe?" Katharina said, realizing with a start that he was humoring her. Anger sparked. "You don't believe a word I've said, do you?"

Accustomed to dealing with volatile members of his own family, Kane repeated, "I do if that is what you want me to believe. Katharina, against my will and better judgment, I will love you even if you tell me you can fly."

Katharina pulled herself free of Kane's arms and crossed to where her torn gown lay at the foot of the bed. She jerked it up and wiggled into it. Holding the unfastened bodice demurely over her breasts, she shot him a heated looked. "Damn it, Kane. For your information, I have flown before. And I didn't have to sprout wings to do it. Anyone can fly wherever they like in my time."

The unfairness of his position sparked Kane's own anger. He glared at the madwoman who claimed his heart. Bloody damn! He loved her, but he'd not give in to her madness himself. "Pray tell, madam, how do these people in your twentieth century fly without sprouting wings?"

Tears of frustration sprang into Katharina's eyes. "By airplane, damn you." She swiped at her eyes and her lips began to tremble as she looked at Kane. "I wanted to tell you the truth, and now you think I'm as crazy as a bedbug. But I'm not, Kane. By some strange quirk of fate, I've ended up in your seventeenth century."

Like a breath of icy winter air, a chill rippled down Kane's spine. When he'd first questioned this woman, he'd believed her story. Again he felt the truth in her words, even though he knew the truth was an impossibility. No one could travel through time. That was as mad as believing a person could fly without wings. "What proof can you offer to substantiate your story, Katharina?"

Katharina slowly shook her head. "I have only my word."

"Your word, my lady, seems to lack the truth. If you recall, you told me that you had lost your memory and didn't know how you had come to be in my home."

"I didn't know how I had gotten from 1993 to 1651. But I never said I had lost my memory. You assumed it when I said I only knew my name."

"But you didn't deny it."

Katharina's cheeks heated and she nodded. "That is true. But as I've explained, I didn't know what else to do. I was afraid, Kane. Can't you understand what it is like to be afraid? I come from a world where they haven't burned witches in nearly two hundred years, a world where women have the same rights as men. What would you have done had you been in my place?"

"I would at least offer some proof of what I claimed."

"I have nothing to offer. You took my only possession the night I arrived. I now have only my word to give you."

"You came with nothing but the gown on your back."

Katharina again shook her head. "No. I also had my nightgown and my tote bag with me when you took me to the dungeon."

Kane's face lit with recollection. He remembered tossing the bag aside as he strode down the passageway. It would still be where he'd dropped it, because no servants ever entered the family wing without his express permission. And had Joshua or his mother found it, they would have brought it directly to him.

Kane crossed the chamber and jerked on his pants. "Wait here until I return." He strode toward the door.

A moment later Katharina was left alone to wonder at his sudden departure. Her knees seemed to turn to water beneath her, but she managed to cross to the high-backed chair in front of the fireplace before they completely gave way. Breathing deeply, she laid her head back and closed her eyes. She didn't know what Kane intended. He had rushed from the chamber without any explanation. He could even now be summoning the guards to come for her.

Before even worse thoughts could evolve, Kane

strode back through the doorway, tote bag in hand. He crossed to where Katharina sat and held it out to her.

"My lady, provide your evidence."

Katharina's hand shook slightly as she reached out and took the tote bag Sidney had made her pack. She murmured softly beneath her breath, "Please let there be something here to convince him of the truth."

"What is it you say?"

Katharina shook her head. "I was only praying that I would find something in this mess to prove the truth to you."

Kane chuckled humorlessly, "So, even three hundred years into the future, people still seek to use God to get their way?"

Katharina shot Kane a quelling look. "People will always need divine intervention when they run into such formidable foes."

Her words sent a chill down Kane's spine, but his voice didn't reflect any of the turbulent emotions sweeping through him as he said, "Then we are enemies, my lady?"

"No," Katharina said, her hands stilling on the half-opened bag. "Never. No matter what you decide to believe of me, I never want us to be enemies, Kane. I have come back in time some three hundred years to find you, and I would travel another three if only I could make you believe what I say is true. I want no lies between us. Call me mad, but I want everything that happens between us to be based upon honesty."

Another shiver shot down Kane's spine as the thought of his misshapen sixteen-year-old brother clouded his mind. She spoke of honesty, yet he could never reveal the truth that lived only a few doors away, even to the woman he loved. Neither his love nor anything else would be able to keep her at Sedgewick should she ever learn of the Sedgewick vampire.

Her attention back on the contents of the tote, Katharina failed to see the pain in Kane's eyes. She plunged her hand into the bag and pulled out her travel hair dryer. She looked up at Kane as she held it up. "Ah-ha! See."

Jerked away from his morbid thoughts, Kane looked at the strange thing in her hand. Brow furrowing, he asked, "See what?"

"This. My hair dryer. You don't have anything like it in the seventeenth century."

Kane took the object from Katharina and carefully held it up. He turned it from side to side, upside down and peered down the round cannon-like nozzle and then looked back to Katharina. "I agree with you, my lady. I've never seen anything like this. However, there is much in this world I've yet to see. I can't see how you can get even a curl wrapped about the contraption. It must take a long time to dry your beautiful hair, lock by lock."

What a fool she was! In her rush to make Kane believe her, she'd forgotten that an electric hair dryer wouldn't mean anything to him. It was only a smooth gun-shaped device connected to a long cord. A cord that was meaningless without twentieth-century electricity.

Turning her attention back to the bag, she began to rummage in earnest for something that would make Kane believe her. It would have to be something simple, something that would work properly in his time but had as yet to be invented. At last she spotted several small red packets that she'd absently dropped into her tote to carry home as a souvenirs: matchbooks from the hotel in London. Smiling, she held one up. "This will prove it to you."

Kane arched a skeptical brow.

Katharina's smile didn't waver as she flipped open the flap and pulled off a match. She drew it across the rough surface and laughed as the flame flared. She held it up for Kane's inspection, only to see a look of horror cross his face.

"Mother Mary, you are a witch," he muttered as he took a protective step back and made the sign of the cross.

Panicking, Katharina jumped to her feet, sending the tote's contents spilling across the floor. She shook her head as she took a step toward Kane, but he moved away again. She paused, not wanting to add to his fright. "Kane, it's only a match. Nothing more. I am no magician or witch."

Suddenly uneasy, she held out the matchbook

to Kane. "Try it. You can make it light just as easily as I."

Kane hesitated, eyeing her skeptically.

Fully understanding that her future could be determined within the next few minutes, Katharina reached out and took Kane's hand. She could feel the tension in his muscles as she placed the matches in his palm and looked up at him. All the love she felt was reflected in her eyes as she said, "I would never harm you or yours. Nor will I allow anyone else to do so if it is in my power to stop them. This I vow to you and God, Kane."

Kane's hand closed about the matches. He held them as he stood gazing down at Katharina for a long, indecisive moment. Then he smiled as he held out the matches to her. "Show me again this miracle you have wrought."

"It's no miracle, Kane. Only an invention that took place in the eighteenth century." Seeing the look of wonder on Kane's face as he watched her light another match, Katharina felt suddenly awed by the overwhelming love she felt for this strong man—this man who found such wonder in such a simple thing.

Chapter Eight

Kane's strong fingers struck the match against the sandpaper strip several times before he managed the miracle of fire. In awe, he watched the match burn down to his fingertips and swore under his breath when the flame scorched his skin. He dropped it on the floor and watched it slowly extinguish itself before he looked back at Katharina.

" 'Tis a wonder that you bring, my lady. Yet 'tis still hard to believe what you say is true. My heart tells me you are no witch, but I know not what you truly are."

A tender smile curled Katharina's lips as she looked at Kane. "What I am is a woman who has found that she is willing to give up all the conveniences of the twentieth century to remain here with you. Earlier, I left my chamber to find my way back to my time. Now, to my own amazement, I find myself at home here. And I now know why I always felt out of place in the modern world. This is where I belong—if you will have me."

Kane's heart leapt at her words, yet he forced himself to remain still. He looked down at the matchbook in his hand, focusing his attention on it as if was the most important thing to him in the world. He wanted Katharina more than anything else, but he couldn't give way to his emotions again. He would be blessed if she did not already carry the Sedgewick heir. And he'd not place her or her happiness at risk again just because of the weakness of his own flesh. He loved her too much. He wanted her to stay at Sedgewick if that was her desire; however, they could never have any physical contact again. It wouldn't be an easy way to live. In truth, it would be hell on earth, but he'd not bring the curse down upon another he loved. Nor could he blame Katharina should she choose to leave him. She was too vibrant, too beautiful to accept such an arrangement for very long. She needed to live life, not just observe it as he'd done for the past sixteen years.

When Kane didn't answer immediately, Katharina began to sense his tension. She noted the strained lines about his tightly held lips, the furrows across his brow as he concentrated on the matchbook. Swallowing uneasily, she asked quietly, "Do you want me here, Kane? Or did the truth about me change your feelings? Can you not love me now?"

Kane cleared his throat. His ebony eyes reflected his misery as he raised his gaze to Katharina's face and uttered a lie. "I fear there are many things that keep us apart, my lady. I will not say 'tis because you come from a different time and place. Or that my feelings at the moment are in a quandary because of that. Still, I must have time to consider this and what we are to do."

"To do? There is nothing *we* can do. Fate has decided my future. You can't send me back like an unwanted package, but you can ask me to leave your home. Is that what you want, Kane? Do you want me to leave Sedgewick?" Katharina asked, unable to avoid the question. All she wanted at that moment was for Kane to take her into his arms and reassure her that she'd not made a fool of herself by falling in love with him.

"I have no wish for you to leave Sedgewick. I find wonder in this simple invention of fire on a stick, yet 'tis still a great deal to accept. I cannot readily believe what you tell me is true, even though my heart tells me again that you do not lie."

Katharina released the breath she'd not realized she'd been holding. She could well understand Kane's dilemma. Had someone told her that time travel was possible two weeks ago, she'd have laughed in his face. Now she was expecting this man, who had never seen a match, to accept what even she, born in a time when men had walked on the moon, could barely believe herself.

"You're right, Kane. I should not expect you to accept what I say so easily. I still have a great deal of trouble believing it myself. Yet I haven't lied about where I come from. And I pray that in time you will be able to accept me."

Kane couldn't stop himself from reaching out and caressing Katharina's cheek. He wanted nothing more than to take her into his arms and tell her that he didn't really give a bloody damn where she came from as long as she never left him. But common sense prevailed. He would protect this wonderful creature by giving her a place under his roof; he would give her everything she desired in life except the one thing she wanted the most, himself.

Kane stroked Katharina's cheek one last time before letting his hand fall to his side. "Katharina, you are welcome at Sedgewick for as long as you wish to make it your home. And I welcome your presence here as I welcome your friendship."

A chill ran up Katharina's spine as she looked into Kane's dark, shuttered eyes. She could no longer see the passion within them, only a look of kindness.

"Friendship," Katharina sputtered before managing to recover a smidgeon of her composure. She'd opened her heart to this man, and now he was welcoming her friendship as if nothing had transpired between them on the great four-poster bed. She cleared her throat and straightened. "I also welcome your friendship and understanding, Kane. And you have my gratitude for allowing me to remain here. I don't know what I would do without your kindness."

The pain in her voice made Kane feel as if he'd been kicked in the gut. He felt her pain as his own and knew he was responsible for it; yet he also knew he had no other choice. He had to put some distance between them in order to survive himself.

"Then I will bid you good night. It's been a long night and I'm sure you have much to consider now that you know the truth about me," Katharina said. Before Kane could reply, she turned away and began gathering up the spilled contents of her tote. She picked up her nightgown and draped it over her shoulders to hide the ravaged front of her gown. There was already enough gossip about her at Sedgewick without creating more by going about half naked. She gave Kane one last tremulous smile before she opened and closed the door silently behind her.

Left to ponder the strange events of the night, Kane crossed to the side table and poured himself another drink. He downed the amber liquid in one gulp and gratefully accepted the burning sensation that filled his gut. The heat of it helped ease the pain in his chest. He set the glass aside and ran his long fingers through his hair in frustration. He turned to look at the rumpled bed where he'd found so much pleasure and wiped at the sudden moisture that dampened his long lashes. He couldn't give in to the despair filling his soul. He had to go on. Too many people depended upon him. And now a new burden rested upon him: He had to protect Katharina from the outside world as well as himself.

Fighting to withhold the wail of agony rising in his throat, Kane grabbed up his shirt and coat and jerked them on. He strode from the chamber possessed by the need to be free of the burdens crushing him. He strode to the end of the hallway where the secret entrance led down through the tunnels beneath Sedgewick. Instead of going to the meadow where the curse had begun, he climbed the stone stairs that exited in the stables. He needed to ride, to clear his thoughts, to cool his blood.

From her chamber window, Katharina watched Kane ride through the gates and whip his mount into a gallop across the open fields. As she watched him, she wondered how he had been in his room when she had seen him ride off earlier. There were yet many mysteries about Sedgewick to solve, she realized. But one thing she understood: his need to ride like the wind. She, too, was far too restless to sleep. So much had transpired in such a short time. She had found her soul mate, accepted the fact that she felt at home in the seventeenth century, and had been told that there could only be friendship between herself and Kane.

"You lie, Kane," Katharina murmured into the night as his shadowy figure disappeared into the woods beyond the field. "I'm no innocent. I've experienced enough fizzled relationships to know when one is special—unique. We both want more than friendship between us, but until I find a way to make you realize it, we will just have to be friends as you asked."

Encouraged by her thoughts, Katharina smiled and turned away from the window. It might take time for him to accept that she'd traveled back in time, but while he was coming to that realization, she'd not let him forget the ecstasy that they'd found together. It was the only way. She had no other choice. She couldn't live under the same roof as Kane with only friendship between them. She had traveled three hundred years into the past to find her soul mate, and she'd be damned if she'd allow anything to keep them apart.

Smiling, Katharina crawled into her small bed and snuggled against the down pillow. She'd learned from Sidney that perseverance had its rewards. The experiments she'd performed in Herbal Health's lab didn't often give immediate results. To achieve success you had to keep trying.

"Dear Sidney, you taught me so much about life. I pray that fate will also give you what you need to be happy. It has given me a chance at something I never truly believed I'd find, and I intend to do everything in my power to make Kane love me," Katharina said as if writing in a journal. It had become a nightly ritual during the past week. The verbal diary to her aunt about the trials of each day seemed to make Katharina's sleep more peaceful. Katharina yawned and closed her eyes, secure that fate would not cheat her out of the happiness that she had sought for so many years.

Chole's knock awoke Katharina. She stretched and sat up as the maid opened the door and bobbed a slight curtsey. The maid's bright smile and deferential treatment puzzled Katharina for a moment. The girl had always been polite, but she had never been overtly friendly.

Arms laden with clothing, she crossed the small chamber. "My lady, His Lordship asks that you join him for breakfast downstairs," Chole said, laying the new clothing across the back of the straight-backed chair. She picked up Katharina's tattered gown and disdainfully tossed it aside. " 'Is Lordship has also said that yer to wear these until the seamstress can be summoned from the village." The maid held up a lovely sapphire-blue gown. The material shimmered in the morning light.

"It's lovely," Katharina said, throwing back the covers and sliding her feet to the cold floor. She stood and pulled the nightgown over her head. She needed no prompting from Chole to dress.

She stepped into the gown and allowed the maid to fasten it. The bodice was slightly tight, but Katharina ignored the discomfort. She was too elated to know that Kane wanted to see her to worry about the gown's fit. She turned to the door only to be brought up short by the maid's reminder.

"My lady, yer shoes, yer hair. Ye can't go down to meet His Lordship like that."

Katharina glanced down at her toes peeking out from beneath the hem of her gown and flushed. She turned back to Chole, who stood holding her shoes. She sank down on the side of the bed and allowed the maid to help her put them on. She cast one anxious glance toward the door before settling down to accept Chole's help with her hair. The minutes seemed to stretch into hours as the maid brushed her long locks and then pinned them carefully up on top of her head, allowing only a few stray curls to lie enticingly against her neck.

Katharina glanced at her reflection in the small mirror Chole held out for her. She inspected her image, unable to believe the miracle the maid had wrought. It had been more than a week since she'd last looked at her reflection, and it shocked Katharina to realize that the plain twentieth-century woman had vanished. In her place stood someone Katharina didn't quite recognize. The image staring back at her was beautiful. Her complexion seemed to glow with color, needing no artifice to produce the rose-tinted cheeks. Her eyes seemed a far deeper shade of blue against her translucent skin. Even her lips held more color.

"What has happened to me?" Katharina asked, raising a hand to her cheek in something akin to wonder.

"Me mam says 'tis the way of things when yer in love," Chole said, laying the mirror aside. She gave Katharina a timid smile. " 'Is Lordship be awaiting his lady below."

Katharina gave Chole an impetuous hug and turned once more to the door, all thought of her appearance dissolving beneath her desire to be with Kane.

Kane's breath caught in his throat at the vision that entered the dining room. It took all of his willpower not to sweep her up into his arms and carry her back upstairs. He ground his teeth together and fought to suppress the urge. He crossed to Katharina and took her hand to lead her to the table, which he'd had set for two. "I hope you slept well, my lady."

"As well as you I suspect, my lord. However, I could not go for a midnight ride."

Ignoring Katharina's comment, Kane seated her and then took his chair. He didn't say anything until the servants had filled their plates. "Then you ride, my lady?"

"Not in a long time. I haven't been on horseback since I moved to Utah to live with my aunt."

"Utah?" Kane asked and quickly glanced about, afraid that others had overheard her statement.

Unaware of his concern, Katharina picked up her fork and began to pick through the soft, fluffy eggs. "Yes. I've only lived there for a few years. My original home was in Texas. My father taught at the University in Arlington."

Kane's hand closing over her own, drawing Katharina's attention to him. "Katharina, you must watch what you say here. 'Twould be far easier for those about us to brand you a witch than to believe that you have come back through time. Please, finish your meal, and then you can tell me all about yourself and your time while we ride."

"Will you also tell me about yourself, my lord?" Katharina asked, her heart racing at the thought of spending time alone with Kane.

"As much as possible. There is little to know of me," Kane said, releasing Katharina's hand. He turned his attention back to his plate. "The gown suits you well, my lady. After we break our fast, you may change into the riding habit I had sent to your chamber. It belonged to my mother. You are of the same size. I'm sure she would not protest your wearing her clothes, since you have come to us with so little. She was a generous woman."

Katharina's heart warmed at Kane's generosity. "Then her son must have inherited her kindness."

Kane stilled. He looked at Katharina, his dark eyes mirroring even darker emotions. " 'Twould

167

have been much kinder had she never borne me."

Stunned by Kane's words and the pain she heard in his voice, Katharina suddenly realized how little she truly knew of this man. He had claimed her heart, yet in truth he was a stranger to her. She knew nothing of his past or his present circumstances. They had shared the most intimate part of a relationship, but she knew only what the tour guide had said about the Sedgewick family and the curse that had been placed upon them.

Reacting from the heart, Katharina reached out and placed her hand over his. Kane was a strong man, an English aristocrat, yet his words made her realize that somewhere deep inside, he hurt like any other mortal. "Then I am grateful that she was not too kind. Had she never borne you, we would not now be together, enjoying this wonderful meal before going riding."

Kane seemed to shed the morose manner that had momentarily shrouded him. He smiled at Katharina and squeezed her hand. " 'Tis a bright ray you bring to Sedgewick, my lady." His smiled dimmed slightly as he continued, "And 'tis very welcome. There has been too much darkness in this household for too many years."

Katharina didn't ask his meaning. In her present state of mind, she didn't want to know about the darkness. She was with Kane and nothing else mattered. She was as giddy as a sixteen-year-old in love for the first time. And she wanted nothing to destroy the feeling. She'd not allow anything to shadow the happiness she'd finally found.

Atop a magnificent roan and with Kane at her side, Katharina viewed the seventeenth-century English countryside for the first time and fell in love again with the England her father had taught her to adore from childhood. Though it was nearing winter, the day was warm and sunny as they rode across Sedgewick and along its boundaries. Untouched by modern man's conveniences, the land was stunningly beautiful. The long fields ringed by stone fences and spiked with withered corn stalks stretched to the thick forest, where she caught her first glimpse of a stag watching them warily from his hiding place amid the trees. Along the rutted, narrow roadway, tall, leafless oaks stood like sentinels set to guard travelers who rode toward the small hamlet of Sedgeville.

The villagers greeted them deferentially yet kept at a distance as Kane reined in his stallion in front of a tiny cottage. He tied the reins to the sagging gate and turned to lift Katharina down from her mount. "Forgive me, Katharina. I didn't want anything to interrupt our ride, but I must visit Mistress Remy and her family briefly. Her daughter recently died, and now the babe she left behind is ill. I've sent the physician and I want to see how the babe is faring."

Before Katharina could reassure Kane that she fully understood his concern for his neighbors, the cottage's wooden door squeaked open to reveal several pairs of eyes staring out from the shadowy interior. A moment later, an elderly woman shuffled forward. She made an attempt to curtsey, but her back was so stooped that she only managed a hazardous forward move. Kane managed to correct the old woman's stance before she toppled over face first onto the ground. She raised a gnarled hand to clasp Kane's arm for support and looked up at him, her rheumy eyes as beseeching as her words. "Bless ye, me lordship. Ye've come to wish me babe a fare-thee-well as ye did the mam."

"Mistress Remy, I've come to see what may be done, not to say farewell. Has the physician come?"

"Aye, yer lordship. He came, he did. But he can do nothin' fer him. It's now in the 'ands of God."

"I'm sorry to hear that, mistress. Your family means much to the Sedgewicks."

"Bless ye, yer lordship. Ye've always been a kind lad."

"Is there anything I can do for you?"

"Nay. Me babe will soon be at rest. I just pray that the wee ones don't come down with the illness. To lose the wee babe is enough to break me old heart, but should I lose the others, I'd die with 'em."

Kane turned back to his mount to retrieve two large bags that had been strapped behind his saddle. "I've had cook prepare some food. She also sent down a few of her own herbs. Perhaps they will be of help."

"Thank ye, yer lordship. Me babes will enjoy a good meal. 'Tis been hard of late to keep the older ones' bellies full. Tell Mistress Brumby, we're grateful to her for thinking of us."

"Should there be anything more I can do, send one of the children to Sedgewick," Kane said, handing the old woman the bulging bags.

She clutched them to her chest. "Bless ye again. No better men ever lived than ye and yer father."

"Kane, may I see the baby?" Katharina asked, swallowing back tears. She had thought she understood the meaning of poverty and suffering until that moment. But looking at the elderly woman clutching the bag of food and calmly accepting the death of her grandchild, Katharina realized how naive she was. She had come into a time when illness was an unconquerable foe. Science had as yet to invent weapons to arm man against it. But she could possibly help in this instance. She didn't have the chemicals to make twentieth-century medicines, but she had been trained in knowledge of the medicinal plants and herbs from which many of the medicines had come. That knowledge could be of benefit to this woman and her family.

"I fear now is not be best time, Katharina. As you heard, the physician has already visited and said there was nothing to be done. 'Tis best to leave Mistress Remy and her family to grieve as they see fit."

"Kane, you don't understand. I don't want to visit Mistress Remy. I may be able to help the baby."

" 'Tis a kind thing to suggest, Katharina. But I'll not risk your becoming ill. I have given them food and the cook's herbs. There is nothing more to be done." Kane took her by the arm to lead her back to their mounts. "Now come. The day wanes and there is still much I would have you see."

Katharina jerked her arm free. "Blast it, Kane. You're not listening to me. Remember the matches. I'm saying I may be able to nurse the child back to health. I know things about herbs and medicine from my time."

Kane flashed an anxious look around. His congenial tone disappeared as he once more grasped Katharina firmly by the arm and turned toward their mounts. "Woman, I have warned you. Watch your tongue. 'Tis dangerous to speak of such things or to know more than the physicians. It takes little to be accused of witchcraft."

"I'll heed your warning, but please let me see if I can help Mistress Remy's grandchild. Don't make that poor woman suffer to protect me. I can't live with the knowledge that I might have been able to save a baby's life but didn't do it out of fear for my own well-being. Nor do I believe you could live with that on your conscience."

"Mistress, lower your voice. You draw attention to yourself."

"Will you allow me to see the child?"

Kane cast another cautious glance about, noting the old woman's curious stare. "You test my patience, Katharina. A woman should obey the commands of her lord."

Katharina flashed Kane an obstinate look. "And a man should have compassion for those who serve him. Look about you, Kane. These people barely survive on your beneficence. Mistress Remy is grateful for your charity even while her grandchild lies dying because of the poverty in which they live."

Kane flushed and his eyes sparkled with ire as he looked down at the woman accusing him of neglecting his people. He had always been far more generous than other lords. He didn't allow his people to starve when the harvest failed, and he had sent the physician to see to the old woman's grandchild. What more could he do— bring them into his own house? Death and hunger often visited those who were not born into the aristocracy. It wasn't a good thing, but it had been their lot for centuries.

"Have you no wit in that beautiful head, Katharina? I am trying to protect you. You risk your own life by what you ask."

"It is my life to risk, Kane. You do not own me as you own these people. My love for you is freely given, not yours to command. Nor can you demand my obedience. I am no child. I have a mind of my own. And I can make my own choices, whether they be right or wrong."

Kane drew in a steadying breath in an effort to regain control over himself. This vexing, impossible woman held his heart in the palm of her graceful hand, and she expected him to watch her destroy herself and say nothing about it. Kane's nostrils flared as he inhaled another deep breath. He wanted to turn her over his knee and swat her bottom for such disobedience. In the same instant, he wanted to draw her into his arms and ravish the lovely lips that spouted such nonsense. However, he did neither. " 'Od's blood. You test me. But you are right, I do not own you. Do as you wish, madam. I pray we all do not suffer the consequences of your folly."

Katharina placed a hand on Kane's arm. She could feel the tension in his muscles through the thick velvet sleeve of his coat. "I don't wish to cause you trouble. But I can't walk away when the knowledge I possess might save the life of a small child. Please understand, Kane."

Kane nodded in resignation. "I do understand, yet I cannot stop myself from fearing the worst. You may know many things, but you are an innocent here. 'Tis easy to be condemned for your compassion, Katharina. You may help the child, only to find that the people will turn against you out of fear that you used witchcraft."

Katharina stood on tiptoe and placed a gentle

kiss on Kane's cheek. "I will do my best not to rouse such suspicions."

"Then go if you must. May God be with us all."

Katharina gave Kane's arm a loving squeeze before she turned toward the old woman who stood near the door. For Kane and Mistress Remy's benefit, she concocted a reasonable tale as she paused upon the threshold to the shadowy interior. "Mistress, may I see your grandchild? I come from a large family and have some knowledge of childhood illness."

Mistress Remy glanced toward Kane and saw him nod his approval before she stepped aside to allow Katharina into her home. She watched anxiously as the beautiful stranger crossed to the small pallet where the babe lay burning with fever. A chill of apprehension shivered down her crooked spine as Katharina bent and touched the tiny, hot brow.

Katharina glanced past the old woman hovering over her to the tall figure standing in the doorway. "Kane, this child is burning with fever. We must bring it down or the baby will die. Have someone bring in several buckets of water." Ignoring the expression that crossed Kane's face at her command, she turned to the old woman. "Mistress, let me see the herbs the cook sent. Perhaps one of them will cool the fever."

Intimidated by the younger woman, Mistress Remy fumbled in the bag for the herbs. She finally found the small packets after dumping the contents onto the rough-hewn table. The sight of the food drew a small, dark-eyed boy and a tiny, blue-eyed girl out of the shadows. They crept forward, their gazes locked on the loaf of crusty brown bread. Unmoved by the look of hunger in the children's eyes, the old woman growled, "Be gone with ye. When the babe is tended, then ye'll get a bite to eat."

She turned her attention back to Katharina as the two small children scurried back into the shadows. "Mistress Brumby has sent sage and featherfoil as well as garlic."

"Featherfoil?" Katharina questioned before she remembered the history of the herb and the change of name that had occurred when it had been brought to America in the eighteenth century. "Feverfew? Good. That should help reduce the fever. Put some water on to boil so we can make a tea for the baby," Katharina ordered as she lifted the tiny form and began to unwrap the swaddling that still bound its limbs and generated far too much heat for its fevered body.

Kane reappeared a few moments later with a bucket of water. Katharina dipped her free hand into the icy liquid. "Set the bucket near the fire to warm."

"Lady, the babe is much too ill to worry about bathing," Kane said as he did her bidding.

Naked and free from the restricting swaddling, the tiny baby began to squirm, kick and scream. Quickly wrapping the red-faced infant in a tattered blanket, Katharina held it close, comforting it as if it were her own child. "The water isn't for bathing. It's to bring down the fever."

Kane seemed to ponder the thought for a moment and then accept the new idea without further comment. Claiming a stool by the hearth as his own, he said no more. He watched Katharina as she moved about the sooty interior as if he'd never seen her before. He marveled at the ease with which she took charge of the situation. Unlike the ladies of his acquaintance, who would have found it distasteful to touch a peasant's babe, she held him tenderly, cooing sweet-soothing baby talk as she gently lowered the infant into the tepid water. By the time she had administered the featherfoil tea and gotten the babe to sleep, Kane found himself deeper in love than he had ever imagined possible—and also far more troubled. He saw a woman that any man would be proud to call his own, a woman who cared for others without thought of herself, a nurturer of life and goodness. But he also saw a torturous future for himself. Even now he felt his body stir in longing to take her again. His heart cried out to know the sight of her with his child in her arms. Yet it could never be.

Kane's eyes stung, whether from smoke or emotion, he didn't know. He abruptly rose to his feet and turned toward the door and said, "I'll await you outside, my lady."

Puzzled by Kane's expression as he left, Katharina gave the old woman instructions on how to administer the tea to the baby before she followed Kane. She found him standing by their mounts, staring out across the winter-barren fields. He seemed not to note her presence as she paused at his side.

"The baby's fever is down. I hope it will have enough strength to survive."

"Then it is time for us to return to Sedgewick," Kane said without preamble. He helped Katharina to mount and turned his own steed in the direction from which they had come.

Unable to read his mood, Katharina waited until the village lay far behind them before she asked, "Are you still angry with me?"

Kane glanced at her before turning his attention back to the roadway ahead. "I'm not angry that you chose to help the infant, Katharina."

"Then what is troubling you? And don't deny that something is wrong. I know it by your expression."

Kane refused to look at Katharina. It was hard enough to speak with her without revealing the agony in his soul. "I truly don't know what you mean. I have been merely reconsidering a few things. Today has shown me how truly naive you are to the dangers surrounding you. And I must take action to assure your safety for as long as you are with us."

The warmth left by Kane's concern for her welfare dissipated abruptly with his last statement.

Frowning, Katharina asked, "What do you mean, for as long as I am with you?"

Kane gave a nonchalant shrug. "My lady, we have no reason to believe that your visit will be permanent. By some strange act of fate, you have traveled three hundred years into the past. I still find it hard to accept this time travel, but since it happened once, it may happen again."

Having no way to deny his assumption, Katharina fell quiet. The very thought of going back to the twentieth century was abhorrent to her. She had found her time and place, as well as the man of her dreams. Yet how could she expect this man to plan a future with her when neither knew what the next moment would bring? Katharina shook her head. She'd not give in to such depressing thoughts. She loved Kane Sedgewick, and she'd be damned if she'd allow anything to keep them apart. No one in the seventeenth century, or the twentieth, knew what the next moment would bring. At any time, lovers could be separated by a quirk of fate or by a million other things.

Determined to make Kane understand that there were no guarantees in life during any century, Katharina drew her mount to a halt and slid to the ground. She would not wait until they'd returned to Sedgewick, where Kane could so easily avoid her. Here on the open road, she'd have her say without the worry of eavesdropping servants.

Sensing that Katharina was no longer at his

side, Kane drew his mount to a halt and turned to look for her. His lips tightened and he frowned at the sight of her standing in the roadway, head held high and arms folded across her full breasts. "My lady, 'tis growing late. At this pace, we will not reach Sedgewick until after the dinner meal is served."

"I want to talk to you, Kane. I don't care if we miss our dinner. In fact, that is the one thing I've yet to appreciate in your time. My palate has learned to like only a few things that you call food."

Kane didn't dismount. "I regret that you find my hospitality so unpalatable, my lady. Perhaps it will be as much of a relief to you as it will be to me when you return to your time."

Stunned by his disclosure, Katharina felt her heart break. Her knees grew weak and tears burned her eyes, but she refused to give way to her emotions. Drawing in a deep shuddering breath, she looked at the man who had just shattered her heart and then slowly turned her back to him. She started walking in the direction from which they'd just come. Her only thought was to get as far away from Kane as possible before she gave in to her misery. She had been hurt in the past, but never had she felt such devastation of the soul.

"Katharina," Kane called as she continued to walk away from him. "My lady, cease this childish behavior at once."

Katharina didn't answer, nor did she look back.

"Katharina," Kane called, urging his mount forward. He had meant to hurt her, to make her realize that there was no future for them. The words had been painful to say, but he'd had no other choice. It was the only way he knew to make her understand, to keep them apart, to keep the vow he'd made so many years before.

Kane dismounted and hurried to catch up with Katharina. No matter how hard it was to be near her, he couldn't allow her to walk away from him. It was far too dangerous. "Woman, don't you realize that I can't allow you to do this? While you are here, you must remain at Sedgewick, where you will be safe."

Her heart hammering against her ribs, her eyes glistening with unshed tears, Katharina turned to face Kane. "Lord Sedgewick, my welfare is of no concern to you. I don't need your protection. I am capable of taking care of myself."

Kane swore under his breath. " 'Od's blood. You have no understanding of how you will fare without my protection. You are far too innocent and too beautiful to survive alone. I know not what dangers lie in the future. However, I do know what you will face should I allow you to walk away from me."

"What does it matter how I fare? You don't want me, and I'll not stay where I am not welcome. My fate is in my hands, not yours."

"It would seem your fate has been thrust into

my hands. The moment you entered my chamber, you became my responsibility. And I do not shirk my duty to those under my protection."

"I free you of your duty to me, Lord Sedgewick. Now leave me be," Katharina said, turning away.

Kane reached out and caught Katharina by the arm. "No. I will not allow this. You will return to Sedgewick with me. And you will remain there until I can decide what is best for you."

Suddenly furious with herself and Kane, Katharina turned on him, eyes flashing. "Unhand me. I'll not be forced to return to Sedgewick against my will. Nor will I allow you to decide what is best for me. I have been your prisoner for the last time. I surrendered to you last night, but never again. You may be the lord of Sedgewick Castle and command all that you survey, but I am not your property. In my time, a woman belongs only to herself."

Katharina tried to extricate her arm from his viselike hold, only to find herself held captive by both arms. Kane pulled her against him, so close that their breaths mingled. Time seemed to stretch into eternity as they both became aware of the warmth spreading between them.

"Blast it, Katharina," Kane ground out. "What I do is for your own good."

Katharina looked up into Kane's ebony gaze and swallowed hard. Every nerve in her body responded to his nearness. The rush of heat in her blood vanquished the heat of her anger. She moistened her suddenly dry lips with the tip of her tongue and waited expectantly as she saw the fire flare in the dark depths of his eyes.

A low moan of anguish escaped Kane as he surrendered to the torrid hunger that pushed all thought aside. The heat of his need for her incinerated everything in its path as it swelled him. He took her tempting mouth, ravishing her lips, savoring their sweetness as he enticed them to open for him. He slid his arms around her, his wide palms cupping her bottom and pressing her against his pulsing body.

Unable to resist his allure, Katharina also surrendered. It didn't matter that they had argued only a moment before and now stood entwined in the middle of the lane. She knew only that she was once again where she should be: in Kane's arms. She broke free of his mouth and gasped. "Love me, Kane. Love me now."

No power could have stopped Kane as he lifted Katharina into his arms and carried her to the thick, leafy bed beneath a large oak. Its draping boughs shielded the lovers from view, guarding them as they disrobed each other and lay together as God had made man and woman. The afternoon sunlight dappled their bodies through the bare limbs overhead. A late autumn breeze stirred the great branches, yet the lovers did not feel the chill. The heat of their desire warmed them as they came together on the bed of golden leaves.

The intensity of their union left them breathless

with wonder. Hearts pounding, bodies still melded, they clung to each other, unwilling to allow even a breath of air to come between them.

"Never leave me," was Kane's throaty plea as he buried his face in the curve of Katharina's neck.

"Never, my love," Katharina answered. Her eyes filled with tears of joy as she stroked the dark head pressed against hers. How she loved this man. Had she meant to leave him before, she knew now she could never go through with it. This was where she belonged.

Kane raised himself above her and looked down into her glistening eyes. "I beg of you, no matter what you learn about me, Katharina, never leave me."

Katharina raised her hand to his cheek and smiled up at Kane. "Never will I leave you of my own choice. We have spoken of fate taking me away and the uncertainty of the future. But there are no guarantees in life, even had I been born in your time. I promise you here and now, I will never leave you freely. I vow I will fight to my dying breath to stay at your size, whether you desire my presence or not."

Kane stroked Katharina's flushed cheek lovingly before he rolled away from her to retrieve their clothing. With her vow, she had freed him of the worry of her leaving, yet his own vow kept him shackled. Forcing a smile to his lips, he held out his hand to Katharina. "Come, my lady. The hour grows late and the air now has a distinct chill to it. I would not have you become ill because of my passion."

Katharina took Kane's hand and allowed him to help her to her feet. "You worry far too much about my health, my lord. As you will learn, I am very healthy and quite capable of bearing strong babies." Unaware of the sudden tension that made Kane stiffen, Katharina pulled on her riding habit and continued dreamily, "I wonder what our children will look like? I know they will be beautiful if they take after their father."

Clearing his throat, Kane said, " 'Tis far too late in the afternoon to consider such things, my lady. We must hurry or cook will give our dinner to the swine."

"Your cook could use a few lessons in cuisine. Though I suppose eventually I will grow accustomed to it. I've even adjusted to the lack of indoor plumbing."

"Indoor plumbing? What manner of thing is that?" Kane asked, shrugging into his coat. He wanted to keep the conversation as far away from the idea of his and Katharina's children as possible. It was too torturous to contemplate.

"It is where you have hot and cold running water for your bath and kitchen needs."

"Why would you need that when you have servants to bring your water?" Kane asked, draping Katharina's cloak about her shoulders.

"It makes life far easier, especially for those not

fortunate enough to have the wealth to hire servants."

Kane conceded the point. However, he didn't see any need for it himself. If he wanted a bath, all he had to do was call for it. "Do all people in your time have hot and cold water in their baths?"

"Nearly everyone does."

"Hmm," Kane said, lifting Katharina back onto her mount. "You know of so many wonders, my lady."

"My wonder is you, Kane. The things I've told you about are only common, everyday things that have come about to make life easier. Those don't give you happiness. It wasn't until I came to your time that I truly felt I belonged. And I know now I can do without everything else except you."

Kane's heart swelled with love. He would be willing to give his own life to protect Katharina.

Chapter Nine

The afternoon sun cast long shadows across the barren garden. Sitting amid the leafless rose-bushes, Katharina snuggled deeper into the soft woolen cloak Kane had loaned her. Autumn would soon give way to winter. Soon the icy winds from the North Atlantic would bring snow to blanket the landscape. Katharina shivered and pulled the cloak tighter about her. The thought of winter chilled her, yet the deepest winter couldn't be any colder than she now felt inside. The weather could freeze the wind in the trees and still the mountain streams, yet it would seem warm compared to her relationship with Kane over the past two weeks.

Katharina glanced toward the tall tower that

had become her home. Perhaps the tower was her rightful place, after all. The Sedgewick family had used the tower to house all of their mad relatives, and in her present state of mind, she thought she had lost what little sanity had been left to her after fate had thrust her three hundred years into the past.

Katharina pursed her lips. The cause of her sudden dementia was the man who had also stolen her heart. Annoyed with herself for her lack of control over her life, Katharina shifted on the stone bench. Kane had been avoiding her since their ride to the village. It seemed he never had any time for her. Had she not heard him beg her to stay with him, she could have sworn he didn't want her near him.

Gentleman that he was, he sent his apologies for his absence, using the excuse that his duties kept him far too busy even to partake of his meals with her. The few times she had encountered him in passing, she'd had no opportunity to question him because they had been surrounded by servants.

Katharina plucked a shriveled bud from the rosebush and crushed it in her palm. She opened her hand and allowed the chilly breeze to scatter the remains across the garden. Her heart was like the dried blossom: It shattered far too easily.

The sting of tears burned Katharina's eyes. She swiped furiously at them, determined not to cry. She'd had enough of crying her heart out over relationships that went sour in the twentieth century. This was a new time and a new life for her, and she'd be damned if she'd repeat the same behavior in the seventeenth century, no matter how much Kane's desertion hurt her.

Wiping away the betraying droplets, Katharina squared her shoulders. Kane had begged her not to leave him, and she'd keep her vow to stay. However, her vow didn't mean she'd allow him to act as if she didn't exist. Glancing at the ever-vigilant Chole, Katharina asked, "Chole, do you know when Lord Sedgewick will return?"

The maid shook her head. "Nay, my lady. 'Is Lordship don't tell me when he's coming nor going. But I 'spect he'll be returning soon. 'Tis nearing eventide."

A cunning little smile curled Katharina's lips up at the corners as she braced herself for the battle ahead. Tonight she intended to see Kane, whether he liked it or not. They could not go on living together yet never seeing one another except in passing. Tonight Kane would have to accept her completely into his life or tell her to leave Sedgewick. There could be no gray area where her heart was concerned.

"Chole, I think it's time for me to retire to my chamber. Will you have a warm bath prepared for me and then lay out the burgundy velvet?" Katharina said, rising to her feet. She wanted to look her best when she confronted Kane about the way he'd been ignoring her. Dressed in her borrowed finery, she would see how well he could deny the feelings they shared.

"Aye, my lady," Chole said. With a quick bob of her head, she turned and hurried inside.

The girl was an excellent maid, Katharina mused before realizing how her notions about servants had been changing during the past weeks. In the twentieth century, it would have been abhorrent to her to have someone to serve her every need. Now she had come to accept such ministrations without question. Depending upon the servants seemed as natural as the days she'd spent in the lab at Herbal Health, Inc.

Katharina glanced about the garden, wondering at the things she'd begun to accept in her new life as normal. It seemed that she was slowly but surely letting go of her past.

Katharina took one last look at the garden. She had no regrets for the life she'd left behind. She had gained far more than she had ever hoped. She had found the man to whom she could give her heart; now all that was necessary was to make him accept his fate.

The hood of the cloak fell back as Katharina tossed her head like a high-spirited, thoroughbred filly. She raised her chin and stiffened her spine. She was ready to do battle with Kane for the love they shared. She would fight with every sinew of her body to make him realize that they were meant to be together.

Katharina walked purposefully back inside. Tonight she would confront the demons that kept Kane from her, and she would defeat them with her love.

Frustrated with himself and fate, Kane ran his fingers through his thick hair. The tortured expression in his dark eyes revealed the emotions tearing at him as he watched Katharina determinedly stride out of view. Afraid to do otherwise, he'd become a voyeur. How many times during the past weeks had he hidden himself from view in order to watch her? Each time he'd paid dearly for the pleasure. His body had responded, making him fully aware of his need for Katharina.

Turning away from the window, Kane sank down into the leather monk's chair sitting before the mahogany chess table. He leaned back and let his gaze travel over the opulent room. Rows of twelve-foot high shelves were filled with leather-bound volumes. The crystal chandelier overhead provided good lighting for those who sought the quiet of the library to read or study. Few possessed such an impressive library. Only Sir Winston's could compare in size, yet Churchill's library lagged behind in the number of books. Kane's gaze came to rest on the large mahogany desk where he did his accounts and correspondence. The desk had been a gift from Queen Elizabeth to his great-grandfather. Like himself, his grandfather had been loyal to the crown when others thought to usurp the beautiful Bess.

Kane dropped his chin to his chest and closed his eyes to shut out the elegant chamber. His lips thinned at the thought of his ancestors. The wealth and grandeur of Sedgewick Castle was his heritage. However, he felt pride of family or name, no haughtiness over his station in life. There was no happiness to be had from possessing the Sedgewick blood. It had been tainted since the fifteenth century, when the first Richard Sedgewick had allowed the woman he loved to be burned at the stake for witchcraft. With her last breath, she had cursed him and all future generations of Sedgewicks.

The curse had come to life again in the young man upstairs. A streak of guilt careened through Kane. Here he sat belaboring his own misfortune when his brother was not allowed to walk about in the light of day. Richard's world was of the night, where no one could see his face. He lived on the edge of life, like some evil thing that only came out of hiding to steal men's souls.

As if to stay his tears, Kane pressed the bridge of his nose with thumb and forefinger and drew in a deep, steadying breath. Richard had been cursed at conception, and he knew no other life. Kane was different. Before Richard's birth, Kane had lived his youth to the fullest, enjoying the sports that every young man tried before settling down to a man's responsibilities. It had been a carefree life, one in which only his own pleasure meant anything to him. He had been a Sedgewick, the privileged heir to the family wealth and name. He had anything he wanted because of his standing. Charles II was an intimate friend, and together they had plundered the countryside, learning of women and life.

Sadly for both, their youth had been short-lived. The revolution had made Charles an outcast from his own country, while Kane had become a recluse because of the nightmare that had been born to his stepmother. Soon after Richard's birth, his mother had died, still unable to look upon the misbegotten face of her infant. His father had taken the child and closed off the east wing. Giving the care of the babe over to Nanna, he had promptly forgotten about his youngest offspring. At first, Kane had been unable to be near his brother. However, as time passed and he grew accustomed to the babe's deformity, he found himself loving the child. At the age of sixteen, Kane had held his tiny brother in his arms and vowed never to allow the curse to affect another Sedgewick. He would care for his brother, love him, protect him, but with them, the Sedgewick line would end.

Kane stood, his face troubled and pale. He had broken his vow twice because of his weakness for Katharina. He could never allow himself to let it happen again. He strode toward the door. He had to escape the temptation by riding into the cold night.

Twilight was already encroaching upon the day

as Kane urged his mount through the gates. Shadows crept into the valleys and forest, eradicating any warmth left from the sun. Kane looked up at the deep purple sky. Soon the moon would rise to illuminate his path as he tried to cool the heat in his blood and keep the madness at bay—the madness that possessed him when he was near Katharina.

The fire crackling in the grate was the only sound in the great dining room. Katharina's food sat cold and untouched as she stared at the empty space across from her. Kane's place had been set, but the master of Sedgewick Castle had not seen fit to join her for dinner. Katharina looked down at the fat congealing on the roast beef and vegetables on her plate. She'd had enough of waiting for Kane to come to her. If the mountain wouldn't come to Mohammed, then Mohammed would go to the mountain! Tossing her napkin onto the polished mahogany table, she pushed her chair back. Kane Sedgewick would not escape her by missing a meal. Tonight she would know the truth of how things stood between them.

Sparks shimmering in her eyes, she got to her feet and strode up the stairs to the east wing, ready to do battle. Perhaps women in the seventeenth century accepted a man's rejection meekly, but she was finding that she was not of that ilk. Kane would soon learn he couldn't toss her aside so easily.

Her determination to fight for her relationship with Kane surprised Katharina. In the past, she'd never had such resolve. "But in the past, I hadn't found a man like Kane to love," Katharina muttered as she opened the door to the east wing and went directly to Kane's door. She knocked. Hearing no answer, she lifted the latch and stepped inside. The chamber was empty. Irritated that she'd have to postpone the confrontation, Katharina closed the door behind her and turned to make her way out of the east wing. At the same instant, she caught a glimpse of a masculine figure at the end of the hallway. Recognizing the dark hair and height, she turned to pursue Kane. Damn him. He'd not escape this time.

As Katharina reached the doorway she'd seen Kane enter, she paused to get her bearings. The chamber lay in darkness except for the fire in the grate. Standing before the fireplace, hand resting on the mantel, head bowed, was the master of Sedgewick Castle. Her heart lodged in her throat at the sight of his beloved figure. No man in her past had ever made her feel such euphoria just at the sight of him. All her anger dissipated as she crossed the chamber and placed her hand on his shoulder. "Kane, please. We have to talk. I can't remain here if you keep ignoring me. It hurts too much to live under the same roof with you and never be near you."

Katharina realized her mistake as the man raised his head to look at her. The firelight played over his features, illuminating his beautiful dark eyes as well as the rest of his malformed face. She felt her blood drain from her face. She fought back the scream that choked her. For what seemed an eternity, her gaze was locked onto the fangs that protruded below the garish red lips.

Swallowing painfully, she drew in a deep, steadying breath and forced away the natural instinct to turn and flee. Moistening her lips, she determinedly looked up into the second-most beautiful eyes that she'd ever seen, eyes that mirrored the soul of one lost in torment, eyes that looked so much like Kane's. Katharina's shock began to abate as the look in those eyes touched her heart.

Regaining control over her voice, she apologized. "I'm sorry. I thought you were someone else. Forgive my intrusion."

Katharina made to leave.

"Please don't go, Katharina. I've heard so much about you from Kane. And I get very tired of always getting secondhand information."

His slurred plea made Katharina pause on the threshold. She looked back at the young man, saw the eager expression in his eyes and knew that she could not walk away. "Are you certain I'm not imposing upon your privacy?"

He shook his head rapidly from side to side and quickly pulled another chair close to the fire. " 'Tis nearly winter and this old heap of stones grows frigid. Come, warm yourself. I would love to have some company."

He waved a graceful, long-fingered hand, encompassing the entire chamber. "It gets lonely here, especially when Kane is too busy to visit."

Curiosity and pity ruling her, Katharina took the seat offered her and asked, "Then you live here all the time?"

Richard nodded. "I've lived here all of my life. I don't leave the east wing unless it's night. Then I'm allowed to go for a ride."

"I'm new here, so forgive me for my foolishness, but I didn't realize that someone other than Kane and the servants resided in Sedgewick."

A shield of thick dark lashes lowered to hide the pained expression in his ebony eyes, yet he answered her honestly. " 'Tis my appearance that keeps me bound to the east wing. I am, as you see, the cursed Sedgewick. And the sight of me would frighten the servants to death."

Katharina's cheeks burned at the thought of her own reaction only a few moments before. "I'm sorry."

"There is no reason to be sorry. I have lived quite happily here with my books and my brother to bring me stories of his adventures away from these granite walls."

Katharina's breath caught in her throat. "You are Kane's brother?"

Richard picked up the poker and stirred the coals beneath the logs before taking his seat. He stared for a long moment at the leaping flames before answering. "Aye. I am Richard Sedgewick. Kane is the elder of the last two Sedgewicks, but I am the one afflicted by the curse."

"The curse?" Katharina said, recalling the tour guide's speech the night she'd left the twentieth century. It was said the curse always came upon the heir to Sedgewick.

" 'Tis an unhappy love story not worth the telling, my lady. Let us say that what you see before you is the result of the actions of my ancestor Lord Richard Sedgewick and his mistress. I should think I am properly named."

Noting his discomfort about speaking of his affliction, Katharina said, "Then let us discuss something more pleasant."

Eager curiosity quickly replaced his somber mood. "Do you like Shakespeare, my lady? I've been reading *Romeo and Juliet*. 'Tis true it's another tragic tale, yet a great love story. Lovers separated because of circumstances not of their own making. To be loved so much, seems an impossible dream to me."

"Yes, I've read Shakespeare. And I loved *Romeo and Juliet*," Katharina said, fully understanding the wishful tone she heard in his slurred words. He was reading one of the greatest love stories, yet he knew that he was doomed never to have such love himself.

"Does it remind you of your relationship with

my brother?" Richard asked, watching Katharina closely.

His intuitive question took Katharina by surprise. She looked into the dark eyes so much like Kane's and slowly nodded. There was no reason to lie. He understood that there was something more than friendship between herself and his brother. "In many ways it does, but with Romeo and Juliet it was their families that kept them apart. There is nothing standing between Kane and myself except his feelings for me."

"Do you believe Kane loves you?"

Suddenly deflated, Katharina gave a slight shrug. "I thought he did. But now I'm not so certain. He avoids being alone with me."

"My brother has much on his mind, Katharina. He has enemies who want to destroy him and all he holds dear because he does not support Cromwell and his henchmen. I fear that our enemies have already played foul with our Uncle John. He has disappeared."

"When did your uncle disappear?" Katharina asked, recalling Kane's accusations the night of her arrival.

"I believe it was the same night that you arrived at Sedgewick, my lady. 'Tis strange, don't you think? One comes and one goes."

"It certainly is," Katharina said, an uneasy tingle creeping up her spine as she realized that John might have taken her place in the twentieth century. Suddenly needing to tell Kane about her theory, she got to her feet. "I think it's time that I retire. It's getting late."

"Do you really have to go? I was so enjoying your company. Will you come to visit me again?" Richard raised one graceful hand as if to hide his grotesque mouth as he spoke. "Please do come again."

"Of course I will come again," Katharina said and turned toward the door. She came to an abrupt halt at the sight of the huge man standing in the doorway.

"What are ye doing here? No one's allowed in this wing except the master," Joshua growled, casting an anxious glance toward his charge. By His Lordship's order, it was his duty to protect the young master at all cost. He couldn't allow anyone to leave the east wing knowing the Sedgewick secret.

"I was just leaving. If you will excuse me." Katharina made to step past the imposing figure, but she wasn't quick enough to avoid his meaty hand. His fingers encircled her arm and drew her back into the chamber.

Bushy brows shadowing his dark eyes, he growled again, "No one's allowed here by 'Is Lordship's orders."

His menacing tone raised the hair at the nape of Katharina's neck. She flashed Richard a beseeching look as she said, "I was only visiting Lord Sedgewick's brother."

"Release her at once, Joshua. You are frightening Katharina," Richard said, coming to her aid.

Ignoring the order, he looked at the young man he'd come to love like a son. "She be more than frightened when 'Is lordship learns of her trespassing here. She cannot be allowed to leave now that she's seen ye, young sir. Ye know that. She'll start all the tales up again about the vampire."

Katharina shook her head. "No. I won't say a word about Richard. Nor would I do anything to hurt Kane or any member of his family."

Joshua's hand tightened as he shook his head. "No matter what ye say, I have me orders." He began to pull her toward the hallway.

"Where do you think you're taking me?" Katharina said, digging her heels into the thick carpeting in a futile effort to thwart the powerful man.

"Down to the catacombs until I ask 'Is Lordship what's to be done with ye."

Panicking, Katharina looked back at Richard. "Don't let him to this to me, please, Richard."

Helpless tears glinted on Richard's thick, dark lashes and his words became more slurred from agitation. "I have no power to stop him. Joshua will heed only Kane's orders when it concerns the family. Forgive me, Katharina, but I can do nothing but tell Kane what happened."

Hearing the pain in Richard's voice, Katharina desisted. She would not inflict any guilt upon him. He had suffered enough without her adding to his burden. "I understand, Richard."

"Harm a hair on her head and you'll answer to my brother," Richard said, following them toward the end of the hallway and into a small alcove.

"I do only what 'Is Lordship orders. Now get ye back to yer chamber, young sir. Me mam will be bringin' yer dinner along any time now," Joshua said, reaching for a secret latch along the edge of a portrait.

"You'll not be harmed," Richard said as a narrow door swung open in what looked like a solid wall. He gave Katharina one last, helpless look before he turned away.

Breathing rapidly, Katharina allowed the man called Joshua to lead her through the opening. A small lantern hung on a peg just inside the doorway. Joshua struck a flint to the wick, and in a moment a tiny light illuminated the narrow stone stairs that led downward. Joshua pressed on a stone near the peg and the door swung closed behind them. He held the lantern high and looked at Katharina. " 'Twould be much easier to follow me down to the catacombs than be hauled down. But 'tis yer choice, me lady."

Katharina glanced into the dark void at her feet and then back to her captor. Her voice shook as she said, "I'll follow you."

Joshua gave a quick nod and began to descend the stairs. After a moment he paused and looked back up at Katharina, who stood frozen on the narrow landing. " 'Tis yer choice, me lady.'

Dragging in a deep breath, Katharina flashed one last look at the door behind her before she followed Joshua into the cavern where generations of Sedgewicks lay buried in their stone tombs.

At the foot of the stairs, Joshua hung the lantern on another wooden peg driven into a crack in the stonework. He looked at Katharina, who stood poised on the last stair. Wide, frightened eyes stared out of a face so pale that it seemed lifeless. She gripped the wooden handrail as if her life depended upon it. The look in her eyes tugged at Joshua's heart. He understood her feelings. Though he traversed these steps daily, bringing in the young sir's food or taking the young sir out to ride, he had no fondness for the family crypt. All the Sedgewicks lay there, good and bad alike. A shiver crept up Joshua's spine. He would not like being left here alone himself, but he had no other choice. He couldn't take her to the dungeon to keep her quiet. There were too many eyes and ears to see and hear what was going on. And then there would be questions that he couldn't answer.

"I'll leave ye the lamp. It'll give ye some light until 'Is Lordship decides what's to be done with ye. O'm sorry fer having to leave ye here, but I've no other choice in the matter."

Too choked up with terror to speak, Katharina watched Joshua ascend the stairs, leaving her alone in the Sedgewick burial ground. A cool current of air touched the nape of her neck, sending prickles of gooseflesh down her arms. She glanced up at the lantern and watched in horror as the small flame flickered and jumped. Katharina reached up and took the lantern down, guarding the precious light with her hand against the fresh air.

"Fresh air," Katharina said, comprehending the meaning of fresh air in a crypt. There had to be a way out. Turning in the direction of the breeze, Katharina squinted into the darkness. In the distance, she thought she saw a pinprick of light. Heart pounding, she began to walk toward it. Afraid she'd fall into a trap, she held the lantern high to ascertain her footing. Cold sweat beaded her upper lip as she slowly ascended the tunnel and came to an opening. Breathing a sigh of relief, she pushed her way through the heavy brush that had been carefully laid over the entrance to conceal it from prying eyes. Glancing about, Katharina quickly blew out the lantern and looked at the moonlit meadow. She immediately recognized it as the meadow that she had watched Kane ride across so many nights.

Katharina drew in a deep breath of the refreshing, cold night air and glanced back in the direction she'd just come. The entrance to the tunnel was so well hidden, had she not known of its existence, she would not be able to find it. Katharina knew that had been the intent of those who used it to enter Sedgewick Castle. In times of war, many fortifications had been constructed with tunnels. It was a means of escape should an enemy breach the castle walls.

Katharina's gaze swept past the thick brush and back to the stone walls towering over her. Sedgewick Castle. Tonight she had learned that there were secrets within its granite walls, secrets that could destroy the man she loved, secrets that kept one young man a prisoner because nature had cruelly robbed him of the beauty it had given to his brother.

Trembling from the terror of being left alone in the catacomb and the emotional upheaval of the last hours, Katharina sank to a tuft of dried grass and drew her knees up to her chest. She hugged them tightly and pressed her face against the burgundy velvet. Tonight she had stumbled upon something that Kane had not wanted to reveal to her, the Sedgewick curse. Unfortunately, she couldn't be certain of his reaction when he learned of what she had discovered. After the way he'd avoided her during the past two weeks, this might be all he needed to rid himself of her. However, now that she knew of Richard, he couldn't just allow her to leave Sedgewick. No. He'd have to insure that she'd never reveal what she'd seen.

Katharina shook her head, trying to deny her morbid thoughts. Her heart told her that the man she loved would not harm her. But in truth, she didn't know what Kane would do. He could keep her imprisoned in the tower for the rest of their lives without anyone telling him nay.

Katharina raised her head and looked out across the moonlit meadow. Or would she be the next mistress to be burned at the stake to protect the Sedgewicks?

Shaking the horrid thought away, Katharina leaped to her feet and dusted away the grass clinging to her velvet skirts. She had no other choice but to trust her heart. She couldn't click her heels and wish herself back to the safety of the twentieth century. Nor could she leave Sedgewick without learning whether she had made another mistake in giving her heart to Kane.

Chapter Ten

"My lady, what are you doing here?"

Katharina jumped and swung about to face the man who consumed her thoughts. He was standing with his back to the full moon, and Katharina couldn't read the expression on Kane's night-shadowed features.

"I-I—" Katharina stuttered, seeking an explanation for her being in the meadow without telling him about her meeting with Richard.

"Lady, I asked why you are here? Do you not realize the danger of being outside Sedgewick's walls without an escort?"

"I—" Katharina tried again. Unable to look at Kane and admit that once more she had invaded his private quarters in the east wing, Katharina lowered her eyes to the ground at his feet and accepted what was to come as she answered honestly, "I found myself in your family crypt with no other way out than through the tunnel."

Kane jerked visibly, his gaze going directly to the clump of brush hiding the entrance. Slowly he looked back at Katharina. His voice held no emotion as he asked, "How did you come to be in the crypt?"

"Your man, Joshua, took me there when he found me in the east wing with your brother."

Kane's quick intake of breath was audible. Even in the dim moonlight, Katharina could see him stiffen. The tension between them seemed like a tangible object as they looked at each other for a long searching moment. Unable to bear the distance growing between them, Katharina asked softly, "Why didn't you tell me about Richard?"

Kane turned his back to her, unable to look at Katharina and see her revulsion for him and his family. "Why do you ask such a foolish question? You know the reason I didn't tell you about Richard."

"No, Kane, I don't know why you kept him a secret from me."

Her words seemed like a whip that cut into Kane's flesh, making him tense and square his shoulders against the all-too-familiar pain. "Do not lie, Katharina. You have eyes. You saw Richard: the cursed Sedgewick."

"What I saw was a young man with beautiful

eyes who has suffered a horrid birth defect."

"You are too kind, Katharina. Why not say you saw the beast of Sedgewick, the cursed Sedgewick, the vampire that is born to us because of what happened here in this meadow over a hundred years ago."

Her heart aching for Kane and Richard, Katharina closed the space between them. She wrapped her arms about Kane's waist and laid her cheek against his tense back. He jerked at her touch, yet didn't pull away. "Kane, I saw a boy who is tortured with the knowledge that he can never live and love as other men. He is no more a beast than you or I."

Kane's shoulders sagged as he removed Katharina's arms from about his waist and drew her in front of him. He looked down into her moonlit features and marveled at her beauty again. She looked as fragile as a porcelain doll. Gently he raised his hand to cup her soft cheek and looked into her eyes, eyes that confirmed the truth of her words. "Did God send you to me, Katharina? Are you an angel sent to give me comfort? Or did the devil send you to torture me?"

"I am neither angel nor devil's helpmeet, Kane. I am only the woman who loves you and yours."

" 'Tis impossible for you to feel such a way after learning of the Sedgewick curse."

Katharina nuzzled Kane's hand before taking it into her own and placing a kiss on his wide palm. Her eyes reflected all the love in her heart as she looked up at him. "I knew of the curse before I came here. It is part of Sedgewick Castle's history. Legend has it that a vampire is born into the Sedgewick family every few generations because of the woman who was burned to death in this very meadow. The first Richard Sedgewick denied his love for her, and she placed a curse upon him and all the generations of Sedgewicks who carry both Sedgewick and Clive blood."

"Then you understand why I didn't tell you about Richard?"

"No, Kane. I don't. There is no reason to have your brother locked away because of a stupid legend. He is young and lonely. He needs to be freed from his prison in the east wing."

Kane shook his head and let his hands fall to his sides. He stared past Katharina into the ebony night. " "I'm afraid you don't understand, after all. It is for Richard's own good that he is kept in the east wing. It's for his protection. Should the villagers or the witch hunters hear of him, he would be tortured and humiliated because of a curse he can't control. 'Tis not his fault fate chose him instead of me."

"Do you mean to say that even your own people would turn against your brother because of something that is not his fault?"

Kane looked down at Katharina, his eyes solemn. "Aye. They would see him dead. You are from another time, Katharina. Perhaps people in your time do not persecute those who are different from themselves, but in this age, Richard would be seen as evil as the curse that follows this family. He has only goodness in his young heart, yet those who don't know him will only see his grotesque appearance, his vampire features."

Tears brimmed in Katharina's eyes as she thought of the tormented life Richard would always have to lead. He could never be free of the prison nature had created for him. She understood well what it would be like for him. Even in the twentieth century, people gawked at those who were different from themselves. Others who were far more cruel made derogatory comments when they passed. "I may come from a different time, but some things never change, Kane. There will always be stupid, cruel people."

"Yes, but do they burn those who are different in your time?"

The thought of Hitler flashed across Katharina's mind. "I wish I could tell you that in the future, everyone treats others as equals, but I'm afraid I can't. It seems evil always exists. Even in the twentieth century, men are still fighting over land and religion, just as they are doing now."

" 'Tis sad to think that man has not changed in the ways that would make life better for all."

"Life is much easier for the average man, and people have worked to improve the lives of the poor. But even in my time, hunger still exists, there are homeless people begging in the streets and children are killing children because their parents have been too self-centered with their own lives to teach them how to be civilized. Times have changed, Kane, but in many ways things remain the same, because man remains the same."

Kane pulled Katharina into his arms and hugged her close. He stared up at the granite walls towering over them. " 'Tis a relief to know you understand why I must do the things I do to protect my family. The Sedgewick curse has afflicted Richard physically, yet I, too, am damned because of the blood in my veins."

Fully comprehending the true extent of the burden Kane had lived with since his brother's birth, Katharina understood why he had kept the secret of Richard from her. He was a man loyal to those he loved, and that made her love him even more. She wanted to take some of his burden upon herself, to share every part of his life. "Let me help you, Kane. Let me share your burden."

Kane looked down at Katharina. "I only wish that you could help me, Katharina. But I fear only time will put an end to this damnable life. When Richard and I are gone, then the curse will be no more."

Puzzled by his statement, Katharina said, "Gone? I don't understand."

"The curse will end with Richard and myself. There will be no more Sedgewicks after us. We are the last, Katharina. I have vowed that no other will suffer the same fate as Richard."

Katharina's heart seemed to still. Ice crept

through her blood as she looked up into Kane's tortured eyes. She shook her head in an effort to deny the meaning of Kane's statement and said, "Surely, you can't mean what I think you are saying."

"Forgive me, Katharina, but I do."

"But you love me and I love you," Katharina said, gripping his arms as if to shake some reason into him.

"Aye, 'tis true. I love you with all my heart. I have never met another woman such as you. I believe you stole my heart the moment you walked into my chamber that first night," Kane said, his voice husky with the emotions that were tearing him apart.

His honest answer shook Katharina to the core. She clutched Kane for support and whispered, "You can't do this to us."

"It is something I have to do, Katharina. Don't you see, it is the only right thing to do. No matter how much I love you, I can't give in to my emotions. I had rather see the pain in your eyes now instead of hatred later. What I do is best for both of us."

"Don't tell me what is best for me, Kane. I can make my own decisions. You have no right to deny us our time together because you believe that some stupid curse exists. It is only a legend, nothing more."

Kane pointed toward the castle walls. "Look yonder, Katharina. 'Tis no legend that lives in the east wing. 'Tis my brother. He exists and I'll have no other suffer the same fate, no matter how it hurts me to deny myself your love."

"Kane, listen to me. There is no such thing as a curse. It is all superstition. Richard's condition is a birth defect. The woman your ancestor burned didn't have the power to save her own life, much less put a curse upon your family."

"Say what you will, but I know better. I am a Sedgewick. I have read the history of our family. Richard is not the first to suffer from the curse." Kane turned away from Katharina and gathered up his mount's bridle. "But he will be the last. Come, the hour grows late. I must see Richard and assure him that you are safe. Then I must speak with Joshua."

"Will you allow me to see Richard again?"

Kane gave Katharina an assessing look. "Do you truly want to visit Richard, or is it only pity making you speak?"

"It is pity and love, Kane. I pity Richard his caged existence, yet I love him because he is your brother. I could not live knowing that I had refused to help ease his burden because of something no one could prevent. And, strangely, I feel that in the short time we were together tonight, we became friends. Friends help one another no matter their appearance or circumstances."

Katharina's words seemed to give Kane a measure of peace. He nodded and smiled sadly. "You have my permission to visit Richard as long as I have your word that you will never mention his existence outside the east wing. He is young and needs someone other than myself in his life."

Feeling that she had won one small battle, Katharina walked at Kane's side as they left the meadow and entered the granite walls of Sedgewick Castle once more. There was little more to be said at the present time. She didn't know how she could make Kane understand that no curse existed, but she prayed that in time she would find a way to break through the years of superstition.

Katharina bid Kane good night at the foot of the stairs and made her way back to her tower room. She tried to sleep, but oblivion eluded her. Alone in her narrow bed, she tossed and turned, unable to put from her mind thoughts of what she had learned about the Sedgewick family.

Dawn lightened the cobalt sky to sapphire and then slowly blended it into a melody of pinks and golds before the first rays of the morning sun crept over the trees to spill into her chamber. Dust motes danced in the sunlight as Katharina hit her pillow and flopped onto her side, disgusted with herself for her failure to convince Kane that no curse existed.

"I will not give up," Katharina ground out, her tone full of determination. "I will find a way to make Kane see the truth if it takes me the rest of my life."

Satisfied with her resolution, Katharina yawned and closed her eyes.

An urgent knock at the door awoke Katharina less than two hours later. A moment later the door eased open and Chole's bright head peeped around the edge of the thick oak panel. "Mistress, they've sent for you from the village."

"Tell them I'll be right down, Chole," Katharina said, concerned that Mistress Remy's grandchild's fever had returned. Katharina yawned and threw back the warm covers that had protected her against the icy chill of the late-autumn morning. She slid her feet to the cold floor and suppressing another yawn, stumbled out of the bed. Lethargic after her sleepless night, she managed to dress herself and pin her hair up in an untidy French twist before throwing the borrowed cloak about her shoulders and making her way downstairs.

A gaunt-faced man awaited her with cap in hand. He smiled at her, revealing a row of rotten teeth. He bobbed his head respectfully and said, "My lady, Mistress Remy said if I'd come and ask ye, ye'd help me girl."

"Is your daughter ill?" Katharina asked.

"The physician says it's all in 'er head. Says she's tetched. But she's not, me lady. Me girl knows as much as the rest of us. 'Tis her eyes that's giving her the worry."

"What do you here, Paddy?" Kane asked from the stair landing.

Paddy Shadford glanced up at the man standing above them and bobbed his head again. "A good day to ye, lordship. I've come to ask yer lady's help with me girl, Misty."

Kane took Katharina's breath away as she watched him descend the stairs, the perfect picture of an English aristocrat. Dressed in a red velvet riding coat with white lace at his throat and wrists, black leather britches and shining knee boots, he was magnificent. It took a concentrated effort to force herself to look away from him and turn her attention back to the man called Paddy.

Kane paused beside Katharina and asked, "And what help does your daughter need, Paddy?"

"She be in a bad way, yer lordship. She says she's losing her sight. The physician says nay but I've no faith in that leech. Mistress Remy said he done give up on her babe and that it was yer lady that saved its wee life. And she said if anyone could help me Misty, that it'd be her ladyship."

"My lady knows about herbs to help lower a fever, but I fear she can be of no help to your daughter, Paddy."

The man seemed to sag. He looked forlornly from Kane to Katharina. "O'm sorry to have bothered ye, me lady. I had hope that ye could do me Misty good." He shook his head sadly and turned away. "Now 'tis left in the good Lord's 'ands. 'E's the only hope she has left."

Katharina looked at his stooped back as Paddy Shadford turned and walked toward the door. Her heart went out to the man. She knew she couldn't cure the man's daughter with herbs, but it would not hurt for her to visit her to see exactly what was wrong with her. She'd not been trained as a physician, yet she suspected her knowledge of disease was greater than a seventeenth-century physician's. Flashing Kane a challenging look, she called out, "Mr. Shadford, I may not be able to help your daughter, but I would like to meet her. Would you mind if I walked back to the village with you?"

"Katharina, I forbid you to do this," Kane ground out, his voice only audible to Katharina.

"And I refuse to obey such an order. This man needs my help, and I intend to give it if at all possible."

"Your heart knows too much pity, Katharina. These people would turn on you in a moment should one of their own die after you've treated them. And I will not risk your welfare."

"You do not risk my welfare. It is my decision to use my knowledge to help those who can't help themselves."

"I will have you locked in the tower, Katharina."

"Will you keep me there for the rest of my life, Kane? Because once I am free, I will go to Paddy's daughter. She needs my help."

Paddy Shadford stood in the open doorway, watching Lord Sedgewick and his lady. He couldn't hear what was being said, yet he knew that something unpleasant was taking place between them. The look on His Lordship's face would put fear in many a strong man's heart. Paddy suppressed a shudder. He'd not like that look turned upon him, nor would he want to face her ladyship either. It seemed that Lord Sedgewick's lady was giving as good as she got. Again Paddy suppressed a shudder. 'Twas fortunate that Lord Sedgewick was a strong man, after all was said and done.

"Katharina, you are placing yourself in jeopardy again without thinking of the consequences. You were fortunate with Mistress Remy, however you may not be so again. I can't allow you to do this," Kane growled, his face flushed with anger.

"And I can't allow you to stop me," Katharina said, jerking up the hood of her cloak. The day was fair and did not warrant a hood; however the action served its purpose: to shut Kane out.

Kane looked at the stubborn set of Katharina's chin and realized he had only two choices left to him. He could accept her decision or have her thrown into the dungeon. The thought of the latter left a bad taste in Kane's mouth. He couldn't do that to Katharina again. Throwing his hand up in the air in exasperation, he stalked off down the hallway, his early-morning visit to Churchill already forgotten in the anger that Katharina's headstrong attitude created. The slamming of the library door echoed throughout the castle as Katharina followed Paddy Shadford down the wide steps and to the gate.

Katharina's temper had long cooled by the time

they reached the tiny cottage where Paddy and his daughter, Misty, lived. Unlike Mistress Remy's shadowy home, the Shadford cottage was filled with light. The mud and stone walls had been whitewashed on the inside. Fresh thatch covered the roof and gave off a clean odor. Sparsely furnished like the majority of tenant homes, the main room held only a chest, a food safe, chairs and a rough hewn table. However, a bouquet of dried wildflowers had been placed in an earthenware pitcher and set in the center of the table to add color. That small touch made the entire cottage seem warm and homey.

"Misty, me girl. Come here. O've brought her ladyship," Paddy called out as he stepped through the doorway. No answer came. Frowning, Paddy crossed to the small door that led out of the back of the cottage. He opened it and called his daughter's name again. Again no answer came. Worry etched his worn features as he turned to Katharina. "If ye'll wait here, me lady, I'll go find Misty. She has a bent toward taking care of the animals, and 'tis hard at times to pry her loose from 'em should they need her care."

"I'll come with you, if you don't mind, Mr. Shadford. I'd like to see Misty's animals."

"Yer welcome," Paddy said, marveling at the way Lord Sedgewick's lady treated him. She acted as if he were her equal, not just a tenant who ofttimes couldn't grow enough to pay his rent. Leading the way through the narrow door, Paddy stepped out into what in spring would be the garden. A narrow path wove through the patch to an opening in the twig fence that protected the summer vegetables from the wandering cows and pigs. The sound of a squealing piglet drew them to the small shed that lay only a short distance away.

Katharina and Paddy paused at the sight of the girl down on her knees in the mire, trying to free a greedy piglet from between two planks where he'd become lodged while trying to usurp his brothers at the feeding trough.

"Misty," Paddy called out over the clamorous, wiggling little beast's squealing, "I've brought her ladyship to see ye."

Paddy's daughter raised her head and absently brushed a blond curl out of the way to reveal tear-filled, pale blue eyes. She gave Katharina a wobbly smile before she said, "Papa, I can't get him out. Help me before he hurts himself."

"Girl, leave the pigs alone. Come and see Her Ladyship. I'll take care of 'em," Paddy said, crossing the few feet to his daughter. He bent and assumed Misty's hold on the squirming piglet.

Getting to her feet, Misty tried to dust the dirt from her worn skirt. She blushed as she bobbed Katharina a curtsey. "I'm sorry that you find me in such a sorry state, me lady. But I couldn't just let the little beast be hurt."

"I would do the same," Katharina said, smiling at the beautiful young girl. Katharina guessed her age to be about fifteen. Tall and slender, her young body just beginning to blossom into womanhood, she had outgrown the gown that she wore. Her budding breasts stretched the old faded fabric of her bodice taut, and the hem of her skirt lay several inches above her ankles.

"Will ye take tea, my lady?" Misty asked as they made their way back through the garden.

"I'd love some tea, if it's not an imposition." Katharina's stomach growled in agreement. "And while you make the tea, perhaps you can tell me of the problems you've been having with your sight."

Before Misty could reply, a fat tabby roused herself from her bed in the morning sunlight and stretched gracefully before joining them. A moment later several kittens, in a variety of colors, followed, meowing for their mother's attention. Paying no heed to her offspring, the tabby slowly wove itself around Misty's ankles, impeding her steps. Misty lifted the fat cat into her arms, cuddling her for a brief moment before giving her a scratch beneath her chin and setting her back down. "Go, Sis. Take care of your brood. I have company and canna pet you now."

"I'm sorry, me lady. Sis thinks she's queen here."

"There's no need to apologize. I once had a cat that thought he was a dog. He followed me about and met me at the door when I returned home every night."

The young girl laughed as she stood back to allow Katharina to enter the cottage. "I do love me animals. They ask nothing more than a bit of food and love to be content. And they love ye no matter what people say about ye."

Seeing a look of pain cross Misty's face before she turned away and busied herself filling the kettle, Katharina realized that a seventeenth-century adolescent was no different from one of the twentieth. They all needed approval to build self-esteem. Her own memories of her earlier years had faded, yet Katharina sensed from the tightness that gripped her heart at Misty's expression that she'd not gone easily down that youthful path.

"Misty, tell me about the problem you're having with your eyes. Paddy said at times you can't see, but the physician can find nothing wrong with you," Katharina said.

Misty set the tea to simmer before she turned back to Katharina. She shrugged as gracefully as if she had been a tabby herself. "I truly don't know. 'Tis like looking through a peephole in the door at most times. And at other times, especially at night, I can see nothing. If I'm late bringing the cow in from pasture, I get lost because I can't see the path. The physician and the villagers think I'm mad, but truly I'm not. There is just something wrong with my eyes."

Katharina's heart sank. There was nothing she could do to help Misty. Without a modern optometrist's examination to confirm her suspicions, she couldn't be certain, but she feared the girl had retinitis pigmentosa. There was no cure for the disease even in the twentieth century. All she could recommend was a simple eyewash made of eyebright to relieve the strain and inflammation.

Katharina's heart contracted. Misty was just beginning her life. She had been blessed with beauty and grace, yet the disease would eventually rob her of her sight entirely. Katharina wanted to reach out and put her arms about Misty to try to protect her from the future. However, she remained seated at the small rough-hewn table and listened politely as Misty once more turned the conversation to her animals. She couldn't tell the child-woman to savor every sight and store away the memories because of the fate awaiting her. It would be unfair. All she could do was to give her friendship.

Tears swelled in Katharina's throat as she lifted her cracked porcelain cup and drank the dark, bitter tea that Misty had prepared. Since arriving in the seventeenth century, she'd done little else than give her friendship. First to Kane, then Richard and now this beautiful young girl. Unfortunately, for Richard and Misty it was all she could do for them.

Suppressing the urge to lay her head down upon the table and weep out her misery, Katharina smiled and carried on the conversation about the different pets that she could remember having had as a child. Misty giggled and laughed, her youth making her forget the reason for Katharina's visit.

A loud knock on the door interrupted their conversation. Eyes bright with happiness, Misty opened the door and quickly dropped a curtsey before stepping back to allow the new visitor into her home. "My lord. 'Tis happy we are to welcome you to our home. We have been enjoying yer lady's visit greatly."

Unsmiling, Kane only glanced at Misty before his eyes went directly to Katharina, still seated at the table with her cup of tea. "Thank you for your hospitality, mistress, but I fear I can't tarry to visit. I've come to escort my lady back to Sedgewick."

Misty's smile faded as she glanced back at Katharina. She'd been enjoying the lady's visit. It had helped relieve some of her loneliness. Because of the strange malady of her eyes, and the belief that she had been bewitched, the villagers had little to do with her. Her father had done his best to be a companion to her since her mother's death when Misty was ten, but she needed the company of other females. She'd never been able to talk to her pa about the things that had been happening to her body the past few years—especially about the illness that came upon her once a month.

Seeing the resolute look in Kane's eyes, Katharina rose to her feet. In her present state of mind, she didn't feel like doing battle with him over a few minutes. There were things far more important in life. Turning to Misty, she said, "Will you thank your father for inviting me to meet you, Misty? And I must thank you for the wonderful cup of tea. Will you allow me to visit again?"

Misty's face lit with happiness. She smiled, revealing even, white teeth. "I would love to have you come anytime, my lady."

"Since we have become friends, will you call me Katharina?"

Misty glanced uncertainly at Kane and saw him give a reluctant nod. Her smile widened. "Yes, my lady. I would be honored to address you as Katharina."

"Then it's settled. Will you come to Sedgewick to pick up the herbs for your eyes? It will not stop your problems, but it will ease the irritation."

Misty nodded quickly. "Thank you, my lady." Seeing Katharina's arched brow, she blushed and said hesitantly, "Thank you, Katharina."

Katharina smiled and preceded a visibly annoyed Lord Sedgewick out to the small, two-wheeled cart he'd driven to the Shadfords' cottage. Without a word, he lifted her up onto the padded burgundy velvet seat before taking his place. He snapped the reins against the sturdy Shetland pony's back, and the animal set off at its own unhurried pace. Kane flicked the reins harder, making the little beast strain to increase its pace.

"You don't have to beat the pony to death because you're angry with me," Katharina said calmly, suppressing the angst that Kane's disfavor created. She had read the furor in Kane's face when Misty opened the door. She'd also heard it in his voice. And she knew it was only increasing at his restraint.

A muscle in Kane's cheek twisted as he tightened his jaw and fought to suppress the urge to turn Katharina over his lap and spank her like the child she was acting like. Did she have no sense in that beautiful head of hers? Was her need to help others going to be the death of her? Not if he could prevent it!

Kane released a long breath and felt his anger begin to dissipate. He knew the answers to his own questions. She was different from the selfish women of his acquaintance. She was willing to give of herself to help others. She was willing to ignore the Sedgewick curse and love his brother, no matter his appearance. Kane drew the cart to a halt in the bend in the road that sheltered them from view of the Shadfords' cottage. He stared for a long moment at his hands grasping the leather reins. He had physical strength enough to prevent Katharina from jeopardizing her own life, yet did he possess the strength to allow her to do what her heart demanded?

Slowly, he turned his head to look at the woman at his side. "Katharina, I am angry with you for putting yourself in danger. Yet I find myself in a dilemma where you are concerned. I admire your need to help others, but I fear that need will endanger you. I've tried to make you understand that in this time, you could easily be called a witch, and the witch hunters would see you dead. I love you too much to risk that, even for those you can help."

The tears she'd hidden so well from Misty formed in Katharina's eyes, brimming over her thick lashes and trailing a path down her cheeks as she looked at Kane. Her lower lip trembled with emotion as she said, "I love you, Kane. And I don't want to upset you. But I'm afraid I will keep upsetting you should I be needed. As I've told you, I can't turn my back on people in need. Especially those like Misty. She is only a young girl, but I fear she is going blind. The sad thing is, I can't help her with my herbs. I can only be her friend."

Katharina fell against Kane's chest and wept for the young girl in the small cottage, as well as for the young man in the east wing of Sedgewick Castle. Both were doomed to a future of loneliness. She also wept for herself and man who held her so tenderly. They, too, were doomed to loneliness, living together but not as a normal couple in love.

"Hush, my sweeting. There are things in life that none of us can change, no matter how much we want to. And I fear Misty's blindness is one of those things. You have to learn to live with it or you'll die from the pain."

Katharina gripped his coat and buried her face deeper into the cascade of white ruffles on his shirt. She shook her head and said, "I don't want to live with it. I want to do something to stop it. I feel so helpless. At home I could have called a doctor, gone on the Internet to find help. There are medicines to relieve the symptoms, if not to cure the disease. And with Richard I could have had the best surgeons in the world fix his face so that he could come out in the light of day." Katharina drew in a shuddering breath before she said, "And with us, I could have found proof that no curse exists to keep us apart."

"God curse us all for giving you such pain," Kane said, his husky voice revealing his anguish. It was as if her tears melted away the wall he kept about himself. His emotions escaped their tomb, and his arms tightened about her. Too late, Kane realized that he had passed the point of no return. The woman he loved lay against his chest weeping for the pain that he had inflicted upon her.

Gently, Kane tipped up Katharina's chin and looked into her tear-bright eyes. "I love you, Katharina. May God forgive me, but I can't help myself. I have tried to make you understand, but I can't even make my own body understand why we can't be together. I want you, Katharina. More than anything on this earth. Love me, my sweet Lady of the Night."

Katharina's breath stilled in her throat and her heart soared as Kane lowered his mouth to hers. She wrapped her arms about his neck, pressing herself to him, answering his request in the only way she knew. A moment later, she found herself being lifted down from the cart and carried to the sheltering trees. Kane took his cloak and laid it over a pile of leaves, making them a soft bed.

There was no need for foreplay. They became as wild as the land about them. Their lovemaking was untamed and unhindered by propriety. A moment of surrender and triumph. Greedily they devoured each other, insatiable in their quest to know every inch of each other's body. Surrounded by the heat of their passion, they felt no cold.

Naked in the afternoon sun, Katharina felt no shame as Kane raised himself above her and looked at her body. Each place his eyes rested his hands soon followed, warming her with his touch. He stroked the curve of her throat and then cupped her breasts. He held them as if they were treasures to be savored, his gaze never leaving them as he flicked her nipples and watched them grow into hard little peaks. Downward he moved, stroking from rib to hip, soothing his hands across her round little belly, admiring each inch of her flesh as he slowly roamed down her thighs. Katharina opened to him, unconsciously arching toward the warmth of his touch, needing to feel him explore her depths, to claim her as his own.

She watched with pride and passion as he enjoyed her body. She denied him nothing and nearly swooned from the pleasure he gave her in return.

Unable to take and not give, Katharina became the aggressor. She raised herself, wrapping her arms about him, forcing him to his back. He lay before her, his body swollen and hard for release. She straddled his middle, stroking his shoulders and chest, circling his flat nipples enticingly. Her hair fell over them as she captured his mouth with her own and temptingly rotated her hips over him. Empowered by the sensations her own movements gave her, she began a slow descent, stroking, caressing his hard, flat belly until she reached his desire. Slowly she took him into her mouth, sliding her tongue caressingly over him. She heard him moan his surrender and again felt a swell of pleasure rush through her. Unable to deny her need any longer, she came up and impaled herself upon him, driving him deeply into her femininity, taking all of him, greedily. She moved on him, thrusting her hips, making him moan again with pleasure. A wild woman now, needing only to appease her own hunger, Katharina rode him, clutching his shoulders, digging her fingernails into the tanned flesh as Kane clasped her buttocks and brought her down even harder against him.

Together they moved. Their sweat-beaded bodies joined in the quest for fulfillment. United, they exploded into a myriad of sensations. They cried out in unison the universal sound of ecstasy. Every muscle in her body quivering, Katharina fell forward, lying against the perspiration-damp chest of the man she loved. She could feel him throb inside of her, and savored the knowledge that she had a part of him deep within her. Moisture beaded on her thick lashes.

Kane rolled on his side, taking Katharina with him. He propped himself on one elbow and looked down at her love-flushed face. With one finger he gently touched a stray tear. "I had hoped your tears would now be gone."

A wobbly smile curled Katharina's lips as she raised her head and kissed the finger holding her tear. "My tears now are from happiness."

Kane smiled down at her. "I'm feeling quite pleased myself. 'Tis not often a man finds himself being bedded. 'Tis most oft the other way round. And now I'm wondering why we go to so much trouble to be the instigator when it's far less work and just as enjoyable to let the females have their way."

A teasing light sparkled in Katharina's eyes, and she laughed softly as she trailed a provocative finger down the middle of Kane's hard chest. "Surely, sir, other women have had their way with you. You are far too handsome and too much of a temptation to deny."

A shade seemed to be drawn down over Kane's eyes, covering the carefree expression. He drew in a deep breath and eased away from Katharina. He sat up and reached for his discarded clothing. "At one time the ladies could not keep their hands off me. But that was before Richard was born."

A mixture of emotions—jealousy, pity, anger—shot through Katharina. Life had been so unfair to this man. She knelt behind Kane and wrapped her arms about his neck. She laid her cheek against his and looked at the forest surrounding them. "There is a saying in my time that you can't always see the forest for the trees. Some things are too close to you for you to see them clearly. But I'm not so close, Kane. I know there is no Sedgewick curse and I will prove it to you, one way or the other. I will see you look at me one day without fear. And we will live our lives together, and have the children that I know you want but are too afraid to sire."

Kane unwrapped Katharina's arms and forced a laugh. "Then I fear, my lady, you have your life's work cut out for you. 'Tis hard to visit my brother and not know we Sedgewicks are cursed." Kane changed the subject. "Now get yourself dressed before you take ill. I need no other life upon my conscience."

Katharina didn't disobey his order. The chill of the afternoon had invaded the warmth left by their lovemaking, and she shivered from the cold breeze as she quickly dressed. But she couldn't resist one last promise as Kane lifted her into the cart. She looked down at him and said, "I will make you happy, one way or the other, Kane. You have suffered enough because of that stupid legend."

Kane gave her a rueful smile and reached up to pick a dried leaf from Katharina's hair. "I fear I'm not the only one who has suffered. 'Twould be far better of me to offer you a decent bed rather than a pile of leaves."

Katharina caught Kane's hand and placed a kiss on it. "We do seem to have penchant for leafy bowers instead of feather beds, don't we?"

Kane's smile faded. "Aye. 'Twould seem I can't be close to you without losing all control."

"I don't mind," Katharina said and smiled.

Kane climbed into the cart and picked up the reins. He snapped them against the pony's back before he said, " 'Twould be far better for all concerned if I minded more."

Katharina laid her head against Kane's shoulder as the small cart carried them along the road toward Sedgewick. She would find a way to prove to Kane that he had nothing to fear by loving her.

Chapter Eleven

Richard laid the leather-bound volume on the side table and stretched out his long legs to the warmth of the fire. He thoughtfully tapped his fingers together and watched the flames dance over the charred logs. He was the happiest he'd ever been in his entire sixteen years. He now had a friend other than his brother, and it was wonderful. Katharina visited him daily, and they would talk and laugh together as if everything within the Sedgewick household was normal. She told marvelous fairy tales of little girls in red capes and of princes and princesses in love. She also told outrageous stories of flying machines and other impossible things that were truly entertaining. Indeed, it didn't matter what Katharina said or did as long as she stayed with him to offset the loneliness of his existence.

Richard released a long breath. He was the happiest he'd ever been, yet he was also the saddest. His visits with Katharina served to remind him that he would never have a wife or family of his own. Doomed by the Sedgewick curse, he would have to remain in the shadows, observing other people's lives for as long as God allowed him to live.

Sudden moisture glistened on Richard's dark lashes. He stood and crossed to the window. Through the blur of tears, he stared down at the meadow as he touched the features of his accursed face. A single tear escaped and trickled down his cheek. He brushed it away with the back of his hand and drew in a shuddering breath. There, in the meadow, his destiny had been cast. And because of his ancestor's cowardice, he would never know the love of a woman or the companionship of men outside his household.

Richard shook his head and abruptly turned away from the window. He couldn't allow himself to dwell upon such melancholy thoughts. Nor could he surrender to self-pity. He had to keep strong, to look toward the light of life instead of the darkness. If he didn't, he'd lose what sanity he possessed. It was also the only way to keep from becoming the monster that his face made him appear to the outside world.

"Joshua," Richard called, needing to escape his

thoughts, "have the horses brought to the tunnel. I need to ride tonight."

A shuffling sound came from the dressing room, and a moment later Joshua's huge frame filled the open doorway. He scratched his head and yawned as he looked at Richard and said, "Ye called, young sir?"

"Aye. I want you to ready the horses. We will ride tonight," Richard said. He raised his hand and shook his head to still Joshua's objection before it could be verbalized. "No. Don't try to deny me this. I will ride tonight. I *must* ride tonight, and I'll have no one say me nay."

Seeing the look of determination in Richard's dark eyes, Joshua merely nodded and turned toward the door. " 'Twill take a few minutes for me to get to the stables and saddle the horses. O'll meet ye in our usual place near the entrance to the crypt."

"Be quick, man. I need to feel the night air against my face. I need to feel free and alive," Richard said as he began to unbutton his doublet. He cast it aside and changed into the black coat and britches he wore outside the castle walls. Tall black boots, black hat and black cloak finished his riding habit. Dressed entirely in black and riding a black horse, he was like a phantom crossing the countryside in the darkness, nearly invisible to those who might chance a glimpse of him. Like a mysterious black cloud with his mount's hoofs creating the thunder, he rode through the night.

Moments later, Richard entered the alcove and pushed the latch behind the portrait frame to open the passageway to the family burial tomb. He lit his way with the tiny oil lamp, though he knew the passage by heart. He needed little light to show the way to the tunnel's exit, where Joshua awaited him, already mounted. Together they set off into the cold night.

In his need for space and freedom, Richard left Joshua and his slower mount far behind. He raced through the night, galloping over freshly cleared fields and leaping his horse over stone walls. Wildly he rode, savoring the pleasure of the cold wind against his face and the feel of the powerful animal beneath him. The horse's speed helped Richard put the misery of his life at a distance. Alone in the night, he was a normal man enjoying life as one with the earth and sky.

His tension easing and common sense prevailing as he reached the outskirts of the village, Richard drew his mount in and turned back toward Sedgewick. He didn't press for speed. The animal had served him well during the past hour and he'd not mistreat him further. Allowing his mount to cool at a steady trot, Richard first heard the weeping as he neared the meadow. A warning chill tingled up his spine as he drew his horse to a halt and listened intently. The heart-wrenching sound reached out to him, wiping away all thoughts of his own welfare.

Drawn forward as if by an invisible hand, he

eased his horse toward the soft crying. Quietly he slipped from the saddle and moved through the trees until he could see a young girl, who cried as if her heart was breaking. Sitting at the edge of the clearing, she wept into her hands.

The sight tugged at Richard's heart. Unconsciously, he closed the space between them and knelt at her side. Gently he asked, "Are you hurt?"

Trembling visibly, the girl shook her head and looked up at Richard.

"Then are you lost?"

Drawing in a shuddering breath, she nodded and let her hands fall forlornly into her lap. "I lost my way to the castle. I'm going to see Lady Katharina. I need her help."

A pale sliver of a moon gave enough light to allow Richard to see the girl's features clearly. His breath caught in his throat. She was beautiful. Suddenly realizing that she could also see his features, he ducked his head out of fear and shame. He didn't want to frighten her with his horrid face. Swallowing back the pain, he said, "You are only a short distance from Sedgewick. Look there, you can see the walls from here."

The girl turned her golden head in the direction of Richard's voice, not in the direction he pointed. "Sir, I fear I can't see the way." She paused and drew in a steadying breath. "That is the reason I became lost."

"What would make you come for Lady Katharina when you cannot see?"

"Please, sir. Help me reach Sedgewick. My Papa has taken ill, and I've come to ask Lady Katharina's help."

"Surely a physician would be far better than Lady Katharina in this matter."

Misty struggled to her feet and shook her head. Blindly staring in the direction of Richard's voice, she pleaded again, "Please, sir. Show me the way to Lord Sedgewick's home. I have need of Lady Katharina's help. She is the only person who will come to my aid, because she does not think me bewitched."

A wave of relief swept over Richard as he realized that the beautiful girl could not see him. Then a surge of pity assaulted him, squeezing at his heart. This lovely creature could not see his deformed face, nor could she see the beauty of a sunset or the full moon reflected in a pond at night. Sympathy for her overshadowing his own demons, Richard reached out and took her hand. "Mistress, may I show you the way to Sedgewick Castle?"

"God bless you, sir. I am in your debt for life."

"Then pay your debt by telling me your name, mistress."

"My name is Misty. I am Paddy Shadford's daughter. He is Lord Sedgewick's tenant."

"The name is as beautiful as its owner," Richard said. Placing Misty's hand on his arm, he walked her toward the castle.

"May I know my rescuer's name, sir?"

" 'Tis of no consequence now. I am merely passing through."

"Then I will call you my gallant knight, for you have rescued me like a knight of old. And like a knight of old, your kindness will save my father's life."

Richard paused in the shadows near Sedgewick's gate door. "I fear I must leave you now, Mistress Shadford. But you are only a few feet from Sedgewick. Should you call out, the guards will hear you and allow you to enter."

Misty reached out and clasped Richard's hand. She squeezed it gratefully and said, "Thank you, my gallant knight. May you reach your journey's end safely. Godspeed."

"Good eve, Misty. I will offer a prayer that your father recovers from his illness soon."

"Bless you, my gallant knight."

Richard watched as Misty crossed the few feet to the gate. It took her a few moments to feel her way to the thick timbered entrance and find the chain to the bell. It tinkled inside, and a moment later he heard a guard's gruff voice call out to ask who was about at such a time of night. Misty answered and then the heavy bar was lifted and the portal swung open to allow her to enter.

Satisfied and bemused by his meeting with the lovely girl, Richard left his mount with Joshua and made his way back to the east wing. All through the night, he thought of the girl, wondering at her easy acceptance of him, wondering if he dared meet her again.

Katharina closed the heavy volume and absently ran the tip of her finger over the letters embossed in the oiled leather. It read SEDGEWICK. Katharina laid her head back against the high-backed chair and closed her weary eyes. They burned from hours of reading. Within the family ledger, written on parchment grown yellow and crinkled with age, was the name of every Sedgewick who had been born into the family since the year 1400. Events of importance had also been recorded. Marriages, dowries, grandchildren, land holdings, visits from kings and queens, heads of Parliament and deaths had been meticulously written down.

Katharina rubbed at her burning eyes. It hadn't been easy to decipher the handwritten entries. Reading the ledger had been like plowing a sun-hardened field with a toothpick. She'd had to learn how to read the English language again, since the ledger had been written with a quill pen in Old English. Much of it she'd managed to guess, though there had been certain passages that she'd had to translate to ensure that she'd not misunderstood their intent.

The only odd thing she'd discovered in the family history was the disappearance of certain children shortly after birth. It seemed as if they were born and then vanished into thin air. The deaths of other children who had passed away shortly after birth had been recorded, as well as a brief description of the cause of each death and the family's ensuing grief over the loss of the child.

"So why weren't the other children included if they died?" Katharina asked aloud.

"Did you say something?" Kane asked, glancing up from the pile of papers in front of him. He'd spent a pleasant afternoon sharing his library with Katharina. She'd wanted to see the family ledger and had quickly become engrossed in the thick volume. Instead of asking her to leave him, he'd returned to his work, enjoying the peace and quiet, and Katharina's silent company. It seemed as if Katharina and he were truly man and wife. Kane shook the thought away. He didn't even want to contemplate a thought that could never become reality.

Katharina glanced over at Kane. The sight brought a smile to her lips. Illuminated by the candelabra, his face was even more startlingly beautiful than usual. One stray curl tumbled over his brow as if he'd run his fingers through his thick dark hair. His eyes sparkled with warmth and love as he looked at her and smiled. She had the sudden urge to touch the tiny dimple that indented his craggy cheek. But she suppressed her desires. She'd enjoyed their time together too much to allow a display of affection to ruin the moment. Hiding her feelings, Katharina said, "No. I was just thinking aloud."

Kane relaxed back into his chair. "Do you often think aloud?"

"Only when I'm puzzled about something. Aunt Sidney has always said I have a tendency to talk to myself when I am trying to work something out in my mind."

"What have you found in that old tome that has you so puzzled?"

Katharina glanced down at the large book lying in her lap. Kane's question was innocent, yet she knew what his reaction would be when she told him what she'd discovered. Resigning herself to the destruction of their quiet moment together, she asked, "I was wondering why some of the children born into the Sedgewick family seem to vanish soon after birth. There have been several during the last two hundred years. The record book meticulously records the lives of every man, woman and child that has ever been born in or involved with the Sedgewick family. All except those children. They just disappear."

Kane's lazy expression vanished. A muscle in his cheek twitched as he drew in a deep breath. "I should think you already know the reason, Katharina. You have met Richard. And as I've already explained, he is not the first Sedgewick to be cursed."

Kane pushed his chair back from the desk and stood. The temperature in the library seemed to have dropped several degrees as he looked at Katharina. " 'Tis time to put away the family history,

Katharina. No matter how much either of us wants to believe that there is nothing in our lives to keep us from being together, we both know different. And there is no reason to keep trying to find something other than the Sedgewick curse to blame for our misery. I will not change my mind about my decision, no matter how much I love you."

Katharina laid the heavy volume on the mahogany table and stood. She closed the space between them, determined not to allow Kane to increase the distance he had put between them since her visit to the Shadfords. She took his hand and pressed it to her cheek as she looked up into his tormented eyes. "I love you, Kane. Curse or no curse. Don't push me away. Let me at least share your burden. You may not want me as your wife, but allow me this much. I need to be with you."

Kane's fingers closed about Katharina's. Every muscle in his body tensed as he stood so near yet so far from the woman he loved. He warred with himself to keep from taking her into his arms. The muscle twitched in his cheek again and his eyes held a desperate look as he said quietly. "Don't do this, Katharina. Don't force the issue further. I will not, *cannot* change my mind."

Kane drew his hand away from Katharina and set her away from him just as the knock came at the door. A look of relief crossed Kane's face as he crossed to the library and opened the double door to find the maid Chole standing sheepishly with hand raised to knock once more against the oak panel.

"What is it, girl?" Kane asked brusquely.

" 'Tis the bewitched girl, me lord. She's come to see my lady."

"Bewitched girl. Blast it! Don't babble such nonsense in my household if you want to remain in my employ," Kane said, finding the maid a convenient way to vent his own frustration.

"I-I'm sorry, yer lordship. I didn't mean to be repeating gossip," Chole stuttered, backing away from the door. "I-I meant ter say that Paddy Shadford's girl is here to see Lady Katharina. And she can't see her way about. As blind as a bat, she be."

"Misty is here?" Katharina asked.

Chole glanced hesitantly around Kane and nodded her curly head. "Aye. She be here. Says her Da is taken bad and needs yer help."

Kane rolled his eyes heavenward before running a hand through his already tousled hair. "Bloody damn! Has everyone forgotten there is a physician who is supposed to be called when someone becomes ill?"

"He'd not come because of me, yer lordship," Misty called out. "He said it was because he had to go to London, but Mistress Remy said she saw him ride through the village just this morning."

Kane glanced down the hallway to see the lovely young girl, her hands held out in front of her to protect her against bumping into anything that might be in her path as she made her way toward the sound of their voices.

"Please, yer lordship, will you allow Lady Katharina to help Papa? He's in a bad way. He canna walk because his side pains him too bad and he's burning with fever."

Katharina stepped past Kane, taking Misty's hands within her own. "Of course I'll do what I can for your father, Misty. How long has he been ill?"

Misty looked toward the sound of Katharina's voice. "He's been down for two days. At first he thought he'd be better after a good rest, but he's gotten worse. His fever is making him talk out of his head, and at times he thinks I'm me Ma."

Katharina gently steered Misty toward a tall, hand-carved chair that sat beneath a portrait of Kane's father. "Wait here, Misty. I'll go get my cloak."

"Katharina," Kane said as she turned toward the stairs. She paused and looked back over her shoulder at him. Seeing the look in her eyes, he surrendered without a fight. "Will you allow me to escort you to Paddy's?"

The smile Katharina gave him was recompense for all his worry. It bathed him in warmth and love. "I would be pleased to have your company, my lord."

Kane glanced at the footman who stood at the end of the hallway. "Have my carriage brought round." Kane glanced back to where Chole stood nervously fidgeting with her white, starched apron. "Have cook prepare her herbs. I fear we'll once more have need of them."

Kane glanced from the stairs where Katharina had disappeared from view back to the girl sitting quietly in the huge chair. He again ran his fingers through his hair and slowly shook his head. For the life of him, he didn't know how he could protect Katharina from herself. She seemed determined to help everyone but herself. And damn it to hell, he loved her even more for it.

"I'm ready, my lord," Katharina said from the foot of the stairs.

"I expected nothing less," Kane said, taking Misty by the hand and escorting her down the hallway and out the tall double doors to the shining black carriage that awaited them.

The carriage wheels ate up the miles along the rutted roadway. The driver pulled it to a halt in front of the thatch-roofed cottage. Kane helped Misty down the steps before lifting Katharina off her feet and swinging her to the ground. He looked down at her as Misty made her way to the cottage door. "What am I going to do with you, Katharina?"

She smiled back up at him. "Love me."

" 'Tis already done," Kane said softly before adding, "Now be about your healing, my lady. The girl has much faith in you."

Katharina's smile faded. "Pray that I will be able to do what she believes of me. I know of plants and herbs that heal, but as you've so often reminded me, I am no physician."

"She and I have faith in you, my love," Kane said softly before dropping a light kiss on her lips.

The light from the open doorway illuminated Katharina's face as she reached up and gently touched Kane's cheek. The love she felt for him glowed softly in her eyes. "Thank you, Kane. You have given me a great gift, and I love you for it all the more."

She turned away and followed Misty into the small cottage. Kane might have said something more, but his throat was filled with emotion. It welled up in him until he felt tears sting his eyes and wet his thick black lashes. He was grateful that there was no moon to illuminate his face, damp with tears of joy and grief.

The moment Katharina saw Paddy lying on his narrow cot, his thin body doubled up with pain, his face beaded with perspiration, she knew the herbs at her disposal would not be enough to help the man. Kneeling on the rough floorboards, she touched his brow. It burned to the touch.

Paddy opened glazed eyes and squinted up at her. He moistened his fever-dry lips and gasped for enough breath to speak. His lips trembled from the effort it took to whisper, "Me lady, will ye see to me Misty? She be all alone once O'm gone. Yer the only one to befriend her. Yer all she's got now."

"Hush, Paddy. You're not going anywhere," Katharina soothed. "You need to rest in order to recover."

Something akin to a weak smile touched Paddy's pale lips. "O'm wise enough to know this pain in me side is killing me just as surely as Cromwell did our king. It's eating away me life, but before O leave this world, O want to see me girl safe. She be too good and sweet to be left to the villagers. They be a hateful lot when they don't understand somethin'."

"Paddy, you mustn't think like this. You need to fight. I've brought the featherfoil for your fever. You'll be much better when it's cooled."

Paddy looked past Katharina to the man who had quietly entered his home. "Me lord, O'm afraid I won't be yer tenant much longer, but I pray ye'll look kindly upon me girl. And—" Paddy's words faded away as he gave in to the tearing pain in his side. He gasped for breath and turned his face into the pillow, stifling his groan of agony. He stiffened and then shuddered before suddenly going limp.

Tears flooding her eyes, Katharina looked up at Kane. "I fear only God can help Paddy now."

Kane closed the space between them and placed a comforting hand on Katharina's shoulder. He wanted to take her into his arms and comfort her until he glanced at the young girl sitting quietly at the small table. Kane's throat tightened at the sight. Death was as much a part of life as birth, yet that didn't make it any easier to accept.

Kane moved to Misty's side and put his arm about her slender shoulders. "You will come back to Sedgewick with Lady Katharina and myself, Misty. You'll be welcome there."

"Thank you, my lord, but I cannot leave Papa. He needs me," Misty said, fighting against the realization that she could no longer hear her father's agonized breathing. She jerked as if struck when she heard Katharina's quiet sobs. Misty shook her head and her lower lip trembled uncontrollably as she said, "Papa. Papa?"

Kane's arm tightened about her for support. "We were too late to help Paddy. Your father is now at rest, child."

Misty shook her head violently and abruptly struggled to her feet. She pulled free of Kane's arm and stumbled toward the silent cot. "Papa, Lady Katharina will make you better. Papa, answer me. Papa, don't do this. Don't leave me. You're all I have."

Misty sank to her knees and fell across Paddy Shadford's still form. She buried her face in his chest. His lifeless body still held the warmth of the living as she sobbed brokenly. Katharina wrapped her arms about the girl, her own tears streaming unheeded down her cheeks as she, too, wept for the old man.

Kane again found himself strangled by emotion. He'd seen many a man die, had attended many a death bed. Yet he'd never felt the pain of other deaths as much as he did this one. His love for Katharina had awakened him to feelings that he'd never recognized he possessed. And it was torture for a man striving to kill off all feeling in order to survive in a life that denied him nearly every emotion except anger.

"I'll go for Mistress Remy. She'll attend Paddy and see to the laying out," Kane said, fleeing from the emotions tearing at him. He escaped into the night and hid himself away in the darkness of his carriage as it traveled along the road to the village. Desperate to regain some control over himself and his wayward heart, he tried to force his feelings back into the steel compartment where they had once been contained. He failed.

Chapter Twelve

Paddy Shadford's funeral was the talk of the village. Generous souls marveled at the compassion of their landlord, remarking upon Lord Sedgewick's kindness to escort the man's daughter to the funeral, even treating the girl as if she, too, were gentry. Less kind individuals made snide comments that birds of a feather flocked together. They reminded all who would listen that the Sedgewick family had also been bewitched. And if people didn't believe what they said, they should just look at the woman who had come to Sedgewick in the dead of a stormy night—the same night that Lord Sedgewick's cousin had disappeared. It was all the devil's work. Old Nick had taken one to make room for his helpmeet.

The gossip swirled through the village, fueled by the retelling of Paddy's sudden death. The rumors spread across the countryside, eating their way into households like insects that begin at the roots of a plant and travel upward until they have covered the leaves at the top.

"Damn me. I can't believe that Kane has allowed things to get this far," Churchill grumbled. Standing with hands folded behind his back, he stared out across the expanse of the winter-browned lawn, which looked even more gloomy because of the overcast day. "This foolishness could jeopardize everything for us."

"Surely you jest. 'Tis only rumors, Winston. We both know Kane would never make an unholy alliance with the devil, nor would he allow any woman to bring harm to his family," Elizabeth Churchill said, straightening the soft woolen shawl about her infant son.

"I had once thought as much. But you haven't seen the way he is now that she's come to Sedgewick. He doesn't act the same man. I catch him staring off into space like some dreamy youth who hasn't had his first woman."

"I think you are jealous. After all these years of friendship, you never have had to compete for Kane's attention. You have been his best friend for the last few years, and now it hurts to know that someone else may come first in his life."

Churchill looked over his shoulder and glared at his wife. "Don't be ridiculous! I've no concern for our friendship. I only fear that his interest in this woman may interfere with the future of England."

Elizabeth smiled at her husband, loving every inch of his tall frame. There wasn't an ounce of evil in his entire body. He was a good man. Loyal to friend and family, church and country. "Does our relationship interfere with your work? Or do your feelings for your family interfere with it?"

"Damn me, Elizabeth! You know this is different. This woman appeared out of nowhere and has worked her way into Kane's life. He doesn't believe her to be Glenville's spy, yet I'm not as sure. Nor am I as certain as Kane that she isn't bewitched. I've overheard his servants talking about her odd ways."

Elizabeth Churchill slowly rocked the cradle holding her sleeping son. "Then perhaps you should speak with Kane about your feelings. 'Tis far better to have everything out in the open. 'Twill save you a great deal of worry. You have enough to trouble you without fretting over your friend's welfare."

Churchill considered his wife's advice for a long moment and then nodded. "You're right, of course." He smiled at the woman lovingly attending their sick child. "As usual."

Elizabeth returned her husband's smile. "Perhaps you should speak with the lady Katharina yourself. You have always been able to judge people fairly. And no matter what has been said, you'll make up your own mind about her."

Churchill crossed the chamber to where his wife sat next to the cradle he'd made for their son. He drew her to her feet and wrapped her in his arms. He held her close as if to absorb her serenity and strength. "What would I do without your faith in me? You always know what is best."

Elizabeth looked up into her husband's handsome face. "I don't always know what is best, Winston. But I listen to my heart. Perhaps that is too feminine for a man to understand, but I've found it makes life far easier." A mischievous twinkle entered her blue eyes. "And you do enough worrying for both of us."

"Wench!" Churchill chuckled before capturing her soft lips with his own.

A small gasping cough interrupted the couple. All other thoughts forgotten in their concern for their child, they turned in unison to the cradle. Churchill lifted his son and laid him on his shoulder and began to pat his back. He and his wife had found it was nearly the only thing that would help ease the infant's breathing. He had spent many long nights walking the floor in order to help his son draw in the life-giving air.

Elizabeth turned frantic eyes to her husband and child. Each day she feared she would lose the battle against the grim reaper. He seemed to hover stealthily in every shadow, awaiting the moment that she or her husband let down their guard. She knew if she did for even one moment, he would slip in and steal the life of their son.

Elizabeth hurried to the salon door and ordered the physician summoned. He came nearly daily, yet he'd done little to help John's illness. She was losing faith in his ministrations, but when the angry coughs racked her son's small body until his tiny lips turned blue, the physician was her only hope. In her present state of constant worry, she'd be willing to summon the devil himself if he would help John.

Less than an hour later, a pensive Elizabeth held her son while Dr. Johnson mixed another vile-smelling concoction that he said would alleviate the severe coughing. Her husband stood beside her chair, a comforting hand resting upon her shoulder. She glanced up at Winston and saw him nod reassuringly as the physician poured the thick mixture into a glass bottle.

"This should bring some results. Young John's breathing should be much easier with the mint and oil."

"That is what you said last week," Elizabeth said, eyeing the evil-looking liquid with distaste.

"Lady Churchill, I've done my best for your son. As I've said in the past, young John will either grow out of this ailment or he will worsen and die from it. In all honesty, what I do is only to help give him some ease in the hope that he'll gain some strength. The rest is in God's hands."

"Then what you are saying, sir, is that you can

offer no hope for our son?" Lord Churchill said, his voice brusque.

"I am not saying to have no hope. I am merely trying to make you understand that I have no power to do more than I am doing at this moment. I am well versed in the arts of healing, but I am not God. There is only so much any man can do."

Tears welling in her eyes, Elizabeth looked up at her husband. "What are we to do, Winston? What are we to do?"

"We'll do as Dr. Johnson says and give John the medicine," Lord Churchill said, giving Elizabeth's shoulder a reassuring squeeze. "Everything will be all right. I promise you."

Elizabeth looked down at the small, pale face framed by the soft blue blanket. Her tears dampened her cheeks as she whispered, "I would die should we lose John."

"No more such talk, Elizabeth. As Dr. Johnson has said, John will outgrow this illness. God would not be so cruel as to take him from us."

Dr. Johnson closed his medical bag. "Your husband is right, Lady Churchill. You must not give way to grief when your son still sleeps within your arms. He has lasted far longer than I first believed. He's a strong little mite." Dr. Johnson set his round-brimmed hat back on his head. "Now I will bid you good day. I have other patients I need to see before the lady at Sedgewick decides to use her spells on them."

"The lady at Sedgewick? Do you mean the Lady Katharina?" Elizabeth asked.

"Aye. The woman sticks her nose into my business at every opportunity. From what the villagers say, she was even at Paddy Shadford's side when he died."

"Do tell?" Lord Chuchill said. "What reason had she for being there?"

"They said the girl, Misty, went and asked her to attend him. You know the girl is bewitched, and 'tis said that the Lady Katharina is also."

" 'Tis only silly rumors," Elizabeth Churchill said, annoyed with the physician for spreading the slanderous accusations.

"Perhaps you are right, my lady. But I know for a fact that the Lady Katharina gave help to Mistress Remy's grandchild. The woman will not let me forget it. She swears the lady is a healer."

"A healer?" Elizabeth said, glancing up at her husband and then back to the physician. "What do you think of her, Dr. Johnson?"

"I believe there is far more to this mysterious newcomer than meets the eye. The woman bears watching. There have been too many strange happenings since her arrival. Now I'll bid you good day. Send for me should John have another spell."

"Of course," Lord Churchill said, escorting the physician out of the room. He closed the door and turned back to his wife. The look on her face said what he feared. He shook his head. "No, Elizabeth. Lady Katharina is no more a healer than myself. She is closer to being a witch than anything else."

"Can we not just try?"

Again Lord Churchill shook his head. "No, we can't. I'll not risk John's soul just to have him for a short time longer."

"This is madness!" Elizabeth said, frantic to do anything to help her son. "The woman is not a witch."

"How can we be so certain, Elizabeth? She is shrouded in mystery. We can't risk John and our own eternal damnation by asking her aid."

"But you don't know that she is a witch, Winston. 'Tis only a rumor. You said you would speak with her before you made your decision about her. Don't deny our son a chance at life because of Dr. Johnson. You must speak with her first."

Wearily, Churchill rubbed at his eyes and then looked back at his wife. Slowly he nodded. "Very well. I will ride to Sedgewick the first thing in the morning."

"And will you ask her help should you decide she is merely a mortal woman?"

"I will decide that when the time arrives, Elizabeth, and not before," Churchill said, raising a silencing hand when his wife opened her mouth to speak. "No more today, lady. In this matter I am firm. I have agreed to visit the Lady Katharina. Do not ask more of me now."

A soft sound drew Churchill's attention to the leaded-glass window. Snowflakes beat against the panes, announcing the first snow of the winter. Soon a white blanket would cover the landscape, making it as bleak and unwelcoming as the future he saw for the child sleeping in his wife's arms.

"It's snowing, Kane," Katharina said, sweeping in to Kane's chamber, her cheeks rosy from the cold, an impish smile on her lips. She held her hand conspicuously behind her.

"And why does that make you so happy?" Kane asked, rising from his chair and closing the space between them. He was drawn to her like a magnet. Unable to resist, he returned her smile.

"Because I love snow," Katharina laughed. In the same instant, she brought her hand from behind her and smeared the handful of icy white crystals over Kane's face.

"You vixen," Kane spluttered, wiping the snow from his eyes. Without thinking of the consequences, he grabbed her before she could turn and flee. Giggling like children, they wrestled about before coming to rest on the thick Aubusson rug in front of the fireplace. The stronger of the two combatants, Kane lay on top of Katharina, holding her arms above her head so she could not find another way to torture him.

He raised himself above her and looked down into her beautiful face aglow with mischief and happiness. The smile left his face as the feel of her body molded against him awakened all his masculine senses. Aroused, he swelled instantly.

A moan akin to desperation escaped him. "God forgive me," he murmured before he lowered his head to capture her lips.

Their play forgotten, Katharina slipped her arms about Kane's neck as soon as he released her hands to discover the intriguing hooks and eyes that kept her breast covered by her gown. His fingers worked swiftly to undo the fastenings. Her full breasts escaped their prison of velvet, enticing his mouth and hands with creamy flesh and beaded nipples.

"God, you're beautiful," Kane whispered as he lowered his mouth to the globe he held cupped in his hand. Like a man starved, he suckled her, running his tongue over the aroused tip before drawing deeply upon it. All thoughts of the past, present and future were obliterated under the current of passion carrying him toward fulfillment.

Kane quickly disrobed Katharina and then reveled in the pleasure of her disrobing him. He gasped in awed wonder as she kissed and touched, tasting and stroking him with her tongue. He savored the feel of her moist womanhood, delving deeply into the dark, wet passage as she stroked his legs and curled her fingers about his manhood, arousing him even further. With a moan of pleasure, she slid her leg over his and pressed his erection against her femininity as she ran her hand up and down his satiny tumescence.

Seeing that Katharina, too, was nearing the pinnacle of ecstasy, Kane rolled her onto her back and thrust himself deep into her. He felt her quiver of acceptance and knew the time had come. He thrust rapidly, penetrating to the very depths of her silky, welcoming flesh as she wrapped her legs about his waist and accepted him to the core of her femininity.

Kane threw back his head, his features frozen into a mask of agonized ecstasy. He spilled his seed deep within her and experienced a moment of ecstatic rapture. Like the warrior on the battlefield, he conquered death by making his blood eternal.

Katharina cried out her own pleasure, savoring the tiny ripples that caressed the male hardness within her body. She hugged Kane close as he collapsed over her, his breathing hard, his pounding heart beating in time with her own.

"I love you, Kane," she whispered, burrowing her face in his dark hair. She stroked her fingers through the curls, savoring the fleeting moments they shared before Kane allowed the outside world to intrude.

"And, God, how I love you," Kane said, pressing his face against her breasts as he wrapped his arms about her. He hid against her flesh, hoping to keep the world at bay for a few moments longer.

The minutes ticked by as Kane and Katharina lay with bodies joined and limbs entwined. A log burned down and crumbled in the grate, sending sparks up the chimney to cool in the twilight air. And like the sparks, the rapturous moment cooled as well. Thoughts encroached upon the peace left by their lovemaking.

Slowly Kane raised himself and looked down at Katharina. A tiny, humorless smile curled his lips as he said, "I have no power of resistance against you, Katharina. I am tortured by your nearness and I am tortured when we are apart. I know not what to do anymore. I am defeated."

"Our love is not defeat, my darling. It is triumph. We have found what so few others find in their lives. Don't destroy what we have by letting the past taint it," Katharina said, reaching up and gently stroking Kane's beard-shadowed cheek.

"Were it my choice, Katharina, I would stop it. However, it's not in my power. Nor was it in my father's power when he and my stepmother bore Richard," Kane said. He rolled away from Katharina and sat up. Grimly, he collected his pants and pulled them on.

A memory tugged at the back of Katharina's mind, trying to escape. She frowned, unable to understand why the mention of his father and stepmother seemed of great importance at that moment. Putting aside the feeling that she'd just learned something noteworthy, Katharina reached for her gown and tugged it on. She refastened the hooks and eyes that Kane had so easily unfastened and adjusted the wide white

Puritan collar that concealed the low neckline of her gown. Fully clothed, she looked at the man who stood clad only in pants and shirt. "Kane, I want to be your wife, to give birth to your children, yet if moments such as we've just experienced are all I'll ever have, I will be satisfied. I love you too much to force you to go against your own feeling. I don't want to make your life miserable. You have suffered enough in the past sixteen years."

"But don't you see that what we've just experienced is the very thing I must not do! I have vowed to end the Sedgewick curse. I will not bring another child into this world to suffer as Richard suffers."

Katharina knew it was useless to argue. She had not been able to convince Kane in the past. She held out her hand and smiled tenderly at him. "I know your feelings, Kane. And I didn't come here to make you unhappy. I just wanted you to come and walk with me in the snow."

Kane looked at the woman who held his heart and felt his own contract. He ran his fingers through his hair and then nodded. "Gather your cloak and I'll meet you downstairs. I have need of the icy air to cool my blood."

Katharina closed the space between them and stood on tiptoe to place a kiss on Kane's beard-stubbled cheek. She loved his five o'clock shadow. Combined with his tousled hair, it gave him a roguish, sexy look that stirred her senses. Pushing the thought from her mind, she said, "I'll meet you in the library in ten minutes."

Katharina cast one last, loving look at the man standing in front of the fireplace before she closed the door behind her. She grabbed her cloak from the hallway chair where she'd dropped it before entering Kane's bedchamber, and hurried downstairs.

Kane found her absorbed once more in the tome of the family history. "Will you never tire of reading that?"

Katharina closed the book and set it aside. She shook her head and smiled. "No. I want to know everything about our family."

"Our family?" Kane said, his heart warming at the thought that she considered herself already a part of the Sedgewick family.

Katharina came to her feet and turned so that Kane could place her cloak about her shoulders. "Yes. Your family is now my family, no matter what transpires between us."

Kane draped the velvet cloak about Katharina's shoulders and wrapped his arms about her. He pulled her back against his hard body as he whispered in her ear. "I love you, Katharina. You are the one blessing that God has seen fit to bestow upon me. Never leave me, no matter how much I burden you with my tribulations. I could not live if you did."

Katharina turned in Kane's arms and looked up into his dark eyes. "God has allowed me to come into your life for some reason. Perhaps it is to share your burden, I do not know. All I know is that fate brought me here to you, and I will never leave you willingly. I can't change Richard's fate, but I can try to make you happy, even if we can't be together as man and wife. We can enjoy the small things in life, such as taking a walk in the snow together."

"You're a marvel, my lady," Kane said, smiling down at Katharina, his dark eyes kindling with ardor. He set her away from him before the heat in his loins made him oblivious to all else. "Now, I think 'tis time for that nice cold walk."

The night was still and perfect as Kane and Katharina stepped through the postern gate. They paused to take in the beauty surrounding them. The sky had cleared and the light of the full moon glistened upon the white mantle covering the countryside. It turned the forest and fields into a land ruled by fairies and elves. A hare bounded across the path in front of them, leaving its tiny tracks in the pristine blanket. Hands clasped, Kane and Katharina strolled into the night. They succumbed to the beauty and peace surrounding them, allowing the enchantment of the moment to overcome the trials of the day. They talked of everyday things, of life and love, of what their neighbors were doing, of what the spring would bring to the fields and pastures beneath their feet. No mention was made of curses or misery as they shared their time together as men and women had done throughout the centuries.

Engulfed in their momentary happiness, they did not see the drapes fall over the window that looked upon the meadow where they strolled. Nor were they aware of the misery welling within Richard's chest as he turned away from his view of the lovers enjoying their time together.

Jealousy stirred to life within Richard's chest as he jerked the velvet over the window and with a swipe of his arm lashed out at the crystal glasses and wine decanter sitting on the table. They shattered, sending wine and splinters of glass across the floor. He looked down at the destruction and felt a momentary sense of relief. The Sedgewick curse had destroyed his face, and he in turn had destroyed something of beauty.

Roused by the crash, Joshua stood in the doorway. "Sir Richard, is something amiss?"

"Amiss, Joshua? Bloody hell! Can you not see my face? My life is not just amiss. 'Tis in total ruin. I am a monster that can never go into the light of day. I exist, but no one outside this castle knows I am alive. I live in the richness of comfort, but it is a prison that I can never leave. I will be alone until my last breath."

"Ye go for rides. And Lord Sedgewick and his lady do come to visit," Joshua said, trying desperately to calm his young master. Of late he'd begun to worry that Sir Richard's affliction was making him go mad. He had been acting so strangely.

"Damn it, man! Don't talk to me as if I am a fool. My face may be that of a monster, but my mind is as normal as any man's. I know what life is like outside these walls. And I know what a man needs."

Understanding flickered in the huge man's eyes. "Aye. I know ye do. I was yer age at one time meself. 'Tis not easy when ye start craving the things all men want, yet ye canna have them."

Richard looked at Joshua and saw that his caretaker did understand how he was feeling. "You do know, don't you?"

"Aye. I've wanted a wife and family as well, but I've never found a wench like me Annie. After she died, there just wasn't anyone else who could take her place. She was special, an angel put here to give me comfort for a short time."

Richard released a long breath. Every muscle in his body seemed to relax. He had found someone who understood his torment, who had also suffered because of something he couldn't control. "Joshua, I think I have also found an angel. But I have no way to be near her. I can only watch her as she goes about her duties."

"Young sir, 'tis sad to know that ye hurt so. I wish it were in me power to ease your pain, but I fear I can do nothing more than sympathize."

Richard sank down into the chair in front of the fireplace and leaned his head back against the soft leather. He closed his eyes to conjure up the image of his beautiful Misty. Fate had brought her to live under the same roof as he, yet he could only view her from the shadows. Neither Kane nor Katharina was aware that he'd begun to slip out of the east wing to watch Misty as she went about her duties. He hurt for her when her impaired vision made her bump into objects, yet she never wavered. He marveled at the strength she possessed. She didn't whine or cry over her misfortune. She always had a smile for others. And he had grown to love her.

"Why is life so unfair, Joshua? Why do I have eyes to see when my face is monstrous, and Misty has the face of an angel and has eyes that will not let her see? 'Tis cruel and unfair."

"Ye speak of the Shadford girl? Is she the one you've set yer heart on?" Joshua asked.

"Aye. The night we last rode, I met her near the castle. She could not see my face and knew not that I was the cursed Sedgewick. She called me her gallant knight for assisting her to the gates. Imagine that, Joshua. She called me, the cursed monster, her gallant knight."

Joshua felt his heart break for the young man he'd cared for since birth. Richard was an aristocrat, yet Joshua felt as if he were his own son. And he'd do anything to try to make his plight easier, even if it would make Lord Sedgewick angry. "Would ye like me to bring the girl to ye?"

Richard jerked upright and looked at Joshua. "My God, can you?"

"Aye, I can do it, but it'll not be easy. We must plan carefully so she'll never know that ye live at Sedgewick."

Richard leaped to his feet, unable to suppress his excitement. "You could bring her to the meadow, near the tunnel. She'd never know that she was still at Sedgewick since she cannot see."

"Aye. 'Twould work."

"When will you bring her?" Richard asked eagerly, his heart beating furiously with excitement.

" 'Twill not be tonight, young sir. I have to find a way to let her know that the young man who helped her wants to see her again."

"Bless you, Joshua. You are a true friend."

"I do it for me Annie. She always had a tender spot in her heart for others. She'd do anything to help those in need."

"Then may God bless your Annie, Joshua. She taught you well."

Chapter Thirteen

The library fireplace was cold. The servants were late in lighting the hearth. The first snow of the winter had left an icy chill in every chamber, and they were busy attending to the rooms used by the entire household first. Shivering from the lack of heat, Katharina pulled her woolen shawl closer about her shoulders. Richard had not exaggerated when he'd said Sedgewick turned into a great lump of ice when winter arrived. Each chamber possessed a fireplace, but they did little to heat the great drafty, high-ceilinged rooms.

Katharina reached for the tinder and flint box sitting on the black marble mantel. She'd not lost all of her independence. She could light a fire without the assistance of a servant. And she had seen Chole light the fire in the tower fireplace enough times to know how it was done. Katharina took out the soft tinder and placed it beneath the kindling. Next she took the starter and struck it against the flint. Sparks shimmered in the air but the tinder remained untouched. Katharina eyed the flint as if it had turned into her enemy. She could do this. She knew she could.

Again Katharina struck the flint and sparks danced in the air but the tinder didn't ignite. Katharina released a long breath in disgust. This was ridiculous. It was a simple matter to light a fire. Again she struck the flint. Nothing happened. Again she struck the flint, then again and again. The fireplace remained cold.

Five minutes later, Katharina stormed up the stairs to her chamber and retrieved her tote bag from its hiding place beneath her bed. She dug through the contents until she again found the matches from the London hotel. Triumphantly she held them up. "I guess I'll start a fire now. I'll be damned if I'll freeze because there is something wrong with the flint."

Katharina hurried back downstairs to the library. Casting a quick glance about to assure that no one was nearby to see her use the matches, she bent to light the fireplace. She struck the match and smiled with satisfaction as it glowed to life. She held it to the tender and watched it ignite. Triumphantly, she held the match up and blew it out before tossing the remains into the flames licking greedily at the kindling.

Intent upon her conquest of the cold hearth, Katharina had not heard the library door open behind her. Nor was she aware of the tall man who stood watching her ministrations with something akin to terror on his face.

Churchill had been shown to the library when he'd asked to see the Lady Katharina. He'd opened the door, expecting to find her curled up with a book. Instead, he'd found far more than he'd ever suspected. Seeing Katharina in front of the cold hearth, he'd already taken a step forward, ready to offer his assistance in the lighting of the fire. To his horror, he'd seen her conjure the fire from her fingertips and then ignite the tinder. Fortunately, she'd been too absorbed in her conjuring to note his presence behind her. And he'd never be able to forget the look of triumph on her beautiful face as she blew out the fire on her fingertips and calmly watched the flames devour the kindling.

Churchill made the sign of the cross and stealthily backed out of the library. He'd come to speak with the Lady Katharina in order to make up his mind about her. He had succeeded. He knew the truth now. She was a witch, just as the servants had proclaimed.

Sweat beading his brow, Churchill fled Sedgewick as if all the demons of hell were upon his heels. He hurried toward the tall double doors, grabbed his cloak from the dumbfounded servant and departed without a word. Fear made goose-flesh rise at the nape of his neck as he mounted his horse and glanced once more at his friend's home. He knew he had to protect Kane from the woman, but at the present moment, his fright ruled him. He needed to put as much distance between himself and the witch as possible in order to regain control over himself. He had to think. He had to plan what was to be done.

Pale and chilled to the bone, Churchill strode into the small, warm salon where his wife sat playing with their son.

Breathing heavily, he slumped down in the chair across from Elizabeth. "I have the answer I sought."

The smile on Elizabeth's face faded at her husband's visible distress. "Are you all right, Winston? You look as if you've seen a ghost."

"I have." He shook his head, negating his words. "No, I've not seen a ghost. 'Tis far worse."

"Winston, you're frightening me. I thought you had gone to Sedgewick to see the Lady Katharina."

"I did go to Sedgewick. And I found the devil in the disguise of a woman."

"Winston, you're not making any sense."

" 'Tis hard to make sense when you've had the wits frightened out of you. Even now, safe in my own home, I tremble. I have fought battles, have faced enemies upon the field that would chill your heart, but I've never felt as I do now." Churchill stood and crossed to the blazing fireplace. He held out his hands to the warmth of the flames for a long moment before he turned back to his wife, who sat still and pale.

" 'Tis hard to comprehend what I saw at Sedgewick, Elizabeth. But Mathew Hopkins was right. There are such things as witches, women who are in league with the devil to steal men's souls. And I have seen one today. She is the Lady Katharina, the woman who has cast her spell upon Kane."

"Surely you are mistaken."

"I think not. There can be no mistake when I saw with my own eyes what she did." Churchill shivered involuntarily. "No. Elizabeth. There is no mistake."

"Tell me what you saw. There may be a logical explanation."

Churchill shook his head in exasperation that his wife's forgiving nature even now looked for the best in any situation. However, in this instance there was no good, there was nothing but evil. "I could not misinterpret seeing the woman light a fire with her fingers." He held his hand up and fanned his fingers as an example. "The fire came from the tips of her fingers. The flint lay on the floor at her side. No, Elizabeth. I could not misinterpret what I saw. The woman is a witch."

Elizabeth cradled her son closer to her breast as if she could protect him from the evil his father had seen. "What do you intend to do?"

Churchill crossed to the high-backed chair and sank wearily into it. He drew in a long breath and shook his head slowly from side to side. A worried frown etched his brow. "I have no earthly idea at this moment. I know I have to save Kane from this witch, but I know not how. I fear it will not be an easy matter. He has not openly admitted his feeling, but he is bewitched by her."

"Winston, you have to go back to Sedgewick to speak with Kane. He has to be made aware of the danger he's in if the Lady Katharina is truly a witch."

"*If*, Elizabeth? I saw it with my own eyes. Do you doubt my word?"

"Nay. I do not doubt you. You are a far too honorable a man to conjure up such a story. But I remember too well what Mathew Hopkins did with his witch hunting. Innocent women died at his hand because people allowed their fears to run rampant. Had it not been for the Reverend Gaule, the man would still be executing every old woman with a wrinkled face, furr'd brow or hairy lip. We cannot be hasty. Too much is at stake."

"Blast it! I'm not being hasty. The woman is a witch. She has used her herbs about the village as if she were a physician. And she has conjured up fire. What more proof do I need?"

"Has her use of herbs harmed anyone?"

"What does that have to do with anything?"

"A devil's helpmeet would not do good, Winston. There is only evil in the devil's work. From all you've said, she has helped those she's attended." Elizabeth glanced down at her sleeping son. "Far more than Dr. Johnson has John."

"Elizabeth, your woman's heart is too gentle to see the way of those who are evil. They use such things to gain power. You can see the way she has worked her way into Kane's life."

"It has nothing to do with my woman's heart. I just want us to do the right thing without rushing in and destroying your friendship with Kane. You must tread carefully, Winston. A man in love sees only what his heart allows."

Churchill ran his fingers through his hair and nodded in agreement. " 'Tis true. As usual, your calm head rules the day. I will speak with Kane about what I know and then make my decision as to what I should do." He stood up. "And I see no better time than today."

Elizabeth smiled up at her husband, her love and pride shining in the depths of her lovely eyes. "You are ever the wise man, Winston."

A tiny smile tugged at Churchill's lips. "As wise as the woman I love." He bent and placed a kiss upon his wife's brow. "Stay close to the fire today. 'Tis horrid cold out."

"Take care, my love," Elizabeth said as Churchill turned once more toward the salon doors. As they closed behind him, she whispered, "And God be at your side to protect you from evil."

*   *   *

"I thought I might find you here with your nose buried once more in that book," Kane said as he entered the library.

Katharina glanced up as Kane crossed the chamber to the fireplace. His smile warmed her as she said, "There was something you said that keeps niggling at the back of my mind. I know the answer is here, but I just can't seem to find it."

Kane shook his head as he held out his hands to the warmth of the blazing fire. "Will you never give up? There is nothing in that book that will banish the curse, Katharina. You have to accept it as Richard and I have."

"Accept something that doesn't exist?" Katharina asked, dismayed that he could even expect her to do such a thing. She shook her head stubbornly from side to side. Katharina laid her hand upon the thick volume resting in her lap. "I will never accept it. I know the answer is here. And I mean to find it. I'll not allow people I love to live in fear because of a legend that has been passed down through the generations."

" 'Tis no legend, as you well know," Kane said, his tone as frigid as the day. Turning his gaze to the leaping flames, he stared into their depths as if seeing the fires of hell. "Richard is no legend. He exists just as the curse exists."

Seeing Kane's pained expression, Katharina closed the book and set it aside. She didn't want to cause him further pain by arguing the point. She held up her hand to the man she loved and said, "The day is far too cold to do anything but stay close to the fire. Won't you sit with me and share what little warmth there is to be had?"

Kane took Katharina's hand and placed a warm kiss against it. " 'Twould be a pleasure, my lady. And will you entertain me with one of the stories that Richard so enjoys? He can talk of little else."

Katharina felt her breath leave her as her gaze locked with Kane's. Her heart began to beat a rapid tattoo in her breast and her hand tingled where his lips had touched. A wave of excitement coursed through Katharina and settled in the very core of her being. However, she forced herself to act as if her blood hadn't turned to lava in her veins at Kane's touch. She was too pleased to share the afternoon with him to allow her emotions to intrude and destroy their time together.

Katharina curled her legs beneath her. "I would be pleased to tell you a story. What would you like to hear?"

"I would love to hear the tale of the two men and the flying machine."

"Oh, Richard has told you of Orville and Wilbur Wright?"

"Aye. From his description, 'tis truly a wonderful fairy tale."

"All right," Katharina said, smiling secretively. The stories Richard thought were fairy tales concocted from a vivid imagination had been actual, historical events. But she would not try to convince Kane of the truth and ruin his entertainment.

"In a land far across the sea, there is a place called North Carolina. It is a wonderful place with high mountains and deep rivers. Where the ocean touches the shores of North Carolina, there are barrier islands with mountains made of sand. That is where two brothers named Orville and Wilbur Wright flew their flying machine for the first time. No one believed them when they said they were going to fly. People ridiculed them, telling them that they were insane. They laughed at the Wrights behind their backs as the two brothers worked on their dream. Then one day, at a place called Kitty Hawk, the two brothers rolled their invention out onto the sand and Orville took his place on the winged, motor-powered Flyer 1. No one laughed at the Wright brothers after the machine they had built rose in the air and flew a hundred and twenty feet. After that day, others began to build machines to fly, and then ordinary people began to travel in them. They flew from city to city and country to country all in a day's time or in just a few hours. The Wright brothers' dream gave man wings to soar like the birds."

" 'Tis a wonderful story, no matter how impossible it would be for man to fly," Kane said, smiling. "And I thank you for Richard and myself."

Katharina bit her tongue to keep from reminding Kane that she'd already told him of flying machines when she'd told him the truth about how she'd come to Sedgewick. "Richard certainly seems to be entertained by my stories."

"Aye. He relates every one to me when I visit."

"I'm pleased that he finds pleasure in my tales. I wish I could do more to make his life easier."

Kane reached across the space between them and took Katharina's hand. "You have been a blessing to both of us, my love. You are the only female other than Nanna that he has ever known. My stepmother died soon after his birth, and he's lacked the gentler touch that a mother can give a young man. I've done my best, but 'tis hard to make hell easier."

Katharina's face lit and her eyes widened with comprehension at the mention of Kane's stepmother. The thought that had been lurking in the shadowy recesses of her mind burst into the light. "Kane, that's it. I know what it was I'd been trying to remember."

Pulling her hand free of Kane's, Katharina quickly retrieved the heavy tome from the table. She flipped it open to the beginning. Richard Sedgewick had married Anne of Clive. The curse was upon those who carried both Sedgewick and Clive blood. The breath caught in Katharina's throat as she quickly turned to the back of the Sedgewick family history. Kane's father had married the daughter of Harold Clive. Excitement making her fingers fly through the age-yellowed pages, Katharina found that the marriage of a Sedgewick and a Clive always produced one of the deformed children. The birth defect came only when Sedgewick and a Clive blood mixed.

Feeling as if a great weight had been lifted from her shoulders, Katharina slowly closed the book and looked back at the man she loved. She had solved the riddle of the Sedgewick curse. Now all she had to do was to find a way to convince Kane of the truth. It was so easy for her to understand, yet she had not been born into the seventeenth century. Kane would find it far more difficult to believe in things such as the chromosomes and genes that caused the recurring birth defect in his family.

Katharina opened her mouth to tell Kane that she'd solved the mystery of the curse, but a knock upon the library door stilled her words. A moment later, the footman opened the door and announced Lord Churchill.

Churchill paused upon the threshold, bracing himself to enter the library with the witch present. He looked at Katharina and fought the urge to make the sign of the cross. He had walked back into the witch's lair with only his love for his friend to sustain him against her evil.

"Winston, what brings you out twice in one day?" Kane said, rising with a welcoming smile upon his face.

"I have a need to speak with you," Churchill said, casting another glance at Katharina.

"It must be of grave importance to tear you away from the fire on such a miserable day," Kane said, stepping aside to allow Churchill nearer the blazing fire.

"Yes, it is of great concern." Churchill pulled his gaze away from Katharina and held his icy fingers out to the warmth of the hearth.

Kane glanced at Katharina and apologized. "I'm sorry, Winston, but I don't believe you have met my guest, Lady Katharina Ferguson."

Churchill drew in a deep breath and turned to Katharina. "No, I fear I haven't had the pleasure of making her acquaintance, though I have heard much of her since her sudden arrival at Sedgewick. The wonders she has performed are the talk of the village."

The look in Churchill's eyes and the tone of his voice froze Katharina's smile before it could be born. A sudden chill crept up her spine, and she quickly pulled the woolen shawl closer about her shoulders. She glanced at Kane for help, but found him smiling widely at his friend, completely unaware of the undercurrent of ill will that had come into the library with Lord Churchill.

"Lady Katharina has been generous with her knowledge of herbs," Kane said, wanting his friend to like the woman he loved. "She has helped several of our villagers when the physician was unavailable to call upon them."

Churchill's gaze never left Katharina's face as Kane spoke. It seemed to search out every nook and cranny as if to find something vile lying within. Katharina shifted uneasily under his scrutiny. Until that moment, she'd never felt the threat that Kane had feared. Now, under Churchill's regard, she knew every action or word could and would be held against her.

She started as Churchill leaned forward and took her hand to raise it to his lips. Her eyes locked with his as he said softly, "I have found you out, my lady." Then he brushed his lips against her hand and turned once more to Kane, who stood beaming happily at them.

"I am pleased to have finally made your lady's acquaintance, Kane. But I've come a long way in harsh weather to speak with you." He cast a brief glance at Katharina as he continued, "I'm sure your lady would not mind if we spoke in private."

Relieved to be free of the man to whom she'd taken such a sudden dislike, Katharina stood and laid the heavy book on the side table. "I will have tea sent in to chase away the chill left from your ride, Lord Churchill."

"Thank you, Lady Katharina, but I would prefer a glass of Kane's favorite brandy. It will warm me far quicker," Churchill said, unwilling to drink anything that the witch might taint with her brews.

"Of course. Then if you will excuse me, I'll go to my chamber."

Both men watched Katharina exit the library before Kane turned to Churchill, perplexed by his sudden arrival for the second time that day.

"The servants said you'd come earlier. Have you

heard from Charles? Is there word of when he plans to sail from France?"

Churchill shook his head. "I've heard nothing more than you have. But with this weather, it will be spring before he can risk crossing the channel again."

"Then what brings you here, Winston? I'm sure Elizabeth and your son are far better company than I on such a frigid day," Kane said, crossing to the side table to pour the brandy Churchill had requested.

"I did not jest when I said I had come to speak with you on a grave matter. It concerns me greatly."

Kane poured the amber liquid into the crystal glass and handed it to Churchill. "What so concerns you that you risk being frozen?"

Churchill glanced toward the library door and downed the fiery liquid in one gulp. He gasped as it burned its way down to his belly and then began to spread warmth throughout his chilled body. He looked once more at Kane as he set the glass aside and braced himself for the eruption of Kane's ire when he broached the subject of the Lady Katharina. "Kane, you know I am your friend. What I now say is only for your own good."

Kane's amicable expression faded. His tone held little warmth as he looked at his friend and said, "I always have doubts about such a statement, Winston. Few people do anything for another's good."

Churchill shook his head and ran his fingers through his hair. He felt awkward and unsure of himself. Still, he had to tell Kane what he'd learned and be done with it. And he prayed his friend would understand that he meant no harm; he meant only to protect Kane from the witch. "Kane, I know I'm going about this badly, but you have to believe I mean you only good. For the past ten years, I have loved you as a brother, and I would not see you harmed because you are blind to the truth."

The lines about Kane's full lips deepened with his frown. He turned to his desk and seated himself in the high-backed chair, putting the mahogany desk between himself and his friend. He arched an ebony brow. " 'Twould be far wiser at this moment, Winston, not to strain our friendship further with such statements. Tell me what you came to say and be done with it."

"I think you already know what I've come to tell you. It's about the Lady Katharina."

Kane's nostrils flared as he drew in a deep breath. The hair at the nape of his neck rose in warning as he asked, "What is it you have to tell me about Lady Katharina?"

Churchill drew in a steadying breath and then blurted out, "She's a witch."

"Bloody damn, Winston!" Kane exploded as he leaped to his feet. "Has the cold outside frozen what little sense you have? Or is it that I've never realized until this moment that you are a fool?"

Churchill stiffened at Kane's insult. He squared his shoulders and eyed his friend coldly. "It isn't necessary to berate me because you don't like what I have to say. You are too bemused by the she-devil to realize what has happened. She has bewitched you, Kane. Can't you see what she is? The villagers are right about her. She is a witch."

"Cease this nonsense or suffer the consequences of insulting the woman I love, the woman I intend to make my wife," Kane blurted out, nearly as shocked by his own admission as Churchill.

Churchill paled visibly. "Surely you jest? You can't possibly mean to make that woman your wife. You are a Sedgewick, the head of a family as esteemed as my own. You know nothing of her. She could have been sent here by the devil himself."

"This conversation is ludicrous, Winston. We are grown men, not frightened schoolboys. We are not children who believe in ghosts and goblins."

" 'Tis what I, too, thought until this morn," Churchill said, giving no ground under his friend's anger.

A prickle of fear tingled up Kane's back. He forced a smile to his lips and feigned a chuckle. "Winston, this has gone on long enough. If you came here just to bedevil me and lighten your day, you've succeeded. 'Tis now time to get down to far more serious matters."

"Blast it, Kane. I didn't come here to bedevil you or to amuse myself at your expense. I came to warn you that the woman to whom you have given your heart is in truth a witch. I have seen it with my own eyes. 'Tis not just some village gossip. I watched her—this very morn, in this very chamber—light the fire without any flint. The fire came from her fingers, and then with a breath she blew it out, unharmed. She did not suffer any pain from touching fire as mortals such as you or I would."

Kane groaned inwardly, knowing what his friend had seen and fully understanding how it would look to see Katharina use the small fire sticks called matches. He couldn't blame Winston for his suspicions. It was still hard for him to comprehend totally the magic of it. However, he couldn't tell his friend the truth about Katharina without further endangering her. It would only confirm Winston's belief that she was in league with the devil.

"Winston, I fear you are mistaken. Lady Katharina was trying to light the fire this morning and managed only to catch her gloves on fire. 'Twas so cold, she'd come downstairs bundled from head to toe."

Churchill shook his head. "Say what you will to protect her, but I know what I saw, Kane. The woman lit the fire from her fingertips."

Kane smiled and shook his head. "You're wrong. The gloves look much like her own hands because they fit well and are the same beige color as the cloak I bought her."

"You protect her because you are bewitched, but nothing you can say will change my mind."

"Winston, no matter what you believe, I pray you'll not speak of this to others. There are other men still alive like the witch hunter, Mathew Hopkins, who follow Cromwell. They would love to hear such a story, especially about the woman I intend to make my wife. It would suit them well to try to injure me by harming her."

"In truth, I know not what to do. I love you like a brother and would see no harm come to you or yours. But, damn me, Kane! I am frightened for you. You can't marry that woman, knowing what I have seen."

"Will you not listen to my explanation?" Kane said, trying once more to convince Churchill that he was mistaken.

"Explanation or no, I know what I saw, and nothing you can say will change my mind. Lady Katharina is in league with the devil, and I know not how to save you from her."

"I don't want to be saved. Have you not listened to a word I have spoken? I love Katharina and intend to wed her as soon as possible," Kane said. Churchill's accusation was forcing him to go against all his vows. He would have to marry Katharina. He had no other choice now if he wanted to save her. His name was all that would stand between her and the hangman's noose should

Churchill decide to report what he'd seen to the authorities.

"I beg you to reconsider," Churchill said, stricken by the thought of what might happen to his friend when the witch became his wife.

"Reconsider? Why should I decide otherwise? Lady Katharina is a beautiful woman and gives freely of herself to everyone who needs aid and comfort," Kane said, remembering her at Paddy's death bed and how she'd cradled the sick babe at Mistress Remy's, as well as the long hours she'd spent with his brother in the east wing. No, he'd not reconsider. Any man would be damned lucky to marry a woman such as Katharina.

Kane looked at his ashen-faced friend. "To go against Katharina is to go against me, Winston. She is mine."

"Either way, I lose a friend," Churchill said. "Should I report what I saw here this morn, then you will turn against me. Should I keep it to myself, then you will suffer through eternity because of her. 'Tis not an easy decision."

" 'Tis one I would suggest you go home and think over, Winston. As you said, we've been like brothers for the past ten years, yet I will not give up the woman I love, any more than you would give up Elizabeth."

" 'Tis not the same. How can you even suggest such a comparison? My Elizabeth is an angel."

"And I believe the same of my Katharina. Now I will bid you good day, Lord Churchill. When you have made your decision, you are welcome to come again," Kane said, giving a curt nod of dismissal.

Churchill flushed a dull red with anger. The presumption! How dare Sedgewick dismiss him as if he were a servant! Still fuming, Churchill turned toward the library door without a word of farewell. Head held high and chin thrust out at a belligerent angle, he didn't look back.

Kane released a sigh of relief when he heard the library door close behind Churchill. He crossed to the side table and poured himself a brandy. Downing the contents, he refilled the glass before taking his seat once more at his desk. He stared blindly at the richly appointed chamber and wondered what he was going to do if Churchill chose to go against him. He had managed to protect Richard for sixteen years, but should Churchill make charges against Katharina, he feared all would be lost. The stories of the Sedgewick vampire would be rekindled along with all the other legends of ghosts and goblins that abounded about Sedgewick Castle. It would only take a dead cow or a sick babe to bring his enemies down upon him. They'd swarm over Sedgewick like flies on a carcass in the heat of summer. Like Mathew Hopkins, they'd use the law to gain the advantage over him. And once Richard was discovered, it would not only be Katharina's life in jeopardy, but his brother's and his own.

"God, what am I to do?" Kane said, leaning his

head back on the burgundy leather and squeezing his eyes closed against the future that awaited should Churchill's fear overrule his head and heart.

"Kane," Katharina said from the doorway. She'd seen Churchill ride away as if the devil was upon his heels and wondered if he and Kane had argued.

Kane drew in a deep breath and looked at the woman standing hesitantly in the doorway. A humorless smile touched his lips. "Come in, Katharina. I have something I want to tell you."

Katharina's skin prickled and she absently rubbed her arms as she entered the library. "I saw Lord Churchill ride away. He seemed in a great hurry."

Kane nodded as he set the brandy glass on the desk in front of him. "Aye, he was."

Katharina crossed the chamber to where Kane sat. She knelt beside his chair, sensing the pain that he was trying to hide from her. His lips still curved into a smile, but his eyes held no joy, only the haunted look she'd grown used to seeing when he was troubled. "What is it, Kane? What did Lord Churchill say to upset you?"

Kane cupped her cheek in the palm of his hand and gently stroked her lower lip with his thumb as he looked down into her eyes. "He made me realize that 'tis time that we wed."

Katharina's heart froze. "What did he say, Kane? What did he threaten to do?"

"He saw you light the fire this morning with your matches." Kane raised his hand to Katharina's hair, absently curling a long strand about his finger. "He believes you are a witch."

"That's absurd. I've told you there are no such things as witches, any more than there are curses."

Kane gave a sad shake of his head. "Can I not convince you that it doesn't really matter if there are such things? In truth, it's only what people believe. And Churchill believes you are a witch. The only way I can protect you now is to give you my name."

"I won't marry you if that is the only reason, Kane," Katharina said, pulling her hair free of his hand and getting to her feet. She moved away from him, putting enough distance between them to keep herself from surrendering to her need to be Kane's wife at any cost and for any reason.

"You have no choice. To deny me is to put your life in danger, and I'll not allow you to do that. I love you too much."

Tears welled in Katharina's eyes. She'd discovered the reason for Richard's birth defect and Kane had just proposed to her. Why wasn't she jumping at the chance to be his wife? Katharina turned to stare at the flames leaping in the fireplace. She knew why. She wanted Kane to ask her to marry him without being forced to propose because of a threat to her life.

She couldn't look at Kane as she said, "I do have

a choice, Kane. And I choose not to marry you."

"Bloody damn, Katharina!" Kane exploded as he came out of his chair and crossed to where she stood. He took her by the arms and turned her to face him. "Don't you understand? My name is all there is to protect you from the hangman's noose should Churchill go to the authorities about what he believes. You *will* marry me, and I'll hear no more nonsense."

"It's not nonsense! I said I will not marry you and I won't. And you can't force me to the altar."

"God's blood. I thought you loved me as I love you."

"I do love you, but I'll not be wed to you when I know the only reason for your proposal is your duty to protect me."

"This is foolish. I love you and you love me. But you won't do the very thing we've both wanted because it will protect you from harm. This doesn't make any sense to me."

"It makes all the sense in the world," Katharina said, struggling to pull free of his hold upon her. She was dying inside, and knew she'd not be able to take much more. She had to get away from Kane or she'd end up giving in to his demands. In time, she knew she'd regret it. She wanted Kane to come to her without duty or remorse for the vows he'd broken. He had to come to her free of everything. There could be no shadows from the past to ruin their future.

"Katharina! Stop this madness. We will be wed

next week. It's the only recourse we have because of Churchill. It is the best thing for all of us."

Katharina stilled. She looked up into Kane's ebony eyes and saw the haunted look she'd seen so often in the past when he spoke of Richard. "It's not just to protect me that you want us to marry. It's also for Richard, isn't it?"

"I have no other choice. Should the charge of witchcraft be brought against you, then all the rumors would start again. It is the chink that Glenville needs to pry away at the wall I've built around my family. The authorities would search every inch of Sedgewick to make certain that they had rooted out all the evildoers. That would be the end for Richard. Once they saw his face, he would be doomed."

Katharina trembled at the thought of what might happen to the sensitive young man she'd grown to love as a brother. She stepped into the circle of Kane's arms and buried her face against his shoulder. Kane was right. She had no other choice but to marry him. Drawing in a steadying breath, she wrapped her arms about the man she loved and accepted the fact that they would have to marry for the reasons he'd given her. She had his love, and that was far more than she'd had in the twentieth century.

Kane enfolded her in his embrace and kissed the top of her head. "I love you, Katharina. And I will do everything in my power to be a good husband to you. Everything except give you children."

Katharina jerked as if she'd been hit. She was to marry the man she loved. A man who loved her in return. A man who intended that their marriage be in name only. Even if she could convince him that there were certain times when it would be safe for them to make love, they could never have a child, never be a family the way she'd always dreamed.

Chapter Fourteen

Misty sat by the fire, enjoying the warmth a few moments more before she had to find her way up to the servants' quarters. It wasn't something she looked forward to doing in such weather. The straw mattress was the only thing to protect her from the cold floor up there. Misty released a sigh of longing, remembering the warmth of the tiny cottage she'd shared with her father. There had been times when they had had little to eat as well as little wood for the fire, yet she could not remember ever being cold or hungry.

A wave of loneliness swept over Misty and she huddled closer to the fire. Lord Sedgewick had been kind to her, giving her a place at Sedgewick. And Lady Katharina had gone out of her way to make her life easier as her sight continued to dwindle away. She had taught her many things, had read stories to her and had even given her a cane to help her keep from bumping into things. But no matter the kindness she received, she missed her father. She missed his tenderness and caring. He had been the center of her life for so many years. She was surrounded by people night and day here, yet she had no one who cared about her alone.

Misty wiped at the dampness that moistened her lashes. Her future looked bleak and lonely. No man would want a blind wife. Men wanted women who could care for them, who could see their smiles or their children. She would be too much of a burden to take to wife. Life was hard enough without adding a sightless wife who could not help provide for the family.

" 'Tis time ye be off to yer bed, girl," Cook said, banking the fire for the morning. "The rest are already abed. Ye'll have to find yer way to yer pallet without their help this night."

"I know," Misty said, struggling to her feet and reaching for the cane she'd left leaning against the bench. Finding it, she turned in the direction of the door that led to the narrow flight of stone stairs. She dreaded traversing the stairs alone. They wound unevenly upward, a hazardous climb for even those who could see. The stones were worn from the tread of the servants over the past several hundred years. In many places the mortar had loosened from much use, making the stones unsteady underfoot.

Yet Misty didn't ask for help. She'd learned long ago, when her sight had first begun to vanish, that people had little compassion for those who were different and unable to help themselves. And she was determined she'd not be a burden to anyone for as long as God gave her the strength to help herself.

"Do ye not need a light?" Cook asked, watching the young girl find her way toward the thick oak door.

"Nay. I can find my way without a candle." Misty didn't add that a candle would be useless to her because the tunnel she looked through during the day closed completely at night. No candle or even torch light would be of help to her.

"Then sleep well, girl," Cook said, glad that she'd not have to find the girl a lamp to light her way. She'd been on her feet since five that morning, and she wanted nothing more than to find her own bed. Yawning, she turned toward the small room that housed her narrow bed.

Misty closed the heavy oak door behind her. The tapping of her cane echoed eerily against the stone walls as she made her way toward the stairs. A slight noise made her pause at the foot of the first step. She listened intently. Hearing the sound of breathing, she asked, "Who's there?"

" 'Tis a friend, girl. I come with a message for ye."

"Did Lady Katharina send you?" Misty asked, believing that Lord Sedgewick's lady was the only one who would send her a message.

"Nay. I'm here for a young gentleman," Joshua said, keeping his voice low so no one else would know of his furtive meeting with the girl. Should someone see him, they'd wonder why he'd come to the castle so late and what his business might be with a girl young enough to be his daughter.

Misty frowned. "A young gentleman? I know none. You must have made a mistake."

"Nay. I've not made a mistake. The young gentleman in question sent me to find you. He said you'd know who he was if I told you the message was from your gallant knight."

Misty smiled. "Aye. I know of whom you speak. He rescued me the night Papa died. Had he not been so kind, I might not have reached Sedgewick."

"Then you would be willing to meet with him again?"

Butterflies seemed to flutter in Misty's stomach and she absently placed her hand against her middle as if to stay their flight. "He wants to see me?"

"Aye. He said to say he's not been able to get your memory from his mind since your brief encounter. Your beauty has touched his heart."

Misty's cheeks flushed with warmth from the compliment, yet she couldn't believe what was being said. "Surely 'tis some jest he wants to play on me. He is a gentlemen and I am but a servant."

"My young gentleman does not jest, girl. He awaits you even now. Will you come?"

Misty hesitated, uncertain of what she should do, yet stirred at the thought of once more meeting her gallant knight.

"I don't have all night, girl. Do you come or nay?"

Throwing caution aside, Misty said, "Yes. I will go with you."

"Good," Joshua said, taking her hand. "Hold to me, and I'll lead ye to him."

Misty held his sturdy woolen coat sleeve as Joshua took her out the kitchen door and along the path to the postern gate. From there he led her to the opening of the tunnel, where Richard awaited.

"My lady," Richard said, taking her hand from Joshua's sleeve. "I'm so glad you chose to see me."

"I'm afraid you have mistaken me for some other, sir. I am but a servant; not a lady," Misty said, unable to hide the smile of pleasure that his words gave her.

"Let no one deny my words. You are my lady, Misty."

Misty flushed again with pleasure. "And you are the same gallant knight who rescued me so many nights ago."

"I was sorry to hear of your loss. You must be very lonely without your father's comfort."

Misty suddenly felt as if she'd come home. His words wrapped themselves about her heart, wiping away the loneliness that had chilled her far worse than the cold winter's day. Tears of gratitude brightened her eyes and she surreptitiously tried to wipe them away.

Richard caught her hand, stilling the movement. Gently he touched the tear on her cheek and wiped it away. "I did not mean to make you cry by bringing back sad memories, my lady. I meant only to try to give you some comfort in my own awkward way."

Misty's lower lip trembled as she looked toward the soft, sympathetic voice. She wished she could see his face, to see the kindness that she knew she'd find in his eyes. But that was not meant to be. "You did not make me cry, sir."

"If I did not, then what brings the moisture to your beautiful eyes?" Richard said, savoring the beauty of her candlelit features. She was ivory and gold: a mixture of two of the most precious things on earth.

"Your kindness. Others have given me sympathy, but you are the first to understand what it's like without Papa."

"Do the people at Sedgewick mistreat you?" Richard asked, suddenly furious at the thought that anyone would harm the beautiful, innocent creature who looked up at him with eyes that could not see.

"Nay. I have been treated well at Sedgewick. Lord Sedgewick and his lady have welcomed me into their home. And I should be ashamed that I am unable to consider Sedgewick my home. But a home is where you are loved, not just a place to lay your head at night. And their generosity can't stop the loneliness."

" 'Tis true. I know much about loneliness myself."

Desperately needing to see the man who had looked into her heart, Misty raised her hand to Richard's face. She touched only his brow before he captured her hand and drew it to his sleeve.

"Come, my lady. Let us walk a short ways to the warmth of the fire that I've had my man kindle to chase away the icy night."

Embarrassed by her brazen behavior, Misty allowed Richard to lead her to the small fire Joshua had made a short distance inside the tunnel.

Richard glanced back at the tunnel entrance to see Joshua working to cover it with brush to prevent any passerby from seeing the light. Richard turned his attention back to the girl at his side, satisfied that they were safe from prying eyes. For as long as he lived, he knew he'd remember this night and the man who had made it possible. Joshua was no longer a servant but a true friend.

Richard felt like shouting his happiness aloud

but refrained. He didn't want to frighten Misty to death or to make her believe she'd come to meet a madman. Instead he said, "My lady, will you sit and have a glass of wine with me? I thought we might have a midnight supper together. I have brought a bottle of claret and some bread and cheese."

"I've never tasted wine before," Misty said, accepting Richard's assistance to seat herself on the blanket by the fire.

"Then I am glad I am the one to give you the first taste. And I hope that in the future we may share many other things together. Have you ever ridden a horse?" Richard asked as he poured the glass of wine and placed it in Misty's hand.

"Nay. I have often watched as the lords and ladies ride by and wondered what it would be like to ride."

Richard's brow furrowed as he looked at Misty. "Then you have not always been blind?"

Misty touched the wine to her lips and hesitantly sipped. She made a slight moue as her taste buds adjusted to the new flavor. After a moment she smiled with pleasure at the sweet flavor of grapes. She liked the taste of wine, after all. She took another, deeper sip before she said, "Nay, I can remember a time when I could see like everyone else. Then came a day when the world began to shrink. Now I can see only in the brightest light of day."

Unnerved that the fire illuminated his features,

Richard shifted uneasily. "Can you not see at any other time? Even when the candles are lit?"

"Nay," Misty said, knowing her confession would make this wonderful, sensitive man see her as the burden she was.

"For your sake I am sorry you've lost your sight, Misty," Richard said, yet he was grateful that she could not see him. As long as he did not allow her to see him in the light of day, she'd never know what a monster she allowed to be near her.

"You are kind, and I will understand if you feel my affliction makes you uncomfortable to be with me."

"Your affliction? I fear, my lady, that my own affliction is far worse than yours," Richard said, thinking of his grotesque appearance.

"I find only sweetness in your voice, Sir Knight. Perhaps all your words do not come out as elegantly as others, but they are all beautiful to my ears," Misty said, trying to make her knight understand that she'd noted his slightly slurred speech at times, but that it meant nothing to her.

Richard's heart opened to the girl at his side. She had known all along that there was something wrong with him, yet she'd still come to meet him. His eyes grew moist and he quickly wiped the dampness away. He raised his hand to Misty's cheek, gently caressing her as he said, "My lady, you are the angel I've been searching for all of my life. Never had I hoped that I might find her, yet God has blessed me by sending you into my life."

Misty closed her eyes, savoring his touch. She didn't doubt his words. She had lost her sight but she had learned to hear things in people's voice that spoke far louder and truer than their words at times. And she heard no lies in her knight's voice. She smiled and leaned her cheek into his caress. She was home.

"Will you come to me again?" Richard asked, unable to wait until they'd finished their supper and it was time for her to leave.

"Yes, I will come again if you send for me," Misty answered, knowing that nothing on earth could keep her away from the man she had named her Gallant Knight.

"Then I will send for you until you decide you no longer want to be with me."

"Then we both may be too old and decrepit to meet," Misty said, smiling up at Richard.

"This is to be our secret, Misty. Let no one know of our meetings or they may try to prevent you from coming to me," Richard said, knowing that Kane would stop them should he learn of their tryst.

" 'Tis our secret," Misty said. "I would have no one come between us."

Richard leaned his brow against Misty's, needing to feel her closeness yet daring to do no more. She was his angel and he longed to touch her soft, rose lips with his own, but he could never kiss her. His deformity wouldn't allow him that pleasure.

Together they sat by the fire, enjoying each other's presence without doing anything more than holding hands. They ate the cheese and bread and drank the wine as they chatted about inane matters as all youths do when they are shy and inexperienced in love. The night was beautiful to Richard and Misty, though they sat in the tunnel of the Sedgewick family crypt. The place and time didn't matter. All that meant anything to them was being together, finding someone who understood, finding someone who cared.

The log crumbled in the fireplace, showering sparks up the chimney as the last flames nibbled at the charred remains. Katharina sat once more holding the leather volume that had solved the riddle of the curse for her. She absently ran her finger over the embossed name and wondered what she could do to protect Kane and Richard. Because of fate's wild scheme to thrust her backward in time she'd found the man she loved—the man her mere presence could also destroy.

"Why is this happening? Has not enough damage been done to this family without my arriving to destroy it completely? Have Kane and Richard not suffered enough?" Katharina said aloud to the empty chamber. After his forced proposal, Kane had gone up to his chamber and had not even come down for dinner.

Katharina could understand why he'd not want to see her. She was the reason for all his troubles. He'd managed to make a life for himself and Richard that shielded them from the outside world. That was until she came bumbling into it, her twentieth-century beliefs making her too brazen to listen to his warnings. Now she would be responsible for destroying the very thing she'd come so far to find.

"God, how stupid can one person be?" Katharina asked herself. She didn't have the answer. She had thought she could change things, make Kane realize his seventeenth-century beliefs were wrong. Too late she was realizing she wasn't God. She couldn't change everyone's mind in 1651. She'd been foolish enough to ignore that fact.

Katharina squeezed her eyes closed to try to shut out the vision in her mind of the destruction she'd wrought. She couldn't. She laid the book on the side table and got to her feet. Raising her fist toward the ceiling, she swore aloud, "No! I'll be damned and in hell if I will destroy Kane and his family."

Realizing she had reacted like Scarlett in the turnip patch, Katharina let her hand fall to her side. She'd acted foolishly enough without adding the dramatic effect from the movie *Gone with the Wind*.

Silly laughter bubbled up and spilled out even as tears brimmed in her eyes. Even Scarlett O'Hara couldn't handle the situation she'd created. Katharina swiped at her tear-bright eyes and resigned herself to what she must do. She had only one course of action. She had to make Lord Churchill understand that she wasn't a witch before it was too late for Kane and Richard. No matter what happened to her in the future, it was her only hope to save the two people she loved from destruction.

Katharina's gaze moved over the library and came to rest on the heavy mahogany desk where she'd watched Kane work for so many hours. When she convinced Churchill that she wasn't a witch, all her dreams of marriage to Kane would again vanish beneath his belief in the curse. She would once again be on the edge of his life.

Katharina picked up the leather-bound volume of the Sedgewick family history and turned toward the door. She was going to prove to Kane once and for all that no curse existed to overshadow his life. Even if she wasn't the woman he married, she would give him that gift. She loved him too much to do otherwise.

She strode up to the east wing, her resolve making her steps firm. She knocked on the door and heard Kane bid her enter. He sat in front of the fireplace, his hair tousled, his face bleak. An empty brandy glass lay overturned on the floor by his chair.

He didn't look at her as she closed the door quietly behind her and crossed the chamber. "I have been expecting you."

"Oh?" Katharina said, seating herself in the chair next to his. "Am I so predictable that you already know what I'll do next?"

Kane's ebony gaze swept her face, taking in each feature. He slowly shook his head. "Nay. I never seem able to predict what you will do, but tonight is different. You have taken longer than I expected to come."

"Since you knew I was coming, do you also know why?"

"I suspect you've concocted some scheme to save Richard and myself should Winston go to the authorities with his accusation." Kane arched a brow in question.

Katharina smiled. She would not tell him what she planned to do. It was best to keep that to herself until all was settled. She wasn't lying. She was merely leaving out just a little of the truth. "Then you suspect wrong. I came for another reason."

Wearily, Kane ran his hand over his face and drew in a deep breath. "I hope you've not come here to argue about our wedding. 'Tis settled, Katharina. There is no more to be said."

"For the moment I agree with you," Katharina said as she leaned over and placed the family history in Kane's lap. "I came here to tell you what I found earlier today, before Lord Churchill burst into the library with his accusations."

Kane looked down at the heavy leather volume and then looked back at Katharina, puzzled. "I

312

doubt I have to ask, but I'll do it anyway. What are you talking about?"

Katharina stretched like a well-fed feline and curled her feet beneath her in the chair. She smiled triumphantly at Kane. "I've found proof that the curse does not exist."

"Enough!" Kane said, tossing the family history onto the floor. He got to his feet, his face grim and angry. "I'll hear no more of this nonsense. I've enough on my mind without you badgering me. I may lose all I hold dear. I need no more dreams of denial. I need to find a way to protect those I love!"

"Kane," Katharina said, coming out of her chair. She crossed to where Kane stood and took his hand as she looked up into his haunted face. A muscle twitched in his craggy cheek, and his eyes held the look of the fox during a chase. "My God, I didn't mean to upset you. I just wanted to tell you what I'd found. I wanted to give you a gift that would ease your mind and heart about the future."

Kane drew his hand away and turned toward the fireplace. He braced his hands on the mantle and let his head droop between his shoulders as he stared into the dancing flames. His morose tone revealed his feelings of doom. "There may be no future for any of us."

"There will be a future for you. You can marry and have children without fear once you understand that the Sedgewick curse comes

313

only when Sedgewicks and Clives marry. It's something we call a genetic deformity in the twentieth century."

"Blast it, Katharina! Can't you understand that I don't give a bloody damn about anything but you and Richard? Your safety is all that matters now. I can't worry about children or curses when I must find a way to protect the two people I love most in this world. There can be nothing for me in the future without you and Richard there with me."

"Look at me, Kane," Katharina said. "Look at me."

Slowly Kane raised his head and turned to look at Katharina.

"I love you and Richard. And I will not allow Churchill to destroy you. It's my fault what happened. I was foolish not to listen to you, and I pray for your forgiveness."

"Katharina—my beautiful, naive, Katharina. You still don't understand that there is nothing you can do to stop Churchill. You are but a woman in a time that looks with great suspicion upon beautiful females because of the power they possess over men."

Katharina closed the space between them and wrapped her arms about Kane's hard middle. She pressed her face against his wide chest, burying it in the soft white ruffles of his shirt. "I know my position here. And I know what must be done."

Kane's arms went about Katharina. "As I do. I

will write to Charles immediately and ask that he speak with Churchill. I can only hope that Churchill's loyalty to his king and country is more powerful than his fear. Should Charles fail to make him see reason, then we will leave England."

"You can't leave the place that you love. This is your home. This is your heritage."

"A cursed heritage. No. I will leave to ensure that you and Richard are safe. For I will have nothing but a great pile of stones should I lose either of you."

Katharina raised her head to look into Kane's troubled face. Her eyes held his as she said, "It is not cursed. And in time you will know I speak the truth. But you must promise me that if something should prevent our wedding, you will not marry a Clive. You must make certain that in the future no Sedgewick and Clive blood ever intermingle again. Will you promise me?"

"For hundreds of years our families have been joined by marriage. 'Tis what keeps us strong," Kane said, puzzled by her request.

"And it is what also dooms the children of those marriages to deformities like Richard's. Look back through the Sedgewick history and you will see that I'm right. It's all written down. Each time a Sedgewick and a Clive marry, a child vanishes. If you want to stop the curse that you believe exists, then stop the marriage of Sedgewick and Clive."

"I have already stopped the curse with myself and Richard. We are the last to know such torment."

"But what if I now carry your child? Would you disregard what I have said and allow a marriage to take place between your son and a Clive daughter?"

Kane searched Katharina's face, looking for an answer to her question. Finding none, he asked, "Do you carry my babe?"

Katharina lowered her eyes to the froth of white ruffles at his throat and slowly shook her head. "No."

Kane breathed a sigh of relief and felt a twitch of regret prick his heart. "I love you, Katharina. And should such an unlikely event ever take place, I will do as you ask. The curse, whether it exists or no, will end here, in my lifetime."

"Always remember your promise, Kane, no matter what you believe to be true. It's all I ask of you."

Kane frowned down at Katharina, worried by her tone. "You speak as if you will not be here."

"I made you a promise not too long ago that I would never leave you of my own choice. I will do everything in my power to keep that promise."

Kane smiled. " 'Twould seem this is a night of promises."

Katharina wrapped her arms about Kane's neck and drew his head down to hers. She looked into his dark eyes and whispered, "Let us make it into a night of love and forget all else."

Unable to endure the temptation of her lips, Kane surrendered without any battle. Too much had happened to make him realize how much he truly loved Katharina. He needed her love in that moment as much as he needed breath to live.

Chapter Fifteen

Dawn crept stealthily across the eastern sky. The fire burned low and the candle, its wax creating a curving trail down to the base of the golden candlestick, had guttered out several hours before. Shadows danced across the ceiling and floor as Katharina lay curled against Kane. He slept soundly, his arms wrapped protectively about her even in sleep. She breathed in the scent of him, a mixture of man, herbs and sandlewood from the soap he used to bathe.

Katharina savored his scent. Even the smell of him could ignite her desire. Her gaze moved over Kane's face. She loved every craggy inch of it. The dark shadow of beard stubble did nothing to detract from the beauty of his features. It seemed to heighten the masculine allure he exuded even in sleep. There was nothing soft about Kane. His features were completely masculine. His muscular body, lightly downed with dark silk, was hard and lean.

And at that moment, looking at the man she loved, Katharina knew the true meaning of agony. Drawing in a shuddering breath, she eased out of Kane's embrace and left the bed. She quickly gathered up her discarded clothing and silently left the room. Before the door closed behind her, she cast one last longing look at the man sleeping peacefully unaware of her plans. Before Kane awoke to try to stop her, she had to be on her way to Lord Churchill's estate.

With her bare feet making little sound upon the cold, parquetry floor, Katharina sped back to the tower room to dress. She planned to look her best when she met with Lord Churchill. She'd not arrive at his home looking bedraggled like the witch he thought her to be.

Choosing her warmest gown, a rich royal-blue velvet with a square neckline, she slipped it on and then fastened the wide white linen collar about her shoulders. It was trimmed in expensive French lace that also matched the lace edging the bodice of her gown and waist belt. She brushed her hair and let it fall about her shoulders naturally, forgoing the elaborate curls Chole always urged her to wear.

She turned to look at her reflection in the

cheval-glass mirror. The mirror, like so many other things now in the once-bare tower room, had shown up mysteriously one day while she was taking a walk in the garden. The tower room had become very luxurious over the past weeks. There were now thick Aubusson carpets on the floor, a dressing table, an armoire for her clothing and a thick feather mattress to accompany the new four-poster bed. Kane hadn't moved her to the family's east wing, but he'd seen to it that she had every convenience in her own chamber.

Katharina smiled sadly. Kane had done everything in his power to try to make her comfortable in his world. He had tried to protect her, but her own foolishness now threatened her life as well as all he held dear.

Katharina's nostrils flared as she raised her chin and squared her shoulders determinedly. She would not let Churchill harm Kane or Richard. They were her family now, no matter what might transpire between herself and Kane in the future.

Turning away from the mirror, she collected Kane's mother's woolen cloak and tossed it about her shoulders. She fastened the braided frogs and then turned toward the door. She was as ready as she would ever be to face Lord Churchill. She had to make him understand that she was not a witch, only a woman who loved his friend.

Turning back in the direction of the east wing, Katharina made her way along the hall. She cast only a brief glance toward the door of Kane's bed-chamber as she passed. There was only one way for her to leave unnoted by the servants: the hidden passageway to the family crypt. She hated the thought of entering the burial tomb, but it was the only secret way out. When her absence was noted once Kane awoke, there would be no one to tell him in which direction she'd traveled. He would have to search the entire castle before he finally came to the conclusion that she'd left Sedgewick.

Katharina pressed the lever to the secret panel and it slowly opened to reveal the burly man she'd come to know during her visits with Richard.

"Me lady? What ye doing about at this hour? Is somethin' amiss with the young sir?"

Katharina shook her head and quickly fabricated a story that she prayed he'd believe. "No, I was just going for an early-morning walk."

Joshua's thick brows lowered as he eyed her suspiciously from head to toe. "Ye look dressed up for a party, me lady. Ye don't look like yer going fer just a walk."

"All right, blast it! I'm not going for a walk but to visit a friend. Now will you step out of my way so I may pass?"

" 'Tis an awfully cold morning and 'tis awfully early to go a-visiting, me lady," Joshua said, unmoved.

Katharina rolled her eyes heavenward in exasperation before she looked back at the stalwart man. She'd managed to sneak out of Kane's bed and to dress with no one aware of her actions. Now here was Joshua, determined to know the reason behind her every move. "Joshua, I have business outside the castle and thought it best to go by way of the family crypt so the servants couldn't spy upon me and carry tales. Now are you satisfied?"

"What kind of business do ye have that ye have to sneak out at the break of dawn? I doubt that Lord Sedgewick would approve of it, if he was aware of yer actions. 'Tis dangerous for a woman alone to be about at such an hour."

Realizing the time she needed to convince Lord Churchill was being wasted trying to persuade Joshua to let her leave Sedgewick, Katharina answered honestly, "I am on my way to Lord Churchill's. He believes I'm a witch, and I must talk with him to make him understand that he is mistaken. It's the only way I can protect Kane and Richard. Should Lord Churchill go to the authorities with his suspicions, everyone will learn about Richard."

Joshua paled at the thought of what would happen to his young charge should people learn of his existence. And he understood Lady Katharina's need to try to stop Lord Churchill. However, he couldn't let Lady Katharina travel through the snow on foot and alone. She'd never make it to Lord Churchill's estate. She'd freeze in her tracks before she was halfway there. "Me lady, I canna let ye do this. Lord Sedgewick would skin me alive if I let ye go off by yerself. If ye'll follow me, I'll get the horses saddled and ready fer us."

Katharina had already opened her mouth to protest Joshua's denying her passage when she realized his intent to go with her. "You mean you'll go with me without telling Kane?"

"Aye. 'Tis little enough to do when ye go to protect me young sir. He has the blood of the Sedgewicks in his veins, and I'm but a mere servant, but I love 'im like a son."

"Bless you, Joshua. Let us pray that I'll succeed, for Kane and Richard's sake. I don't want to see them destroyed because of me."

"Ye'll convince Lord Churchill that yer an angel, me lady, not a witch."

"You have far more faith in me than I do, Joshua."

"Aye, I do. And if ye don't want anyone to know where ye've gone, we'd best be on our way before the servants start stirring about."

Katharina reached out and took Joshua's hand. "Thank you for being such a good friend to us all."

Joshua withdrew his hand and blushed. He stepped aside to allow Katharina ahead of him down the narrow stone stairway. "The lantern is lit, me lady, but watch yer step."

Katharina hugged her arms about her as she waited at the tunnel entrance for Joshua to return with the horses. He had been right when he'd said she would not make it to Lord Churchill's on foot. It was far colder outside Sedgewick's stone walls than inside.

It was also a relief to have Joshua's escort. She'd had such grand plans to confront Lord Churchill. But she had no earthly idea how she intended to get to his home when she didn't even know in which direction to travel. She'd planned to ask directions along the way, but had not considered what might happen to her alone on such an icy morning.

Kane had been right about her reckless actions. She didn't stop to consider the dangers to herself or to anyone else. She rushed headfirst into things with no thought at all. No thought that there was no 911 that could come to her rescue. Nor were there telephones she could use to call Kane for help. Her impetuous nature was the reason why she was now standing here with her toes freezing off.

Katharina glanced up at the gray sky. It looked like it might snow again. And she said another prayer of thanks for Joshua's companionship. She knew enough from her life in Utah that if it snowed heavily, she could easily become disoriented and lost in an area that she knew well. Should that happen here, she'd never find her way back to Sedgewick. Kane wouldn't find her frozen body until after the snow thawed.

Catching sight of Joshua making his way through the trees with the horses, Katharina smiled. She'd be safe with him to guide her through the snowy landscape.

Katharina found she was far warmer mounted on horseback than on foot. The animal's heat offset the icy wind that burned her cheeks and made her eyes tear. The snowflakes began to fall heavily soon after they lost sight of Sedgewick's granite walls. At first they were only tiny flurries, barely visible to the eye. But as the minutes passed, they began to grow until the large, fluffy flakes covered her horse's roan coat, her cloak and even her eyelashes. It hid the horses' hoofprints nearly as soon as they were made, making it impossible for anyone to follow their trail.

The falling snow made travel difficult, yet Katharina was grateful for the thick veil of white flakes that hindered sight for more than a few feet ahead. The inclement weather would also impede Churchill's travels. He'd have to wait until the snow stopped before he contacted the authorities about her.

Katharina smiled to herself. There were some benefits to not having telephones or four-wheel-drive vehicles.

It took several hours for Joshua and Katharina to traverse the distance to Churchill's estate. On a clear day, it usually took an hour or less to cross the same distance. When they finally rode up the winding drive of Churchill's three-storied manor house, Katharina's teeth chattered and she was shivering from head to toe. Exhausted, she allowed Joshua to help her dismount. Her knees threatened to buckle beneath her as her feet touched the ground, and it was only with Joshua's steadying hand that she remained upright.

The footman who answered their knock upon the wide double doors eyed them haughtily, as if he'd discovered vermin upon his master's threshold. He gave them no time to say anything and commanded imperiously, "Beggars to the rear of the house."

The order sent heat spiraling through Katharina. She raised her chin and eyed the footman indignantly as she thrust out her arm to keep him from closing the door in their faces. She feigned the most pretentious tone she could muster as she said, "I am the Lady Katharina Ferguson. And I've come to see Lord Churchill."

Her tone made the footman take pause long enough for her to shove the door back and step inside the foyer. Undoing the braided frogs of her cloak, she tossed the snowy garment to him and added arrogantly, "Please inform your lord that I am here to speak with him. Then kindly escort Joshua to the kitchen and see that he has a warming drink. The weather is icy out."

Dumbfounded and suddenly aware that he might have made a severe mistake in his first impression of the lady with the flashing blue eyes, the footman nodded graciously and said, "Yes, my lady. Will you await Lord Churchill in the salon?"

Katharina glanced at Joshua in time to see him smiling broadly before she followed the footman to the salon just off the foyer. He bowed as he closed the door, leaving Katharina to make use of the heat coming from the dancing flames in the grate. She held out her hands to the warmth, hoping to bring the feeling back into her chilled fingers.

Katharina's feet and toes had just begun to warm when the salon doors opened to reveal a lovely woman in her mid-twenties. Dressed in a beautiful brocade gown of pale blue, she smiled at Katharina as she closed the door behind her and crossed the chamber. She extended her hand to Katharina and said, "I'm Elizabeth Churchill. And you're Kane's lady. I've wanted to meet you for so long."

Katharina liked her instantly. There was no guile, only sincerity in her smile and voice. "I'm delighted to meet you, Lady Churchill. Kane speaks of you fondly."

"Please be seated, Lady Katharina. I've ordered tea. You must be frozen to the bone on a day such as this. 'Tis horrid out."

Katharina laughed. "I'm just beginning to feel my toes and fingers again."

"The tea will warm you," Elizabeth said, taking the seat beside Katharina. "Now tell me what was so important that you would chance being frozen stiff. There is nothing wrong with Kane, is there?"

Katharina shook her head. "No. Kane was in

good health when I left him this morning. I've come to speak with Lord Churchill about something he misconstrued on his visit yesterday."

Before Elizabeth could respond, the salon doors burst open to reveal her husband. Hands on each door latch, he stood glaring at them from the doorway. "Elizabeth, what in the devil are you doing?"

"Winston, we have a visitor," Elizabeth said, smiling sweetly up at her husband as if his thunderous look was his ordinary expression.

"I can well see that. Go upstairs and stay with the children," Churchill ordered, his face flushing with fury.

Elizabeth turned to Katharina, her smile never wavering. "I must go up and check on the children. The weather has worsened John's cough, and even our little Arabella has the sniffles today. She's usually as healthy as a little horse. And that's fortunate, because I don't know what we would do should both our children have constitutions like John."

"I'm sorry to hear that your children are ill, Lady Churchill," Katharina said, rising as Elizabeth stood. "It has been a pleasure to meet you. I hope both John and Arabella will soon feel much better."

The thought of her son's worsening condition made Elizabeth's smile fade. She glanced uncertainly at her husband before she said, "I pray for that each day. But I fear for John's life. The physician can find nothing to help his cough, nor is there anything to help him breathe."

"Elizabeth, I said go upstairs. The children are awaiting you," Churchill said, crossing the salon to stand between Katharina and his wife as if his body could shield Elizabeth from harm.

"Please come again, Lady Katharina," Elizabeth said, flashing her husband a censorious look as she turned toward the door.

Churchill didn't speak until his wife had closed the salon door behind her. He looked at Katharina and again felt the need to make the sign of the cross to ward off the evil she seemed to exude. She looked ravishing in the royal-blue velvet gown, with her hair lying about her linen-covered shoulders like a thick silk mantle, yet she was evil incarnate to him. "What do you here, Lady Katharina? I do not recall extending you an invitation to my home."

"No. You did not invite me, but I am grateful that you have seen fit to see me. I need to talk with you, to explain what you saw yesterday morn when you came to Sedgewick."

"There is no need for any explanation. I know what I saw, and nothing you can say will change my mind." Churchill moved across the chamber, putting as much distance as possible between himself and the witch.

"I don't think you do. You believe you saw me light the fire with my fingers and come away unscathed. But you are wrong. As Kane explained to you, I wore the beige gloves he gave me."

"Do you have any proof? Do you bring the gloves with their fingertips charred and burned?" Churchill quizzed. Seeing Katharina shake her head, he continued. " 'Tis as I thought. You have no evidence to discredit what I saw. You thought to come here and use your wiles to convince me that you are not a witch. But you are, Lady Katharina. And I intend to see my friend protected from you even at the expense of losing a friendship I hold dear."

"No. I'm not a witch. And I love Kane. I would never do him harm."

"Humph!" Churchill snorted. "Witches have no hearts. They are in league with the devil to steal the souls of men."

"You are wrong, Lord Churchill. I love Kane and that is the reason I have come here. I beg of you not to go to the authorities. I will do anything you ask. I don't want to see Kane hurt any more than you do."

"Your plea falls upon deaf ears, Lady Katharina. Kane is too blind with love to see you as you truly are, but I am not. I have seen your devil's work with my own eyes. And I intend to make certain that you cannot harm Kane or anyone else. You will not work your spells with your herbs again if I have anything to say upon the matter."

Katharina closed the space between them and looked up at Churchill. Her eyes beseeched his beneficence as she pleaded, "Please, Lord Churchill. Don't do this. Kane has many enemies who would love to use your accusations against me to destroy him. I will leave Sedgewick if that is your wish, but please don't hurt Kane in the misguided belief that you are protecting him. Deep in your own heart, you must know that you are not."

"I do what I must. It is my duty, as a man who believes in God, to root out evil such as yours," Churchill said, unaffected by her plea.

"Then you should join Cromwell. His beliefs are what rule his judgment. They are why Charles the First was hanged and why his son now is in exile in France."

Churchill jerked visibly at Katharina's comparison. He was nothing like Cromwell. The man was a fanatic who wanted to force everyone to believe as he did. No. He was nothing like Cromwell. He had an open mind, one willing to accept new ideas. Except when it came to those close to him. He'd protect them at all cost, even if he had to go against their wishes. Men wrapped up in love often didn't know what was best for them.

The salon doors burst open as Katharina opened her mouth to plead again. However, the words went unspoken as a white-faced Elizabeth charged into the salon with her son clutched to her breast. Tears streamed down her ashen face as she gasped, "John's not breathing. John's not breathing."

In a flash, Churchill had his son in his arms. He

pressed his ear to the small infant's chest. He heard only silence. "Send for the physician," he ordered the servant hovering in the doorway, though he suspected that it was already too late for his son. His heir, his only son, was dead.

"Make him come back, Winston. Don't let him die. He can't die. He is your heir. Make him live, Winston! Please, God. Don't take my baby," Elizabeth cried, crumpling to her knees at her husband's feet.

"Let me see him," Katharina said, holding out her arms to Churchill.

"Stay away from my son, witch. You'll not get his soul for your master," Churchill said. Glaring at Katharina as if she'd suddenly grown two heads, he backed away from her.

"But I might be able to help him," Katharina pleaded. "Please don't let your son die because of your own foolish superstitions. I know CPR."

Churchill shook his head. "Nay. Keep away, witch."

"Let her have John, Winston," Elizabeth said, her tone brooking no argument.

Churchill looked at his wife. "But she will steal his soul. She is a witch."

Elizabeth pushed herself to her feet and crossed to her husband. She took the limp child from his arms. "I don't give a blasted damn if she is the devil himself as long as she'll bring John back to me." Elizabeth turned to Katharina. "Save my baby. Please, save my baby."

Katharina took the small body into her arms and laid him on the seat of the chair. It had been a long while since her last seminar on administering CPR, and she prayed she could remember enough to save John. She opened the tiny mouth and checked to see if the air passage was clear before she covered his nose and mouth with her own. Drawing in a small breath, she filled the babe's lungs with air before she gently pressed down on his chest as she'd been taught. Nothing happened. Again, she breathed into the baby's lungs, then again. At last she felt a tiny beat and then a gasping of air.

The babe stirred. Elizabeth came to her knees beside the chair and lifted her son into her arms. She looked with wonder at Katharina. "You have saved my John's life. How can I ever thank you?"

"I need no thanks. I did what anyone would do in the circumstances," Katharina said, awed by her own victory over death. She'd taken the CPR course at Herbal Health, Inc., because the other employees had been required to do it and she hadn't wanted to appear privileged by avoiding the course. At the time she'd doubted she'd ever have a need for it. Now she understood why it had been required. She had saved a life.

Awed by what she had done, Katharina stood back and watched as Elizabeth hovered over her son, whispering soothing words. Katharina glanced at Lord Churchill, expecting to see the same look of wonder upon his face; instead, she encountered only cold accusation. Katharina swallowed back the lump of fear that rose in her throat. By saving his child's life, she had only proven once again that she was in league with the devil.

"It's not true, Lord Churchill," Katharina said before his thoughts could be verbalized. "Only God gives life. The devil can't."

"So you would have us believe so you can go freely about, destroying lives." Churchill shook his head. "No, witch. You have not changed my mind, only shown me the truth."

Elizabeth looked up at her husband, startled by his words. She lifted her son into her arms and turned to face Lord Churchill. "You would accuse her of witchcraft when your son breaths only because of her?"

"Aye, my lady. She uses what looks like good to gain power over us."

"You are a fool, Winston. For as long as I have known you, I have never seen you act in such a way. You have always been kind and generous, holding no animosity even toward those who have harmed you. Now, with Lady Katharina, you can see only evil when she has done naught but good."

"You know not of what you speak," Lord Churchill said as the salon doors opened to reveal Lord Sedgewick.

Taking in the scene, Kane crossed to where Katharina stood ashen faced. "What goes on here?

Has he threatened you, Katharina?" Seeing the negative shake of her head, he looked at Lady Churchill. "My lady, is something amiss? From the look on all your faces, you've just seen the devil himself."

Elizabeth's lips trembled as she gave Kane a wobbly smile. Tears brimmed in her eyes once more as she looked at Katharina. "No devil, my lord. An angel perhaps."

Kane glanced from Lady Churchill to her husband before he looked once more at the woman he loved. "Something is not right here. I demand that one of you explain to me what has happened. And I would also know the reason you are here, Katharina. Luckily, Joshua woke one of the stableboys before he left, or I might never have found your whereabouts."

Churchill didn't allow Katharina time to answer. "I will tell you what's going on here. Your lady came uninvited to try to tell me she is no witch. Then, before my very eyes, she breathed life back into my own son."

Kane glanced once more at each face in the room before he frowned. "I would think my lady's actions would serve as evidence that she is no witch, Winston. What more proof do you need?"

"None," came Elizabeth's stalwart answer. "Winston was mistaken about what he saw yesterday. Your lady is right when she says only God can give life. It is something far too precious to come from the devil. No. Your lady is an angel, my lord. She has no evil about her."

"Elizabeth! You know not what you say," Churchill burst out.

Elizabeth shot her husband a quelling look that chilled the very marrow of his bones. He swallowed uneasily. In all their years of marriage, he'd never seen her react in such a manner. She had never contradicted him, only supported him in his every deed and word. He was shocked to the core by her defense of the woman he believed to be a witch.

"I know exactly what I am saying. I hold my son because of her. Had she not been here, I would now be readying him for his burial."

At his mother's words, the babe stirred and began to cough and gasp for breath. Elizabeth paled as she looked once at Katharina. "Can you help him? Please. I don't want to lose him again."

Katharina took a step forward but Kane's hand stayed her. "My lady has done all she knows, Lady Elizabeth. The physician should be summoned."

Katharina looked from the man she loved to the child wheezing and coughing as he once more slowly began to turn blue from lack of air. In that moment, she realized why fate had sent her back in time. It hadn't been to meet Kane or to fall in love, nor was it to stop the Sedgewick curse. If her memory served her right, the sick child that now lay in his mother's arms would grow to be the first Duke of Marlborough, the man who built

Blenheim Palace, the birthplace of Sir Winston Leonard Churchill, the Prime Minister of England during World War II. Katharina looked down at the small sick face. Should she choose to do as Kane wanted and the child died, there would be no dynasty to beget the Churchill that would lead England to help defeat Hitler.

The thought was staggering. Fate had chosen her to help this child. Katharina glanced at the man at her side and wanted to burst into tears. She had only two choices: To help Lord Churchill's son and perhaps be condemned to death for witchcraft, or to do as Kane wanted and stay at Sedgewick with the man she loved for the rest of her life.

Katharina looked up into Kane's handsome face and knew she didn't have two choices after all. There was only one to make. She had to help the child, no matter the cost to herself or Kane. John Churchill had to carry on his father's bloodline for the future of the coming generations of all men.

Intimidated by the magnitude of fate's decisions for her, Katharina looked into the face of Elizabeth Churchill and saw the agony only a mother feels when her child's life is in jeopardy. "I will do what I can, Lady Churchill."

Kane's grip tightened on her arm. "If you do this, Katharina, it could well mean your life."

Katharina glanced back at Kane's beloved face and nodded serenely. "I know."

"Then come with me before it is too late. Let Churchill summon the physician for his child. Don't put your own life in jeopardy for a child you may not be able to help."

"I have no other choice, Kane. I now know why I'm here. I've been blessed to know your love, but I was sent here for a reason, and it now lies coughing and straining for life in its mother's arms. John Churchill must live, no matter what happens to me."

Seeing the resolute light in Katharina's eyes, Kane accepted her decision. He didn't want to lose her, but the woman he'd come to love could not walk away from a sick child even to save her own life.

Kane's heart seemed to break as she took the babe from Lady Churchill and then began to give orders to have the kettle filled with water and set over the fire to steam. He watched in silence as she requested the very things that he feared Churchill would call her instruments of witchcraft: sage, comfrey, parsley, horehound, mint and honey from the kitchen. Elizabeth rushed to comply while he and Churchill stood regarding each other suspiciously, each determined to protect those they loved—even from each other if need be.

Chapter Sixteen

The babe slept peacefully. The aromatic steam rose above his cradle, filling the air with the sweet scent of the herbs that Katharina put into the kettle. Elizabeth also slept, her head resting on the side of the cradle, afraid to lie down and leave even a few feet between herself and her son.

Lord Churchill sat gloomily in the chair next to his wife, his arm resting protectively across the back of her chair. He glanced at the woman who now sat next to his friend, her head cradled on his shoulder, their hands clasped together as if afraid something or someone would tear them apart.

Churchill tore his eyes away from the two lovers and looked down at his son, who slept peacefully for the first time in weeks. He didn't know what to do. He'd seen the woman who had nursed his son for the past hours light a fire from the tips of her fingers, yet she had come to plead for mercy, not for herself but for Kane. She had not used her power to bring his son back to life as leverage over him but had freely given her aid to save John.

Churchill stretched his lean frame and ran a weary hand through his already tousled hair. He, like his wife, was exhausted. It was only mid-afternoon, but he felt he'd lived a year during the past few hours. He had lost a son and regained him only to realize that he might lose him again. And he would have, had it not been for the herbs of Lady Katharina.

Churchill released a long breath and looked back at his friend, who was speaking softly with the woman he loved. Did it truly matter if the woman was a witch, if she made Kane happy? If she used her power for good, not evil, should he turn her over to the authorities? Was it his responsibility to decide her fate and destroy Kane's life and their friendship?

Churchill glanced down at his sleeping wife, her beautiful face pale with worry and exhaustion. And should he destroy his relationship with Elizabeth because of his need to protect Kane? Because that was exactly what would happen should he go to the authorities with what he had seen. Elizabeth would never forgive him.

Churchill grimaced and slowly shook his head. He had his wife and his children. He'd let Kane take care of his own house.

Churchill looked once more at his friend and found Kane's eyes on him. He smiled wearily in surrender as he glanced toward the window where the sky had cleared and the winter sun glared blindingly against the white landscape. " 'Tis turning into a fine day."

Hearing far more in his friend's tone than in his words, Kane smiled and nodded. "Aye. 'Tis a fine day after all."

"Will you and your lady stay with us this eve? I would offer you our hospitality. 'Tis little enough thanks for the wonder she has given us this day."

"We accept your hospitality, Winston. My lady is far too weary to make the journey back to Sedgewick this late in the day."

"Do you think you and your lady can ever forgive me? I regret my words and actions."

Katharina listened quietly to the two friends speak. She was relieved and grateful that Churchill had changed his mind about her. All had turned out well. Lord Churchill and his wife still had their son, and Kane still had his friend. She smiled warmly at Churchill. "I see nothing to forgive, my lord. I love Kane as you do. And I would do the same to see him protected."

"I doubt you'd go quite so far, my lady. But I do thank you for your understanding, as well as for the life of my son. Neither my lady nor I will ever forget what you have done for us."

"I did not give you the life of your son. God only has the power to do that, my lord. I merely used the knowledge gained through God's grace to help young John. And I pray he will grow strong and my help will never be needed again," Katharina said, holding tight to Kane's hand. She felt him squeeze her fingers in reassurance and gratitude for accepting Churchill's apology.

"Then we are blessed to have your friendship, Lady Katharina," Churchill said as his wife stirred and looked up. She hid a yawn behind her delicate hand and dreamily smiled at her husband, all her love for him glowing in her eyes.

"As I've always known, I married a very wise man," Elizabeth said, turning her smile to her friends.

Churchill smiled down at his wife. "And I married a woman whose love can overlook my flaws."

Standing in front of the window in Kane's bedchamber with his arms wrapped about her, Katharina felt she was in heaven. She had fulfilled her contract with history by helping Lord Churchill's son; now she could turn her attention to the man she loved and their life together.

She leaned back against Kane and dreamily looked upon the moonlit meadow that had been the scene of the witch burning so long ago.

It was hard to imagine anything so evil happening in the meadow that now looked like a fairy-land with the moonlight's reflection upon the snow. It shimmered as if made of crystal and silver.

Kane rested his cheek against her shining hair and breathed in her scent as his gaze also moved over the meadow where his ancestor had been cursed. He tightened his arms about Katharina as his thoughts turned toward the conversation they'd had before she'd gone to confront Churchill. She had told him so many wonders, had shown him so many things that he could not have imagined before she'd come into his life. Her knowledge astounded him. She knew far more than the most educated of men; could she also be right about the curse?

Kane squeezed his eyes closed and pulled her even closer against him. He longed to believe in what she said, but he had to be certain before he could go on with the life he longed to have with Katharina.

"Do you truly believe that what happened in the meadow has nothing to do with Richard's condition?"

Katharina nodded, savoring the feeling of being totally protected in his arms. She wrapped her hands over the strong arms about her waist. "There is no curse, Kane. The curse came about as a way for people to explain away the afflicted children that were born of the unions of the Sedgewicks and Clives. They had no scientific way to prove that it was a birth defect. They had only superstition to explain the tragedies."

Kane released a wishful sigh. "If only I could be certain of what you say, I would be the happiest man on earth."

"Kane, there is no curse, but I can't prove what I say. The only evidence I have is your family history. Were we in my time, there would be tests that could be done to show you the genetic make-up that creates this abnormality. But we don't have that here. So you have only my word."

"I want to believe you. God! How I would like to live as a normal man again!"

"There are no guarantees in life, Kane. When two people marry, there is always a risk of some genetic disease or deformity coming from their ancestors. But there is far more chance of having beautiful, wonderful, brilliant children. And if life had guarantees, it would be far less interesting. All we can do is to treasure each day we have together and to trust in God."

"It's hard to deny the very things you have believed all of your life."

"But you accepted me. It can't be easy for you to believe I traveled through time."

"It's far easier to believe in you. I can see and touch you."

"Then what are we to do?" Katharina said as she caught sight of two shadowy figures entering the meadow.

"Do as I told Churchill. We will be married as

planned. Winston may have decided against going to the authorities, but you still need my protection. Nothing has really changed."

Katharina released a long breath and shook her head. "No, Kane. Nothing has changed. I won't marry you unless you will be a true husband to me, not just someone who offers his protection. I can't live with you knowing that you come to my bed only when your desire overshadows all else. It breaks my heart to know that making love to me tears you apart. Come to me without the chains of the past, and I will gladly become your wife, but not before."

"Will you give me time?"

"I give you my heart and soul. Time is a small thing, as we have learned."

Kane dropped a light kiss upon the crown of Katharina's shining head. "I love you, Katharina."

"And you know I love you. Perhaps some day, we will be as free as the lovers who now meet in the meadow."

Kane peered over Katharina's head to the white landscape below. "Who would be about on such a night as this?"

Katharina smiled wistfully. "Lovers who care only about being together and nothing else."

Kane drew away from Katharina. He moved closer to the window to get a better view of the dark silhouettes. As he watched, another figure joined them. After a few moments they separated, one moving back into the shadows of the forest and the other two walking back toward Sedge-wick's granite walls.

Kane frowned. Something was not right. A chill of warning raised the hair at the nape of his neck as his suspicions rose. He had thought Katharina a spy at one time; was he now looking at Glen-ville's real hireling?

Ebony eyes flashing fury, Kane turned toward the door. "Stay here, Katharina."

"Kane, what is it? Where are you going? What did you see?"

"I have no time to answer your questions now," Kane said, his hand already on his sword. Taking it from the scabbard, he opened the door and a moment later he was gone.

"Stay here! I'll be damned," Katharina said, quickly following in Kane's wake. Stealthily she kept herself at a distance as he swiftly moved along the corridor and down the narrow steps to a passageway lit by torches. Katharina held back a shudder as she passed the doorway that led to the guard room and dungeon beyond. She had no desire to visit those realms ever again.

The passageway grew wider as Kane strode to-ward the exit where Katharina had found herself tumbling into the mire from the kitchens. He paused briefly as if considering his next move be-fore he opened the heavy oak door and strode out into the night.

Breathing heavily from the rapid pace he set, Katharina closed the door behind her and gingerly made her way down the worn stones and around the huge pool where she'd lost her shoes on her first adventure outside Sedgewick Castle.

Holding her skirts above the slush created by the passage of the servants, she hurried after Kane, suddenly frightened for his safety. Kane had enemies who would like to see him dead, and he had gone alone to meet them.

Katharina quickly stepped into the deepest shadows as Kane hid himself behind a cart left near the postern gate. He seemed to brace himself, preparing to face an unknown enemy as he crouched low to await the intruders. A moment later, the solid oak door squeaked open.

From her hiding place, Katharina couldn't see the two shadowy figures who emerged through the portal. She could only see Kane as he sprang from his hiding place, sword ready to dispatch the intruders.

Realizing there were two against one, Katharina hurried toward the gate where she could only see Kane's towering figure. His back to her, he shielded the others from view until she was only a little distance away. Her breath coming in short gasps, she stopped suddenly at the sight of Joshua and Misty. They stood in front of Kane, bewildered.

"What do you do about at this hour?" Kane asked, eyeing the two distrustfully.

"Lordship, we was but taking a walk in the

snow," Joshua said, trying to protect the secret of the two young lovers.

"Don't lie to me, man. I saw you from my chamber. You did not go to the meadow to take a walk."

Joshua lowered his eyes to Kane's feet, unable to lie while he looked at the man he'd known all of his life. "Nay, me lord. Misty wanted to go for a walk and needed my escort."

Kane's ebony gaze shot to the girl at Joshua's side. "Is what he says true, girl?"

Misty nodded and bowed her head. Something was not right. Lord Sedgewick was acting as if he knew the man at her side, as if Joshua was his servant. Misty's breath caught in her throat. Why had she not realized it from the first time he'd come for her? He had to be in Lord Sedgewick's employ for him to have entrance to the castle. And why was he lying to protect her and her gallant knight?

Kane's heated gaze shot back to Joshua. "Do you expect me to believe all this nonsense? Do you think I have no eyes to see the truth of what you have been up to? Did he pay you well, Joshua? Did you think that you would not be found out?"

"I don't understand. I but took the girl fer a walk, me lord. I've done nothing more. She's but a babe. I'd not touch a hair on 'er head."

"Blast it! No more lies. Admit you've been working for Glenville."

Joshua shook his head, his face draining of

color. "Nay, me lord. I serve only ye and yers. As God is me witness, I have not betrayed ye."

"Then who did you meet in the meadow if you are still loyal to me?"

Again Joshua shook his head. "I took the girl fer a walk, me lord. 'Tis all."

Seething with rage against the one man he had trusted with his deepest secret, Kane ground out, "Perhaps a night in the dungeon will refresh your memory."

Misty stared up at the voice in front of her. She couldn't let Joshua go to the dungeon for trying to protect her and the man she loved. "Nay, Lord Sedgewick. You can't put him in the dungeon when he is only trying to protect me."

"Hush, girl," Joshua said, trying to stop Misty from telling of her tryst with Richard.

Kane arched a dark brow at the young girl, who had taken a tentative step forward. He frowned. Could this child-woman be the one in Glenville's employ instead of Joshua? He flashed Joshua a quelling look as he asked, "Why is he trying to protect you?"

"Misty, girl. Ye don't have to tell," Joshua said, raising his chin belligerently. He couldn't allow the girl to tell of her relationship with the young sir. When Lord Sedgewick learned of it, he would put an end to it. Joshua feared what Richard might do to his brother and himself. The boy had fallen in love with the girl, and love made men crazy.

"He is trying to protect me because I asked him to go with me to meet a friend."

"A friend? From what I viewed out my window, he's more than a friend to you."

Misty raised her chin proudly, unashamed of her love. "I love him, my lord."

Kane's ebony gaze swept back to Joshua. "Who is he?"

Joshua remained mute.

"He is my gallant knight," Misty answered, unaware that the question had not been directed at her.

Again Kane arched a dark brow at Joshua.

Again Joshua ignored the unspoken question.

"Does he have a name?" Kane asked at last.

"I know him only as my gallant knight, my lord," Misty said.

"Surely you mislead me, girl? You say you love this man, yet you know not his name."

"I need no name to know he is kind and gentle. He is unafraid to care for someone like me. He needs no other name but Gallant Knight, for that is what he is in truth."

"Do you know his name, Joshua?" Kane said, turning his ebony gaze back to the burly man standing stiffly at Misty's side.

Joshua again remained stubbornly mute.

"I think you must need a night in the dungeon to improve your memory," Kane threatened again.

"Nay, my lord. Do not imprison Joshua because

of me. 'Tis my fault, not his. Put me in the dungeon in his stead," Misty said, bravely defending her friend.

"So be it," Kane said, reaching to take Misty's arm.

"Kane," Katharina said, stepping from the shadows. "Surely you jest. You can't think to imprison this child. She has done nothing wrong but fall in love."

Exasperated, Kane looked at the woman he loved. "Katharina, this is none of your concern. Go to your chamber. We will speak later."

"I am not a servant to be ordered about. Nor will I allow you to put Misty in the dungeon."

"Allow me, lady?" Kane ground out between clenched teeth. "I am master of Sedgewick, and I will do what I must to protect what I hold. This girl may now be in the employ of my enemies, and I will know their names or she'll suffer the consequences."

"Nay," Joshua burst out. "Misty canna tell ye a name. She knows him only as she has said."

"It would seem the two of you are set to protect each other as well as deny me an answer. Unfortunately, Misty will be the one to suffer. She will spend this night in the dungeon. Perhaps she doesn't know the man's name, yet I suspect you do, Joshua. And until you tell me, she will remain my guest in the bowels of Sedgewick."

"Me lordship, ye make it difficult to keep me vow, but I canna let the girl suffer because of her love. Ye know his name as well as yer own."

Katharina looked from Kane's stern, moonlit features to Joshua. Her eyes widened with comprehension. Kane had suspected the identity of Misty's lover when Joshua refused to answer his questions. He knew his threat to put Misty in the dungeon would be his only leverage to make Joshua tell him the truth.

"Aye, I know his name," Kane said morosely and drew in a slow, deep breath as if to brace himself for the events to come. He glanced at Katharina. "You know this cannot continue."

"Kane, you can't do this. They love each other," Katharina said, taking hold of Kane's arm. She looked up at him. "Please talk with Richard. It may be the only chance that either of them have for happiness."

Kane seemed to age as he looked from Katharina back to the young girl who had fallen in love with his brother. "Go to your bed, girl. We will discuss this matter further tomorrow."

Joshua's hand on her elbow urged Misty toward the oak door that Kane and Katharina had exited a few minutes earlier. He glanced back at Kane and smiled wearily. " 'Tis innocent, me lord. They've done nothing but meet and talk."

Relieved by her momentary reprieve from the dungeon and puzzled by the sudden change in Lord Sedgewick's tone as well as by the name of Richard, Misty didn't ask any questions as she took the worn steps back into the castle.

Kane nodded. He had that much to be grateful for. 'Twould be far worse had Richard bedded the girl.

Katharina rubbed her arms in an effort to warm them as she stood beside Kane and watched Joshua and Misty pass from view. Her feet felt like ice standing in the snowy slush, yet she made no move to return to the warmth of the castle. She waited for Kane to speak, to tell her what he intended for Richard and Misty.

Kane glanced down at her and realized that they both stood in the icy, moonlit night without cloaks. He reached out and put his arm about Katharina, pulling her against him. He dropped a light kiss on her brow as his gaze wandered up the granite castle walls to the east wing where his brother lived. "What should I do, Katharina?"

Katharina huddled closer to Kane's hard body and wrapped her arms about his waist as she also looked in the direction of the east wing. "Talk with Richard."

Kane flashed her a puzzled glance before nodding. "All right. I will speak with him, but I will not guarantee to allow this to continue."

"Give them a chance to live and love as others, Kane. That's all I ask."

Kane smiled down at Katharina. "Before you came to me, I would not even have considered what you now ask. However, I now know what it is like to love and be loved, and I would not deny that to my enemies, much less my brother."

"Richard is Misty's gallant knight, and you are mine," Katharina said, hugging him close as they made their way back to the castle's rear entrance.

"I love her and she loves me, Kane," Richard said, refusing to deny his tryst with Misty. He was no longer a child but a man who didn't need his brother to say him yea or nay. He had his own life and would live it as close to normal as possible for anyone with his face. Misty had been an answer to his prayers, and he'd defy anyone to forbid his love for her.

"I understand your feelings for her. She is a beautiful young woman. But is it right to meet her only in the dark of night? Is it right to keep her unaware of where you live and why?"

"I had no other choice, as you well know. You have created this world for me, and I must live in it the best way that I know. I am not foolish enough to think I can go about like you with your handsome face, Kane. But I still need the same things you need. I need to feel a woman in my arms as much as you need to feel Katharina in yours. I have a normal man's desires and a normal man's heart, no matter the monstrous face that I possess. Can't you understand? I must live or go as mad as the monster I resemble."

Kane felt his eyes burn with sympathy. He understood everything Richard was saying, yet he was still undecided about how to handle the situation. He had agreed to speak with Richard, but their conversation only confused him further because he also knew what it was like to try to deny one's emotions.

Kane ran a weary hand over his face. He'd slept little through the night as he'd gone over what he must do. " 'Tis true that I have created this world for you, but I did it out of love. I have never wanted to see you hurt, Richard."

Richard looked at his handsome brother and nodded. "I know. 'Tis only that I'm now a grown man, not a child to be coddled. I understand why I have had to live here in this dark world. But you must understand that Misty is the sun that has illuminated the blackness for me. She can't see me. She knows only a man who loves her, not a man with a monster's face. She loves me not because I am a Sedgewick. She loves only the true me."

Kane surrendered. He could not take away what little joy Richard had gained from his love of Misty. "Then so be it. As long as you and Misty are happy, I will say no more."

Richard's thick-lashed eyes widened in surprise at his brother's sudden capitulation. "Do you honestly mean what you say? You will allow Misty and me to be together?"

Kane nodded. "I know how it feels to love someone and then be denied that love. 'Tis far more pain than I would wish upon anyone, much less the brother that I love. Love your Misty, Richard.

As long as you are honest with her about yourself and your feelings, you have nothing to fear. 'Tis a lesson that I, myself, have had to learn the hard way."

Excitement coursed through Richard. He jumped to his feet and grabbed Kane's hand to shake it, but instead pulled his brother out of his chair and gave him a robust, brotherly hug. "Thank you, Kane, for your blessings."

The two brothers hugged for a long moment before Kane said, "You are a man now, Richard. And you must consider what life here will be like for Misty. To keep you safe, she will have to leave her world and enter yours. Do you understand the magnitude of what you will be asking of her?"

Richard came crashing back to earth. He'd not considered the choices Misty would have to make to live in his world. He'd hoped that in time they could move far away from Sedgewick, far out into the country where no one would ever see his face. Perhaps there they could live something akin to a normal existence. However, that would be far in the future, if ever. Misty would have to come into his world, perhaps for the rest of her life.

Richard let his arms fall to his sides and turned his back to his brother to hide his feelings. His dark eyes were troubled as he stared out the window into the sunlit afternoon. "I will make her understand before I allow her to choose."

" 'Tis all I ask," Kane said, placing a comforting hand on his brother's shoulder and giving it a reassuring squeeze. "And if you are meant to be together, all will go well."

Richard raised agonized eyes toward the clear blue heavens. "God, Kane. Why did we have to be the cursed Sedgewicks? Why did the first Richard have to let the witch burn to death? Had he been honest about his feelings for her, we would not now be cursed."

"Katharina says there is no curse. She says that 'tis only something that happens when Sedgewicks and Clives intermarry. And in truth, our family history bears her out. Had your mother and my father married others, this would never have happened."

Richard looked over his shoulder at his brother. "Do you believe her? Could I love Misty as a man loves a wife and not pass along the horror of my face?"

"Katharina knows things that few of us know, Richard. She has a gift that comes only with time," Kane said, smiling to himself at his play on words. "She is far wiser than either you or I on matters such as this. And I am coming to believe that she is right. She says it is no curse, but only a birth defect. And that should she and I have children they would not be affected by it because she does not have Clive blood. The same should hold true for you and Misty."

Kane's gaze swept past his brother's dark head

to the snowy landscape beyond the window. He was not completely convinced that there was no curse, but he was convinced that Katharina was right when she said that there were no guarantees in life. You had to live each day as it came and make the most of it. Richard and he had suffered enough because of the past. And he was determined to put the past where it belonged and to go on making the future the best it could be.

"I intend to make Katharina my wife as soon as I can convince her to have me," Kane said, smiling broadly at the thought.

"As I intend to make Misty my wife if she will have me when she learns the truth." Richard turned to Kane and asked, "Will you bring her to me so I can explain why I've kept the truth from her?"

"Aye," Kane said. He could add nothing more, nor give his brother advice. He had his own hurdles to cross where the woman he loved was concerned. Kane turned toward the door. There was no better time than the present to start on the future.

Kane found Katharina sitting with Misty in the small salon. Dark head and gold were bent close together as Katharina tried to teach Misty to knit the woolen yarn that lay on the floor at their feet. He smiled at the sight. He and his brother had good taste in women. There could be no two lovelier females in England. He cleared his throat to draw their attention and watched as a shadow of worry passed over their faces.

"Kane," Katharina said, smiling as she held up the knitting needles. "I've been trying to teach Misty to knit, but I'm afraid I'm not good enough with the needles myself to be a tutor."

Kane returned Katharina's smile as he crossed the room and took the seat beside her. He looked at the snarled yarn and chuckled. "I believe I agree with your assessment, but there are other things you may teach her."

Katharina arched a brow at Kane. "Pray tell, my lord. Please tell me what my best traits are so I may share them with Misty."

"Lady, I don't think you want me to discuss your best traits. 'Twould make such a young thing blush to her toes to know exactly how talented you are in keeping my interest. I was thinking more along the lines of being kind and understanding as well as wise."

Hope glowed in Katharina's eyes as she looked up at Kane. "You have made your decision?"

Kane nodded as he looked past the woman he loved to the young girl, who stared at him as if straining to see his features. "Richard made the decision for me. Misty, will you come with me to meet your gallant knight?"

"He is here, my lord?" Misty asked, smiling.

"Aye. He is here and I will take you to him. There is much you and he have to talk about."

Kane rose to his feet and took Misty by the

hand. He looked down at Katharina. "If you will await me here, there is also much that we need to discuss."

Katharina's heart lodged in her throat. She nodded her agreement, unable to pose the questions she needed to ask because she feared the answers. She watched quietly as Kane escorted Misty from the salon. She loved Kane with all her heart, but she didn't know what she would do should he return to the salon only to tell her that he could never put the past behind him and that they could never be man and wife.

The velvet drapes closed out the bright sunlight as Kane entered the chamber with Misty. He escorted her to the high backed chair in front of the fireplace and glanced at his brother, who stood quiet and tense.

"I will leave the two of you alone so you may talk," Kane said, and saw Richard nod his agreement. He closed the door behind him and briefly leaned back against the heavy oak panel as he sent a prayer toward heaven to give Richard his angel.

"I'm glad you came, Misty," Richard said after a long moment.

Misty turned her sightless gaze toward the sound of her love's voice. She gave him a wobbly smile. "I'm afraid I don't understand what is going on. Are you a guest of Lord Sedgewick's?"

"Nay, Misty," Richard said, closing the space

between them. He'd wanted to keep some distance from Misty in order to calmly explain everything to her, but he found it impossible. She was like a lodestone and he the metal. They were drawn together by a force none could see. "I'm am Lord Sedgewick's brother, Richard Sedgewick."

Misty stiffened. "His brother? How is that possible? I have not heard of you before."

Richard reached out and took Misty's hand. " 'Tis not something known among many. And I must ask you to give me your word never to reveal my presence at Sedgewick to anyone. Will you do that for me, Misty?"

Misty sensed the importance of his request at once. She could also sense Richard's tension. She reached out to touch him, wanting to soothe him in the only way she knew. She found both her hands held by his. "You have my word, Sir Knight—I mean, Sir Richard."

"Please, Misty. I am still the same person who held you only last night. Don't let my identity put a wall between us. I need your understanding now more than anything else in my life."

"I'm sorry. But 'tis hard to think of that man as the same one who now sits beside me. You are a Sedgewick, and I am but a mere servant. I am confused, sir. I do not know what you want of me."

"The same thing I wanted last night, Misty. I want only your love."

"You have that, sir," Misty said, feeling that her heart would break. She'd had dreams of being this man's wife. Now she knew such a thing would never come to pass. It was impossible. He was an aristocrat, while she was a servant in his brother's household.

"I am not sir, Misty. I am Richard to you. I have not changed, nor have my feelings for you. You must understand that there is a reason why I kept my identity secret from you, and it has nothing to do with your status in my brother's household. I would love you should you be a beggar."

Confused by his words, Misty moistened her dry lips and looked in the direction of his voice. "Will you tell me?"

"Aye, that is why I asked you to be brought to me. 'Tis time that I told you the truth. We can do nothing until you know why I always met you at night."

Misty made no sound but waited expectantly for Richard to continue.

He cleared his throat. "I have an affliction that is far worse than just a speech impediment, Misty. It is something that my family has kept hidden from the world. I chose the night to meet with you so you could not see my face."

Richard drew Misty to her feet and led her across the chamber to the velvet-draped window. "I know you can see during the brightest time of day, Misty. And once you see me, you will understand why I am kept hidden away."

Richard jerked the drapes open, allowing the bright afternoon sunlight to spill into the room and fall fully upon his features. He closed his eyes, unable to bear the revulsion he knew he'd see in Misty's eyes once she focused upon his face. He felt her hand tense briefly and then suddenly pull free of his own. He waited, expecting the cry of horror. Yet it never came. He jerked his eyes open as her hand lightly touched his drawn cheek. He looked into her blue eyes, his own filled with the agony of knowing he'd lost her.

"See me now, Misty. I am a monster. Do you not see why I have hidden from view?"

Misty's gaze moved over his features before she looked into his beautiful eyes. She smiled lovingly up at him and said, "I see only the face of the man I love, Richard. I look into the most beautiful, kind, understanding and caring eyes I've ever seen. Perhaps you do not fit the mold of your brother, but you are the man who has claimed my heart."

"Surely you jest? Is there not enough light for you to see me clearly? Do you not see the face of the accursed, the face of a man damned to live in the darkness because others would see me dead because of my features?"

"Nay. I see only you. You have not changed since last eve when you held me close to share your warmth with me."

"Do you realize what will happen to you should you choose to stay with me? You will have to give up everything you have known. You will have to live in the darkness with me."

"I live in darkness already, Richard. You are the only bright light in my life. 'Tis true Lady Katharina has been kind to me, yet others are not. I am as different as you." Misty laughed sweetly as she took Richard's hand and gently rubbed it against her cheek. "We are two alike and we are fortunate to have found each other. I feel God has blessed me by allowing me to have you in my life."

Richard nearly sagged with relief. He took Misty into his arms and hugged her close. "Nay, *you* are the angel God sent *me*. Could you think to share my life? Will you be my wife in all ways, Misty?"

Tears glistened on Misty's lashes as she looked up at the man she loved. True, his face was less than perfect, but that didn't matter to her. His heart was what counted, and it was as beautiful and perfect as any God had ever created. Misty stood on tiptoe and touched her lips to the taut, thin line of Richard's. "I love you, Sir Richard, and will gladly become your wife in all ways. Your world is my world."

Kane found Katharina sitting in the library, staring off into space. "Will you ever obey me, woman?" he said, closing the door behind him.

Katharina jerked at the sound of his voice and turned to look at the man who held her heart. She moistened her lips and shook her head. "I fear I will never obey you, my lord. I will love you, honor you, and be your helpmeet in all ways, but never will I obey you."

"I thought that would be your answer," Kane said, crossing to where Katharina sat. He went down on one knee in front of her, took her hand and raised it to his lips. "My lady, I have come to the conclusion that you and I were meant to be together, no matter the time. And I also realize that the time to look toward the future is also the time to put the past aside."

Katharina stilled. Her breath froze in her throat and her heart pounded against her ribcage as she looked down into Kane's ebony eyes. He smiled up at her.

"Will you be my wife, Katharina, in all ways? Now and throughout eternity?"

Tears of joy sprang into Katharina's eyes. "Yes, I will be your wife in all ways, my love."

Kane rose to his feet and crossed to where the large leather volume sat on the side table. He picked it up and carried it back to Katharina. "Record our marriage in the family history, my love. For I have already summoned the minister. Tomorrow you will be Lady Sedgewick."

Katharina opened the book and took the quill pen from Kane. She wrote the entry on the line below the record of the last visit from Charles II to Sedgewick.

"On this day, Lord Kane Sedgewick took to wife

Katharina Ferguson as fate planned. We are happy. Be happy for us. Signed, Katharina Sedgewick, Lady Sedgewick, in the year of our Lord 1651."

Kane read the entry and frowned. "Why do you write; we are happy, be happy for us?"

Katharina closed the leather volume and set it aside as she stood. She took Kane's hand and smiled up at him. "My lord, I am so happy I want the world to know. I also want the future to know. It is my small way of telling those I left behind."

"Do you miss them?" Kane asked, realizing for the first time that she would have had family and friends in the future.

"Not anymore. I loved my aunt, but I have found what I sought all of my life here in your arms." Katharina gave Kane an impish look and added, "Now come and let me show you some of those traits of which you spoke earlier. I have need to test my skills."

"I am your servant, Lady Sedgewick," Kane said, sweeping her up into his arms and striding toward the stairway.

She wrapped her arms about his neck as they ascended the stairs toward the east wing and his bedchamber. "I love you, Kane."

He returned the smile as he kicked open the door and strode toward the huge four-poster bed. He laid her gently upon it as he bent to take her lips. "And I love you, my mysterious lady of the night."

Epilogue

Reservations had been awaiting them upon their arrival at Sedgewick Castle, and now Sidney and John paused upon the threshold of the room they'd shared several months earlier. Each took in the sight of the bedchamber. Much had changed in the last months, and much had remained the same. The room looked exactly as they'd left it, however John was no longer the man who had come from seventeenth-century England. His roguish personality had quickly adjusted to the luxuries of modern life. He gloried in them, savoring the feel of hot water, the softness of the beds, the excitement that coursed through him when he rode in automobiles or airplanes. It was as if he existed in a fantasy world.

It boggled the mind and sometimes left him bewildered until Sidney showed him what to do.

John glanced at the beautiful woman at his side, marveling at the love he had for her. In all his years, he'd never found another woman who could rouse him as Sidney did. And their life together would be perfect if she could only rid herself of her guilt for falling in love with the man who had taken her niece's place in this time in history.

"Professor Harrogate should be arriving shortly," Sidney said, tossing her pocketbook onto the bed. She crossed to the window and looked down at the winter landscape. Tonight would be the night that Katharina would return, if Dr. Harrogate was right. Sidney glanced toward the overcast sky, wondering for the millionth time why fate had to be so fickle. It had sent her the man she loved, yet had taken her niece into an oblivion where she didn't know if she had even survived the last few months. This was the last chance. If Katharina didn't return tonight during the last conjunction of the planets, she knew she'd never see her niece again.

Sidney looked up at the man standing behind her as John rested his hands on her shoulders. "You're thinking of her again and feeling guilty because of us, aren't you?"

Sidney nodded. "I can't help myself. Tonight is the last conjunction for a hundred-and-seventy-one years. Should Katharina not return, then I will never see her again. Nor will I know if she even survived her time travel."

"You know if she comes back, then I will have to leave you and the baby that you now carry?"

Sidney closed her eyes against the agony of that thought. She leaned back against John's strong body, wanting to bury herself inside him in order to stay with him, no matter what might happen tonight. "I don't want to lose you. I love you with all my heart, and I want our child to grow up with you as his father."

John wrapped his arm about Sidney and spread his hand over her rounding belly. "You know I love you, but I fear this is one thing I will not be able to fight should fate decide to send me back."

"God, this is a mess. I lose you or Katharina." Sidney placed her hand over John's. "I would choose to have you stay. I need you. You are my other half. You make me whole."

"Could you continue to love me knowing the price for our happiness was your niece's life?"

Sidney shook her head wearily. "I could never stop loving you. But I don't know if I could be truly happy. If I could only be certain that she is safe and well! I could live with that. I could go on."

"I am a selfish bastard, Sidney. I don't want to leave you and my child. I don't give a damn what happens to anyone else but us," John said vehemently. The thought of being taken back to the seventeenth century without Sidney was abhorrent to him. She was right; he was her other half, just as she was his. They were meant to be together.

A knock on the door interrupted their melancholy conversation. When Sidney opened it, she found Dr. Harrogate grinning widely at her. He held a large, leather-bound book in his arms. "I'm so glad you've finally arrived. I've found something in the Sedgewick family history that I thought you'd want to see as soon as possible."

Dr. Harrogate strode into the bedchamber before Sidney could invite him. He glanced at John and smiled warmly. "This will be of interest to you as well, John. It has to do with your cousin, Lord Kane Sedgewick. He possessed Sedgewick in the year of 1651."

"I already know that," John said, crossing to the table where Dr. Harrogate had opened the aged book and was flipping through the yellowed pages. He pointed down to a page and said happily, "Here. Look. It's the entry of Lord Sedgewick's marriage."

"Kane has sworn never to marry. He's too involved in bringing Charles back to the throne to think of anything else," John said, peering over the professor's shoulder.

Sidney noted the difference in handwriting first. Her eyes widened and her lower lip began to tremble. She looked up at the man she loved and tried to smile. "It's a message from Lady Sedgewick."

"There is no Lady Sedgewick," John said, bending for a closer look. He tensed and then looked back at Sidney. "It would seem that I am wrong."

Dr. Harrogate nodded. "Yes. It would seem you are. As this reads, Katharina Ferguson was married to your cousin in 1651. And I think this message is for you, Sidney. We are happy. Be happy for us!"

"That's all she said?"

"It would be difficult to try to add more during the seventeenth century. What would the generations after her think should she write missives to the twentieth century? Even if she had, we are lucky to have found this much. Things get destroyed through the years. And it has been over three hundred since this was written."

Sidney looked at John and burst into grateful tears. "She is happy. She is happy."

"She must have been happy," Dr. Harrogate continued. "She had six children—three boys and three girls—and twenty-four grandchildren. Sedgewick's owners today are distant relatives of your niece."

Sidney laughed. It was far too much for her to take in. Her niece was only twenty-four years old, but she had six children and twenty-four grandchildren. Sidney looked at John, completely happy for the first time in months. Fate had taken their lives into its hands and had given them everything they'd ever dreamed of. Both she and

Katharina had found the love that they'd been searching for all of their lives.

Wiping at her eyes, Sidney took John and Dr. Harrogate by the arm and turned them toward the door. They could go over the Sedgewick family history later in the evening. She was content with the message Katharina had sent her. The rest was history. "It's time for dinner, and now that I'm eating for two, I mustn't skip any meals."

Sedgewick's gray-haired hostess eyed the handsome man and the dreamy-eyed woman critically. She didn't know what was happening to the young people today, much less those in their middle years. They were even worse. They were so annoying, trying to relive their youth. They had to gush over each other all the time, even during her speech about Sedgewick's ghosts. She pressed her lips tightly together. The two were devouring each other with their eyes. If she didn't do something to gain their attention, anything might happen right there in the middle of Lady Katharina's salon.

Clearing her throat and drawing in a deep breath, she folded her hands gracefully in front of her and launched into her speech about the paranormal happenings that had taken place at Sedgewick Castle. "There have been many strange goings on at Sedgewick since the first stone was laid for its foundation nearly four hundred years ago. There have been sightings of ghosts, goblins and several other specters about the castle and its grounds. Rumors have been rampant through the centuries. For a couple of hundred years it was even said that the Sedgewick family produced a vampire every few generations.

"However, that rumor was never substantiated and died during the seventeenth century to be replaced by the story of the beautiful, mysterious woman who arrived at Sedgewick on a stormy night to capture the heart of the lord of the castle. No one knew from where she hailed nor recognized the strange manner of her speech. However, the love the lady and her lord shared became a legend unto itself. Throughout the area she became known as the Lady Beneficence, for she also knew much about healing and saved many lives with her knowledge of herbs. It is said she is responsible for saving the life of the first Duke of Marlborough. She gained favor with King Charles when he was restored to the throne, and this salon is named in her memory: Lady Katharina's salon. Here she welcomed the powerful from court as well as tenant farmers."

Sidney and John smiled conspiratorially at each other. They expected no less from their relatives. Like themselves, Katharina and Kane had found a love that would last throughout the centuries.

Heart's Magic

Flora Speer

Bestselling author of *ROSE RED*

In the year 1122, Mirielle senses change is coming to Wroxley Castle. Then, from out of the fog, two strangers ride into Lincolnshire. Mirielle believes the first man to be honest. But the second, Giles, is hiding something–even as he stirs her heart and awakens her deepest desires. And as Mirielle seeks the truth about her mysterious guest, she uncovers the castle's secrets and learns she must stop a treachery which threatens all she holds dear. Only then can she be in the arms of her only love, the man who has awakened her own heart's magic.

___52204-7 $5.99 US/$6.99 CAN

FLORA SPEER

Rose Red

A Faerie Tale Romance

Once upon a time...they lived happily ever after.

"I HAVE TWO DAUGHTERS, ONE A FLOWER AS PURE AND WHITE AS THE NEW-FALLEN SNOW AND THE OTHER A ROSE AS RED AND SWEET AS THE FIRES OF PASSION."

Bianca and Rosalinda are the only treasures left to their mother after her husband, the Duke of Monteferro, is murdered. Fleeing a remote villa in the shadows of the Alps of Northern Italy, she raises her daughters in hiding and swears revenge on the enemy who has brought her low.

The years pass until one stormy night a stranger appears from out of the swirling snow, half-frozen and wild, wrapped only in a bearskin. To gentle Bianca he appears a gallant suitor. To their mother he is the son of an assassin. But to Rosalinda he is the one man who can light the fires of passion and make them burn as sweet and red as her namesake.

_52139-3 $5.99 US/$6.99 CAN

FOR LOVE AND HONOR

FLORA SPEER

Bestselling Author Of *Love Just In Time*

Falsely accused of murder, Sir Alain vows to move heaven and earth to clear his name and claim the sweet rose named Joanna. But in a world of deception and intrigue, the virile knight faces enemies who will do anything to thwart his quest of the heart.

From the sceptered isle of England to the sun-drenched shores of Sicily, the star-crossed lovers will weather a winter of discontent. And before they can share a glorious summer of passion, they will have to risk their reputations, their happiness, and their lives for love and honor.

__3816-1 $4.99 US/$5.99 CAN

Dorchester Publishing Co., Inc.
P.O. Box 6640
Wayne, PA 19087-8640

Please add $1.75 for shipping and handling for the first book and $.50 for each book thereafter. NY, NYC, and PA residents, please add appropriate sales tax. No cash, stamps, or C.O.D.s. All orders shipped within 6 weeks via postal service book rate. Canadian orders require $2.00 extra postage and must be paid in U.S. dollars through a U.S. banking facility.

Name_____
Address_____
City_____State_____Zip_____
I have enclosed $_____in payment for the checked book(s).
Payment <u>must</u> accompany all orders. ❏ Please send a free catalog.

THE LION'S BRIDE — CONNIE MASON

Winner of the *Romantic Times* Storyteller Of The Year Award!

Lord Lyon of Normandy has saved William the Conqueror from certain death on the battlefield, yet neither his strength nor his skill can defend him against the defiant beauty the king chooses for his wife.

Ariana of Cragmere has lost her lands and her virtue to the mighty warrior, but the willful beauty swears never to surrender her heart.

Saxon countess and Norman knight, Ariana and Lyon are born enemies. And in a land rent asunder by bloody wars and shifting loyalties, they are doomed to misery unless they can vanquish the hatred that divides them—and unite in glorious love.

_3884-6 $5.99 US/$7.99 CAN

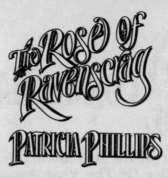

The Rose of Ravenscrag

PATRICIA PHILLIPS

Bestselling Author Of *The Constant Flame*

The daughter of a nobleman and a common peasant, Rosamund believes she is doomed to marry a simple swineherd. Then a desperate ruse sweeps the feisty lass from her rustic English village to a faraway castle. And even as Rosamund poses as the betrothed of a wealthy lord, she cannot deny the desire he rouses in her soul. A warrior in battle, and a conqueror in love, Henry of Ravenscrag is all she has ever dreamed of in a husband. But the more Rosamund's passion flares for the gallant who has captured her spirited heart, the more she dreads he will cast her aside if he ever discovers the truth about her.

__3905-2 $4.99 US/$6.99 CAN

Bestselling Author of *The Mirror & The Magic*

Elinor DeCortenay hails from a world of castles and conquests, sorcerers and spells. So she has no trouble accepting the notion that a magic charm can send her to another time and place, where leather-skinned demons ride noisy beasts. What she can't believe is that the devilishly handsome man she mistakes for Satan's minion is really a knight of the present.

Since the death of his wife, Drew has become a virtual recluse, showing interest in little besides his passion for motorcycles. Then, while riding his souped-up Harley through the California countryside, he chances upon a striking beauty dressed like a resident of Camelot, and despite his misgivings, she wakens his lonely heart to a desire for the future. A medieval maiden and modern motorhead, Elinor and Drew are both trying to escape painful pasts—pasts that will haunt them forever unless they can share a love timeless, tempestuous, and true.

___4273-8 $5.50 US/$6.50 CAN

A Stolen Rose

CORAL SMITH SAXE

Bestselling Author Of *Enchantment*

Feared by all Englishmen and known only as the Blackbird, the infamous highwayman is really the stunning Morgana Bracewell. And though she is an aristocrat who has lost her name and family, nothing has prepared the well-bred thief for her most charming victim. Even as she robs Lord Phillip Greyfriars blind, she knows his roving eye has seen through her rogue's disguise—and into her heart. Now, the wickedly handsome peer will stop at nothing to possess her, and it will take all Morgana's cunning not to surrender to a man who will accept no ransom for her love.

_3843-9   **$5.50 US/$7.50 CAN**

VICTORIA CHANCELLOR

Bestselling Author Of *Forever & A Day*

In the Wyoming Territory—a land both breathtaking and brutal—bitterroots grow every summer for a brief time. Therapist Rebecca Hartford has never seen such a plant—until she is swept back to the days of Indian medicine men, feuding ranchers, and her pioneer forebears. Nor has she ever known a man as dark, menacing, and devastatingly handsome as Sloan Travers. Sloan hides a tormented past, and Rebecca vows to use her professional skills to help the former Union soldier, even though she longs to succumb to personal desire. But when a mysterious shaman warns Rebecca that her sojourn in the Old West will last only as long as the bitterroot blooms, she can only pray that her love for Sloan is strong enough to span the ages....

_52087-7 $5.50 US/$7.50 CAN